W9-CNE-878

The Slowworm's Song

Also by Andrew Miller

Ingenious Pain
Casanova
Oxygen
The Optimists
One Morning Like a Bird
Pure
The Crossing
Now We Shall Be Entirely Free

Andrew Miller

THE SLOWWORM'S SONG

SCEPTRE

First published in Great Britain in 2022 by Sceptre
An imprint of Hodder & Stoughton
An Hachette UK company

1

All characters in this publication are fictitious and any resemblance to real persons, living or dead, is purely coincidental.

A CIP catalogue record for this title is available from the British Library

Hardback ISBN 9781529354195
Trade Paperback ISBN 9781529354201
eBook ISBN 9781529354218

Typeset in Janson Text by Hewer Text UK Ltd, Edinburgh
Printed and bound in Great Britain by Clays Ltd, Elcograf S.p.A.

Hodder & Stoughton policy is to use papers that are natural, renewable and recyclable products and made from wood grown in sustainable forests. The logging and manufacturing processes are expected to conform to the environmental regulations of the country of origin.

Hodder & Stoughton Ltd
Carmelite House
50 Victoria Embankment
London EC4Y 0DZ

www.sceptrebooks.co.uk

For my father, born Belfast 1925.
And for my daughter, new citizen of the Republic.

Take heed, dear Friends, to the promptings of love and truth in your hearts.

Quaker Faith and Practice, Advices and Queries

Our modern world . . . after many centuries of tedious research, has attained a conviction that all things are linked together by a chain of causes and effects which suffers no interruption.

David Friedrich Strauss, trans. George Eliot (1846)

So he rose and led home silently through clean woodland
where every bough repeated the Slowworm's song.

'Briggflatts', Basil Bunting

START

I have had the letter just over a week now and I look at it every day. Sometimes I look at it several times a day. I have shown it to no one. No one other than myself and the people who sent it know it exists.

It did not arrive alone but in its fall from the letterbox it separated itself, glided free of the rest – bills, nonsense – and landed face up just where the mat meets the floorboards. A cool-looking oblong, office white, my name on the front, typed. No logo, no legible postmark, nothing of that sort. I picked it up and turned it over. On the back, printed on the flap, was a return address, Belfast BT2, and a street whose name I did not recognise but that I may have walked down thirty years ago. May well have done.

I carried it through to the kitchen and put it on the table. The room was in shadow. It doesn't get the sun until early afternoon. I was still wearing what I'd slept in, T-shirt and boxers, my feet bare on the lino. Of course, it might have been anything, one of those pieces of junk mail made to look like something else, something personal, or some sort of out-sourcing, the electricity company or the bank writing to me via a sorting office in

Northern Ireland, like when you call to find out the train times from Frome to Bristol and you're talking to a woman in Bangalore who calls herself Julie.

I tore a corner of the envelope then used my finger as a paper knife. Inside, a single sheet, typed on both sides. I read it – scanned it, really – then read it again more carefully and laid it back on the table. God help me, Maggie, if there had been any drink in the house I would have had it. I'm pretty sure I would. There isn't, by the way. Not a drop. Nothing hidden in a gumboot or out in the garden. I could have run down to the Spar and pulled something from those glittering shelves I don't allow myself even to look at when I do the weekly shop. Then, please, picture the scene at the checkout. A middle-aged man in his underwear, clutching a bottle, holding out a banknote. Some of those boys and girls there know me. Not my name but they've seen me often enough, might have passed the time of day with me. Would they sell me a bottle? Would they not have to? Where is it written that you can't buy alcohol in your underwear at ten in the morning? Anyway, I think they'd be frightened of me.

In such moments a wildness appears that is, fairly obviously, linked to self-destruction. I tried to calm myself with the breathing exercises Dr Rauch has taught me. The slow inhalation through the nostrils, the touch of the breath entering the body. Then the out breath, the letting go that you can, if you choose, sound as a sigh. This is ancient wisdom dusted off for a scientific age, for the National Health Service, the Bristol Liver Unit. Someone was teaching it on the banks of the Ganges long before the Buddha was born. It may have saved countless lives.

Steadier – a little – I went to the sink, filled a mug with cold water, drank it, rinsed the mug and went back to the table, picked up the letter again. Perhaps I'd got myself into a muddle reading not what was really there but what I was afraid might be. I read it a third time. There was no mistake. It is, in its way, plain enough.

It comes from an organisation calling itself the Commission and is signed by someone whose name, to me, sounds invented. Ambrose Carville. Ambrose? Is that an Irish name? He is, he says, a 'witness co-ordinator', and on behalf of the Commission he invites me to come to Belfast in October when they will be examining the events of the summer of 1982.

I had never heard of the Commission. I wondered if it was something to do with the Historical Enquiries Team, which is a police outfit that's been working through the Troubles, year by year, 1969 onwards. I don't know where they've got to, how close to my year. I have, at some level I suppose, been listening out for them. But if the Commission is part of the same effort they don't say so. What they do say – what Ambrose Carville says – is that they have no religious or sectarian affiliations, do not represent or work on behalf of any particular community. The word 'legacy' is used twice. The phrase 'an open forum', the phrase 'thorough and impartial'. 'Truth', of course. Truth, justice, peace.

In the last paragraph I am informed, by way of reassurance, that the Commission is not a court of law, that its sessions are private, that it is not their intention anyone's evidence should form the basis of a prosecution. Am I reassured? Not very. The Saville Inquiry reported last year. You must have seen something about it on TV. Perhaps you were curious as to why so much time and money had been spent trying to make sense of fifteen minutes of mayhem in an Irish city forty years ago. (Someone in Parliament, a Tory MP, worked out how many Apache attack helicopters you could buy with the millions spent on the inquiry.) Anyway, the soldiers – those men of the Parachute Regiment involved in the shootings – were offered anonymity and told they could not incriminate themselves, but it already looks like that won't stop prosecutions. It's possible some of those soldiers, men in their sixties or seventies, will go to prison.

I couldn't tell you how long I stood there in the kitchen with the letter in my hand. At some point I realised how cold my feet were, my whole body cold and starting to stiffen. I folded the letter, put it back in the envelope and carried it up here to Dad's study. I put it in one of the desk drawers, then took it out and, after studying the spines of books on the shelves, I slid it between a collection of English songs and poems called *Palgrave's Golden Treasury* and a volume in cracked blue leather with the nice dusty title of *Reform and Continuity in Nineteenth Century Quakerism*. I didn't think anyone was likely to disturb it there. More to the point, I didn't think you were likely to find it, you or Lorna. No one else comes up here.

And this is where I visit it, sit up through the watches of the night with Ambrose Carville and my own odd reflection in the window glass. I could, I'm sure, recite the entire letter now, word perfect. I learn nothing new in these re-readings. It is, like I said, plain enough in its way. The tone reminds me a bit of the letters I get from the clinic in Bristol, respectful as a matter of form but also business-like, direct. Results of the last blood test, the last scan. Date of the next medication review, next appointment with Dr Rauch. Please attend promptly.

By the way, Dr Rauch's first name is Emilia. I only found that out recently, though I've been seeing her for seven or eight years. A joke I've told too often is that she's my most successful long-term relationship. I'm tempted to try it out on her – Emilia. She would let it go, I think, say nothing, though perhaps later note it down as a symptom, one that might, for all I know, be typical of men in my condition. What does she call *me*? I'm pretty sure she never calls me Stephen or Mr Rose. I don't think she calls me anything. Just leans out of the consulting room, scans the ruined faces, sees mine and nods. No need for names.

Another reason for keeping it up here in the study – other than the old trick of hiding leaves in forests – is to have Dad's advice, or at least to ask it. Easy enough to picture him in the kitchen or the bedroom, and certainly in the garden, but this was *his* room. More of his dust in here than anywhere other than the burying ground. This is where he did his reading and writing, made his lesson plans, did his thinking. And this is where he sometimes wrote letters to me, ones I have stupidly lost and would dearly love to have again. So I ask him, out loud, what I should do, then wait for some sort of answer. It doesn't feel any odder than the sitting and listening we do in the meeting house those Sunday mornings we bother going. I ask if I should return the envelope with a line through my name and above it, in bold, NOT KNOWN AT THIS ADDRESS. Or if that isn't strong enough, ADDRESSEE DECEASED, a statement presently untrue but unlikely to remain so for many more years. The liver has great powers of regeneration. It is strangely forgiving. But the fact is I did a pretty thorough job on myself. Not all lizards get to grow their tail again.

These schemes are childish, of course, and in their way dishonourable. Part of being sober is being honest. That might be most of it. I've had that explained to me often enough. For any reformed drunk it's the place he stands, his ground. It may not even be possible to stay sober without it.

So write back with a simple no? I don't think they have any power to force me. They don't say that or hint at it. Even the soldiers at the Saville were there voluntarily. It's not like being summoned to court.

Anyway, Dad so far has kept his counsel. I have not been contacted. No other voice has broken into my thoughts. The ghost in the window is only me. You asked once if I thought I was like him. Do you remember? Last summer in the garden, one of the rare occasions we've sat together and opened the dangerous book of family. I said that my looks (my looks!) probably came from Mum's side, though that's a side of the family I've never seen much of. As for character, I avoided speaking of it for obvious reasons. Neither Mum nor Dad deserves to have that at their door. What I should have said that day, what I wanted to say, is how much of Dad I see in you, and though that is nothing to be astonished about – why shouldn't a girl resemble her grandfather? – it still makes my scalp tingle when I notice some shape or gesture smuggled down the line to you. If you had ever met him I don't think you'd have a problem with that. I think it would please you.

But if not Dad's advice (and, no, I didn't really expect it) whose might I have? The meeting-house elders'? That's Ron Hamm, Ned Clarke and Sarah Waterfall, though to be accurate, Ned's an overseer, which is not quite the same. You've seen them all at one time or another, will have shaken hands with them, heard them close meetings, though you might not have known their names. They might welcome something like this. Something to test them. Sarah's the eldest elder, and having known me a long time, how readily in the past I have made up stories to cover my tracks, she would want to see the letter and read it for herself. And then? Some appeal to conscience, the promptings of my inner teacher, that kind of thing. No 'should' or 'must'. The choice, the decision, would have to be mine.

Do you know they still have the say-so over this house? Sarah and Co? If I don't behave they can put me out of here. It was in Dad's will. An entailment or codicil or whatever the correct term is. The house, and the orchard at the edge of town. I have never resented it. There was a time, not so distant, when left with a house and some land I would have drunk them down to the last red brick, the last green apple. Dad knew that, and I'd have made the same decision in his place. It's slightly strange, though, the feeling of it, as if, at fifty-one years old, I'm still a sort of ward of court.

Will you keep going? To the meetings, I mean, you and Lorna. Other than Tess Douel's kids – and they've more or less moved away now – you're the only young people who turn up. You halve the average age in there. And I won't pretend I don't get a kick out of it, the show the pair of you make with your coats trimmed with fake fur, the jokish rings, the scarlet lipstick, heels of the kind I'm pretty sure nobody ever wore in that space before. I catch them casting deep glances at us and I see the wondering expression come over their faces. I think we're a story they're quite interested in. They're trying to work out how it will end.

What time is it? My watch is somewhere, the bathroom or the sill above the sink in the kitchen. I've heard no cars for a while. The people here are not really country people now – I should think about ten of them actually work on the land – but they still have the rhythms of the country. Early to bed and early to rise. Or else it's just that there's nothing much to do once the pubs close.

If I have a safe place, a sanctuary, then this room is it. The old rug, the shelves of books, the cupboard of Ordnance Survey maps, the painting called *Coming In* or *Coming Home* that Mum and Dad bought the year they were married. The desk itself, country made and probably picked up at an auction in Glastonbury or Wells. All this I grew up with. Almost nothing has changed. I should feel protected in here but I don't, not any more. I was a fool, of course, to drop my guard and forget what I knew very well when I was drinking. How fragile it all is, how we have nothing under our feet, nothing that can be depended on. Did I tell you that story about Peter Irving? I don't always know what I've said out loud and what I've just told you in my head. I heard it from Cheryl, my post lady. She picks up gossip door to door, like a bee collecting nectar. I know Peter a little, or knew him. Our fathers were friends. On Christmas Day last year he was standing at the head of the table to carve the turkey. All his family were there, children, an elderly aunt or two. He stood with the fork and carving knife, a man in his mid-forties, quite successful. He stood and he stood, looking at the bird, looking at the things in his hands. At some point the family must have begun to feel uneasy. Why the delay? Was it a joke? Then – and Cheryl had all this from the wife's sister – he slowly shook his head. He didn't know how to do it. He had carved the turkey every Christmas for years but now he couldn't do it. Whatever had held that knowledge was gone, wiped. In the New Year he was diagnosed with a brain tumour, inoperable. The last I heard he was in a hospice near Bath. A story like that should have put me on my guard. It should have reminded me.

But all this is beside the point – forgetting, remembering, speaking up, keeping silent. There is a reason I cannot go back and the reason is you. Their letter came too late. It wouldn't have mattered before. Now it does. Of flesh and blood and soul you are what I have now. You are all I have. And I know how uncertain it is, this peace between us, your dropping of the old wariness, the old resentments. We have, with days, been building a bridge between us. We have just begun and the bridge is still so frail I hardly dare look at it. A strong wind, a careless word, and it would be gone. And it's not – I hope – only selfishness, not just what *I* would lose. I don't believe you've given up on having a father. I think you need me to make the effort. I have failed in so much! I don't intend to fail in this, not for them, not so they can keep raking over the sorry history of that place. How about raking over some of what their own did? That should give them ten years' work. Why poke a stick in the nest? I was sent there, Maggie, and younger than you are now. That makes me a criminal? And what if you came to look at me like that? If one day you were to look at me as some of the people in that room in Belfast would look at me? Could I survive it?

At last, an easy question!

I could not.

You caught me in bed this morning, not for the first time. Came up and caught me tangled in the sheets, your father, the not so sweet-smelling hulk of him, adrift in sleep at eleven in the morning. I suspect you watched me for a while. Did you? And what went through your head? How well or ill I looked? How odd that you, five foot four and light as a dancer, should be related to such a creature? And then, somehow, I became aware of you and opened my eyes and grinned, and you said, It's past eleven, Stephen, and I said, Is it? Or something equally bare.

You went to put the kettle on while I washed my face and then idled at the bedroom window looking over at my neighbour Frank spraying what was probably weed-killer by the edge of his fence. Plenty of weeds on our side. About, I think, the right amount. Imagine England without dandelions or daisies. Without buttercups! I greeted, as I do every morning, the aspen tree at the bottom of the garden. They say a crown of its leaves allows you to enter the underworld and return safely. Such crowns, or their dust, have been found in burial mounds. The wood is light and the Celts made shields from it. I don't think it has many other uses. It doesn't burn well. For reasons I've never fully understood I have always connected the tree with my mother. Did I sit in its shade with her as a little boy? Was it her who told me about the shields and the crowns? I remember so little about her, but there's some crossover, some muddling of Mum and the tree that I'm grateful for. It means more to me, is more of a memorial, the right sort, than her stone in St John's. She wasn't a Quaker. Dad said she had 'no faith'. I don't think that bothered him.

When I came down to the kitchen the tea was brewing in the pot on the table. You had on the yellow Marigolds and were peering into the fridge where you always seem to expect to find something that shouldn't be there. I sat. I am often a little dizzy in the morning. Sweet tea helps. You closed the fridge door, peeled off the gloves and reminded me it was my day at the garden centre. I said I didn't need to be there until twelve. I said I could get there at one and it wouldn't matter. It might, you said, and I said, No, not really, I don't do much there, I don't have any important jobs. All the more reason to be on time, you said, meaning, I suppose, I should demonstrate my credentials as a keen and responsible employee. I nodded. I didn't feel up to taking you on in that bullish mood, didn't quite have the energy. I checked my hands for steadiness, drew the teapot closer, and poured for both of us.

You served three years in the RAF. If I remember rightly you ended up as a senior aircraftswoman, which might be the equivalent of a corporal in the army, I'm not certain. Anyway, you did better than your father, who never amounted to more than a private soldier. Not that we felt any shame in it. Quite the opposite. As far as we were concerned we were the only part of the army that mattered. We *were* the army. But you often strike me as perfect NCO material. You make things happen, you're a fixer

– you're tough! Or that's one side of you. I'm not going to pretend to be any sort of expert on your character. That would annoy you! I've no idea, for example, how you are with Lorna when it's just the two of you. I wish I did know. I wish I had a book of instructions, had anything at all, a photograph even, something from ten years ago, you on your way to school. Smart and organised? A bit ragged and running for the bus? If you're tough, are you also fragile? And if so, where? What part of you? What button mustn't I push? At twenty-six you seem so competent – a young woman who knows herself and where she's headed. But that can't be the whole story. It may be it's only when dealing with me that you revert to Senior Aircraftswoman Maggie Arden, and then only because you have to, because my life, despite the simplicity of the routines, the careful smallness of it, still looks like trouble, the sort that might bring out the NCO in anybody.

In basic training we had Corporals Wright and Darling, men I fully expect to find leaning over my deathbed, clipboards in hand, checking I'm doing it by the book. Later on, in Ireland, there was John France, Corporal France, who waits for me still at the iron door of the Factory, counting down the seconds.

So this morning you chivvied me, mentioned shaving, mentioned my nails, still black from lifting potatoes yesterday. I promised to smarten myself up and then, before you left, handed you a carrier bag of spuds, my first earlies, Arran Pilots, reliable if not the most exciting. You peered into the bag and said you would give them to Lorna who, it seems, does most of the cooking at the Silk Shed, these days. We stood a few seconds in the hall grinning at each other. Then, suddenly in a hurry, you turned to the door and were gone.

Why do I always grieve at such moments, as if all your departures were final? Because something in me is afraid each might be? That, surely, must have something to do with losing Mum. Childhood wounds never quite heal, do they? Also to do with us, of course. Reasons you might have for coming back, reasons for not. And then a sudden sense of hopelessness that I was trying to win you with bags of potatoes.

I shook myself – and imagined all walls of all houses suddenly glass, what we would see there. I called up the shades of Wright and Darling, climbed the stairs, showered, shaved, scraped under my nails with the point of the nail scissors, then swung back the mirror doors of the medicine cabinet: naltrexone, phytonadione, amiloride, atenolol, lactulose, rifaximin. That's just the prescription half. There's also the stuff I buy from Boots or the health-food shop, the probiotics, the zinc, the fish oil, the milk thistle, the holy basil. I've given up on most of it now. Some of it's been in there for years. Lactulose is the one I've stayed with longest. It's a laxative to help prevent the build-up of ammonia. Too much ammonia in the system and it seeps into the brain. They call it hepatic encephalopathy – HE for short. Confusion, forgetfulness, poor judgement. Then out-and-out craziness. Then coma. Then curtains. But the lactulose has side-effects I've grown very weary of. The last month or two I've taken less and less of it, and when this bottle is done – it's nearly done – I won't hurry on to the next. Dr Rauch would not approve, but Dr Rauch – Emilia! – does not have to take it and is, anyway, a believer in adult responsibility, each of us, suitably informed, making our choices. Well, I'm making mine – though we'll see whether I'm brave enough to tell her about it when I next sit in her office. That's only a couple of weeks away now.

I climbed into my overalls, had some breakfast, checked my face in the mirror in the hall, wiped away a smear of shaving soap – one of the drawbacks of shaving by touch – and finally launched myself into the day's uncertain sunshine, getting to Plant World at twelve thirty, or thereabouts.

Tim Levett, who runs the place, was in the office with the door open. Like many round here I've known him all my life. He was on the computer but glanced over his shoulder when he heard me, treated me to an expression suggesting slight surprise and slight disappointment I was still among the living and still on the pay roll. His sister was in there too, Debbie. She has alopecia and wears a selection of wigs I think she'd be better off without. Today's was the colour of Cooper's marmalade. She does the accounts and other bits of admin. She has no husband or partner, no children. I'm not sure Tim is kind to her. I smiled and she smiled back. Tim said there was a delivery to unpack. Like Dr Rauch, though for different reasons, he also avoids using my name.

I do no heavy work at Plant World. I don't carry bags of gravel around or shift patio slabs or stack bags of compost. There's a lad called Radko who does most of that, a member of some heroic race of horse thieves from the Carpathians, a maker of jokes so dry it's a full week before you laugh. I do some digging and barrowing but even that Tim doesn't like much. We're in a recession. A large, wild-looking employee lying dead among shattered flower pots would not be good for business. People might start going to the place in Shepton Mallet on the industrial estate. What's it called? Dobbs? Dobbies?

I unpacked the delivery. Gardening gloves, garden ornaments made of a sort of imitation stone, hollow and liable to blow away. Bird warblers made in China and perhaps warbling the songs of Chinese birds. Mugs with 'Bloomin' lovely' or 'I'd rather be gardening' on them, also made in China. I priced them and put them out, then crossed to the hothouse – warm rather than hot, and quite shady – where we have the exotics, orchids mostly. Tim likes orchids. He wants us to be known for our orchids – cymbidiums, dendrobiums, vandas, cattleyas. I wasn't sure about them at first. I thought they looked like they were made of wax or plastic, but I've begun to see the appeal. The slender stems, the jewelled flowers. And they have an alertness to them. They look like they're paying attention, like they might be slightly more intelligent than other flowers.

The place was empty. In winter it can be busy in there – somewhere to warm up, see colour – but this time of year people prefer to walk outside. I went round with the spray-mist, prodding a finger into pots to see how dry they were. I was also probably talking to myself, chuntering on, voicing the mind churn, lost in it, when Annie Fuller came in. She might even have heard some of it. I hope not. I don't think it's very impressive material. Annie's a local funeral director, an undertaker. I don't know her well. The business was her father's, Fuller's Funerals, and you might have seen their window on the high street opposite the Spar, with the old-fashioned hand-bier and a selection of urns, some of them looking as if they could be used to store uranium.

Annie likes me and I'm not sure why. Professional interest? In her line of work you must notice the lame dinosaurs, the ones who might not make it to the next waterhole. But I worry it's something else, something to do with politics. I happen to know that she's a card-carrying member of the British National Party. My post lady, Cheryl – as far on the left, I think, as Annie is the other way – told me about it months ago, a leaked list of BNP names and addresses online, Annie Fuller's among them. I found the list myself on the computer in the library. It wasn't difficult. And sure enough, Annie was there and described as an 'activist'. She'll know – it's not a secret, and this is a small, gossipy town

– that I'm ex-army (I'm also an ex-agricultural feeds salesman and did that for longer but somehow it doesn't count). Thanks to the list, I now know there is a fairly strong showing of military, ex and serving, in the BNP. Does she think I might be a sympathiser? A fellow-traveller? Stephen Rose, white supremacist! If I was smarter I could have found a coded way to speak about it in terms of orchids, warned her off. Instead, we small-talked about the town, the unsettled weather, what's coming or going in our gardens. Quite hard to talk to undertakers even when they're not members of a far-right party. (How's business? Did you get many in the winter with all that flu going round?)

She said – out of the blue – that she thought my overalls suited me. She might have said 'dashing'. It made me laugh. She laughed too, became all shiny-eyed, then briefly tongue-tied, and said she had to get back. An odd meeting. I have no idea what to make of it. I should be grateful for any interest, whatever the cause. I've not been fighting women off these last years. But Annie Fuller? The two of us flirting in a pizza restaurant or going for walks along the front at Burnham? I honestly don't have the imagination for it. And anyway, I've probably got it entirely wrong and she's just a friendly soul passing a slack ten minutes with a man she thinks might appreciate a little kindness.

A few more folk came in, ambled round the tables. I know enough about the plants now to be able to answer basic questions, though when a serious buyer shows up Tim takes over and I'm sent to do some sweeping. About two o'clock I went to the centre café, Shrubs, for a sandwich and coffee. As you know, I have to eat regularly, every two hours or so, or I fade. Back in the hothouse I found Tess Douel leaning over a white phalaenopsis as though tempted to dip her tongue into the flower and drink from it. You know who I mean by Tess? Petite woman my age, brown hair to her shoulders – brown with a streak or two of grey in it now. She usually sits opposite us in the meeting house. A green dress last Sunday, a summery blue-linen one today. At sixteen she was my first proper girlfriend. That's what it means still to be living in the place where you grew up. You get to watch your teenage girlfriend become a middle-aged woman. It was an intense enough thing at the time and lasted a year or so. She married her next boyfriend, Colin. They have a business together, Tor Catering, that does posh weddings, festivals and the like. I think it does well enough. I see the van scurrying around town in a way that suggests busyness. We waved to each other. We don't kiss cheeks or anything like that. I asked if she was after an orchid. She shook her head and said she'd come to order lilies for a wedding she was doing over in Chesterblade. Her eldest boy, Nat, was back from university and helping her out (in exchange for a working pass to Glastonbury festival). He was in Shrubs eating carrot cake – apparently he never stops eating – so Tess had come over to look at the orchids and the ferns. She said it was the closest she could get in Somerset to a rain forest. I told her she should visit a real one, take a boat trip up the Amazon. She grinned, said her kids might do it but she'd have to settle for Plant World. She asked after you and wanted to know about the Silk Shed. I said it was Glastonbury's most fashionable tea house, which I believe is accurate. She knows or has a close enough idea what it means to me, your being here.

While we spoke and had the place to ourselves I came close to telling her about the letter. I mean I was tempted to. Tess is one of the two people I have spoken to openly and in detail about what happened. The other was a mate I knocked about with in Crete and who was drowned there the next year swimming at night with a skinful of raki in him. I did – once – try to tell your mother, but during the telling we set our heads on fire with booze so even if I'd managed to get it all out she wouldn't have remembered anything. With Tess it was years later. I was living rough in the orchard, Dad's orchard (mine now, one day yours), going home occasionally but unable to bear for long the shame of Dad seeing me like that. I had a little tent, kept body and soul together with apples and stolen eggs. I have no idea how Tess knew I was up there. Perhaps everyone knew. Anyway, she came up one morning – September time? October? – walked out of the town with a Thermos of tea, a loaf of bread and a pair of thick socks for my knackered feet. I saw her coming and I thought of hiding. No, I *did* hide, lay behind an old apple stump and peeked at her through the long grass. She stopped in the middle of the orchard and called my name. A human voice after days of birdsong! The second time she called I shambled out and let her see me. We sat on the grass. I burnt my lips on the tea. I don't remember if she spoke much or was silent. She's a good Quaker, she knows the uses of silence. Anyway, I gave it up to her – growling, gabbling – astonished to hear it in that place, the true thing, the unfixable thing. It was not a sentimental occasion. She didn't hold my hand. She sat with me as she might with some beast in difficulty, something snared and beyond much useful assistance. She asked one or two questions. She looked at me with her very round, very brown eyes.

I don't know if I would have found the right moment to speak to her today or what would have come of that. The moment never arrived. Her son came in to join us. He is, I'd guess, about five years younger than you, six inches taller than me, a shock of gingery hair that must come from Colin's side of the family. He'll have some vague idea of who I am – a school friend of his mother's, the odd-job man whose past is some undefined zone of trouble. Also, of course, the father of an interesting girl he might have seen once or twice about the town. He's studying French and International relations at Exeter, and is about to head off for a year in Bordeaux or Bayonne or somewhere. I told him I was in the sixth year of a humanities degree with the Open University and eight months overdue with an essay on George Eliot's *The Mill on the Floss*. He glanced at Tess as if he wasn't sure what to make of this. Was I ribbing him? When he realised I was serious he nodded and said it was cool. Cool! I was delighted. To get the nod of approval from a young man like that, a prince among the orchids! And strange, isn't it, how the word has kept its currency when others have come and gone? Hipsters and cats were cool when Dad was young. The sense hasn't changed much. I always lacked the confidence for it myself. The drinking, when it started, could have been my attempt to find it at the bottom of a glass. Your mother had it, that's certain. It came off her like a shimmer. Even her name, Evie Arden, seemed cool to me. I assume she's still an Arden? I don't think she ever married the fellow I met at your passing-out parade, Ray McSomebody. I can't believe she would have changed her name even if she had. You use it, of course. If you had my name you'd be Maggie Rose, and you have to admit that has a charm to it. I allow myself – though strictly rationed – daydreams like that. You as Maggie Rose. You calling me Dad rather than Stephen.

I'm putting all this down on a pad in the library. I bought it in Smith's – a 200-leaf student pad – and I've already made quite a dent in it. I've been in here since finishing at Plant World. I'm still in my overalls, something Tim might not approve of, me as a kind of roving ambassador for the garden centre. Not many people here this afternoon. Two girls and a boy from St Jude's doing their homework. An old fellow poring over a book of photographs of buses. Then there's a girl, a young woman, with brightly coloured tattoos on her very white legs, tapping away fluently at one of the computers. For an hour I was two computers down from her. I should have my own, I suppose. I don't think they're expensive now. But I'm used to coming here and enjoy some of the things I see. I've been here at Baby Boogie Rhyme Time. I've seen the Lego club and mahjong mornings. I once saw the members of the memory group arriving, most of them elderly though not all. The expressions on their faces. Some vacant, some peering around with big smiles, as if hoping no one would come up and ask what day it was. All, I thought, to some degree or another, looked frightened. When I asked the librarian about them she said they sometimes brought in photo albums and used them to piece together the story of their lives. She studied me then, peered up through glasses of the type I think all librarians have to wear even if there's nothing wrong with their eyes, and said the group was full but if I was interested . . . She was thinking perhaps I had an ancient parent at home but I instantly assumed she meant me and was tempted to demand she put me to the test – post-war prime ministers, FA Cup winners, the lyrics of Bowie songs.

What was I looking up today? Things I have looked up before. The Commission, whose website contains very little beyond a mission statement and a photograph of the building in BT2 where they meet, a stranded Georgian townhouse at the side of a roundabout, a place that has managed to dodge the Luftwaffe and thirty years of sectarian bombs. There's a postal address, an email address, but no phone number. On the search results page there are some news stories. One of these, the *Belfast Telegraph* site, shows a wall near the Commission – it may be one of the walls of the building itself – sprayed with the message FORGET THE PAST. Yard-high letters.

When I type in 'The Commission and inquiries into the Troubles', I get most of the same stuff but also sites connecting to the Saville Inquiry and Bloody Sunday. For now, at least, it's hard to avoid. I found myself scrolling through a page of photographs, some of them so familiar they're part of the collective memory of this country, at least for people of my age. The priest, Father Daly, crouching and waving a blood-stained handkerchief as he goes ahead of a group carrying Jackie Duddy, shot in the back and soon to die of his wounds. The body of Bernard McGuigan under a sheet, a great halo of blood around his head. Other pictures were less familiar. There was one of Paras escorting a column of civilians, men and women, with their hands on their heads, which had some echo of Second World War pictures I've seen, though there the soldiers were not British and the civilians not Irish.

I don't want to look at these pictures, Maggie, and yet I do. For years – many – I couldn't have done it. Couldn't have begun to. Now I find it hard to look away, as if some hand gripped the back of my skull and kept me pointed.

Put in 'Ambrose Carville' and I get a whole tribe of them. The name is not as odd or rare as I'd imagined. The manager of a Nissan car franchise in Florida. An Australian cricketer who plays for the Queensland Bulls. A doctor in Essex. Add 'Belfast' and up comes an Irish-history site with a page on the Carvilles of Fermanagh. One of these, Jack Carville, distinguished himself as the commander of a flying column during the War of Independence. The grandfather or great-grandfather of the Carville who signed my letter? How sympathetic would such a man be to ex-British soldiers?

I typed in my own name. This has become an anxious habit, a bad one. The first time I did it was the day after I received the letter. More Stephen Roses out there than Ambrose Carvilles but nothing yet about this one. I can't believe that will last. Some smart or bored journalist will sniff it out eventually, do a little checking and knock at the door.

I almost put your name in today but stopped myself. Too much like spying. I have, of course, looked at the Silk Shed site many times. That picture of you and Lorna holding trays of cakes and cocktails, your faces looking as if you've just stopped laughing, that one I love.

You have to book time on the computer. You get an on-screen warning when there're fifteen minutes left. I used my last minutes searching for answers to the question 'Am I too ill to stand trial?' What I got back was old news articles about General Pinochet. You won't remember him. A Chilean dictator and 'strong man' of the kind who liked wiring up his critics to car batteries in the basements of police stations. He was arrested in Britain on a Spanish warrant when he was already an old man. He stayed here under house arrest for over a year. Margaret Thatcher sent him a bottle of whisky with the message 'Scotch is one British institution that will never let you down'. He was sent back to Chile but never stood trial.

Closer to home, and a little further down the results page, was Róisin McAliskey, who was wanted in Germany for questioning about a mortar attack on the British Army base at Osnabrück. She was pregnant when she was arrested and in frail mental health. According to her lawyer, extraditing her would be 'unjust and oppressive' and in the end (the evidence of any involvement in the attack was also frail) she didn't go. I wonder if for some of the soldiers at the Saville Inquiry the experience also felt unjust and oppressive.

From somewhere a little bell is sounding. In libraries even bells are hushed. It's six thirty and the library is closing. The children doing their homework left long ago to have their tea. It's just me, the girl with the tattooed legs, and the old fellow with his buses. He looks around as though surprised not to be in some oily depot, the lovely machines parked up for the night. The girl stands, stretches, pulls on her denim jacket. The light outside is tender. Cars pass, and a tractor hauling a trailer of cut grass. It might not be true that libraries are the haunts of lonely people but it feels that way tonight. I wish them, old man and pale girl, a night with no terrors, no hard hours. May it be so.

When I told Dad I was joining the army he was, for a moment or two, lost for words. I won't pretend I didn't find that satisfying. He had a manner to him, measured, thoughtful, controlled. He was a teacher for most of his adult life, though he started out at sixteen in Grandpa Rose's boot factory and shop in Langport (there's still a pair of hobnailed boots in the house with 'Rose's of Langport' on the inner sole). At twenty-five or thereabouts he went to a Quaker college up by Birmingham – Westhill? – and got himself a teaching diploma, started teaching at colleges and Workers' Educational Association centres, courses in all sorts from basic literacy to the history of dissenting. He loved being a teacher, felt it was his calling, but he was also proud of his apprenticeship in the boot trade, of beginning his working life stitching leather on a Singer sewing machine in a room over the river Parrot.

The day I spoke to him he was in the garden, down at the raised beds. It was Easter and he was putting in the seed potatoes. I went out and smoked a cigarette, watching him. He was busy and thirty yards away so didn't notice me. I'm not sure what he used to wear when he was younger (though I have seen a picture of him on one of the Aldermaston ban-the-bomb marches in a duffel coat and beret) but by the time I'm speaking of he'd settled on corduroys and checked shirts, the kind you buy in county town men's outfitters or those farmer's stores where, along with a new shirt, you can buy worming powder and axe shafts and lengths of chain. These clothes he would wear on all except the hottest days of summer when he would change into what looked to me like old-style hiking gear and there would be a pair of thin, strong-looking white legs in the gap between the bottom of his shorts and the tops of his socks. I think he was always glad to get back into the cords. He wore them year after year until they had the look of finely beaten metal, bronze or gold.

He knew nothing of what I was up to. I'd made sure of that. He left for work long before the post came so I didn't have to worry about his seeing the two or three letters the army sent as part of the joining process. My trip to the recruiting office in Bristol was done inside a day and needed no explanations. The only time I needed to lie was the two-day assessment in Winchester. I said I was going to a party in London and would stay with a friend. He didn't question it. I was nineteen. I had a job of sorts but so grimly menial neither of us pretended it needed to be taken seriously. He liked to be told if I wouldn't be sleeping or eating in the house. He didn't want to have the food wasted or not know if he could lock the house at night. Beyond that he was careful not to pry.

I wasn't – at least not then – in the habit of lying to him. Lying disappointed him, and I think that's much harder to deal with than anger. But what bothered me more was the prospect of going to the assessment and finding I didn't want to join after all, then coming home and being looked at like a boy who reaches for things without understanding what he's reaching for, who doesn't know his own mind. I expect I was also worried about flunking it. If there was going to be failure I wanted it to be private.

As it turned out the assessment days were a breeze. You must have done something along the same lines for the RAF so you'll know what I'm talking about. We were measured and weighed, read the letters on a chart, checked for rashes, flat feet, lice. We did an obstacle course and played tag. We sat tests of such simplicity I stumbled through the first wasting time looking for what wasn't there. Once I understood that the intention was to identify the genuinely illiterate and those boys who could not tell a rectangle from a square, I finished quickly and handed in my paper. We were shown films about the soldier's life (soldiers abseiling, soldiers at a shooting range, soldiers relaxing in the NAAFI). There were talks about the different trades we might learn. A scrappy boy with grey rings under his eyes wanted to know about the food. There will be plenty, they said, and when he wanted to know how many meals we would have each day, there was nervous laughter from the rest of us. I don't know whether he got in. I never saw him again.

A fortnight later a big buff envelope came with the crossed swords of the army at the top. I was congratulated. I was given my joining instructions, the date of my intake. There was a form to fill in and a Xeroxed sheet of what I should bring and what I was forbidden to bring (more than one change of civilian clothing, valuables, alcohol).

And then it was time to tell Dad. Dad the lifelong Quaker. Dad who, when he came of age in 1944, refused to be conscripted and was sent to do forestry work in Hampshire. (When he fell ill one time, the local doctor, a great patriot, refused to treat him.) His father, Grandpa Rose, was a conscientious objector in the first war and was locked up in Wormwood Scrubs. I think he was treated very roughly there. So I put it off, building my courage until that Easter Monday when I went out to the garden and smoked and watched him putting in the seed potatoes. The old fellows used to have the length of a boot between one potato and the next but we planted them closer and it never seemed to do any harm. For weeks before the planting we had egg boxes of potatoes chitting in the shed, pale shoots sprouting from things that looked like unwashed pebbles or clumps of soil. That still goes on. I still do it.

When at last he saw me he walked up the garden with the spade, frowned at the cigarette and asked if I'd help him finish off. His cheekbones and knuckles looked raw with the wind. I went down to the beds with him and we worked for an hour, earlies and main crop, heaping the earth over them, then giving the ground a good soak and putting up a net to stop the neighbourhood cats digging. I said, I'm joining the army. I spoke clearly so there would be no need to repeat it. And then my reward, if that was what it was, the three seconds in which not just Dad but the whole of that Easter garden was startled into silence.

To his credit he recovered his poise quickly enough. He knew right away that I was serious and that the moment needed to be met properly. He straightened himself, sniffed the sharpness of the air. When do you go? Three weeks. So soon? Yes. Officer or soldier? Soldier. Where? I told him the name of the town. He'd never heard of it. Nor had I a fortnight earlier. Your hair will need to be cut, he said. Do they do it for you? Yes, I said. I think so.

That was about it, for then. If I'd had him lost for words he, in his turn, left me dangling. It certainly wasn't indifference. He was never indifferent to me, never a cold man. And it was Quakerism too, of course. If I'd decided to join up then that, in the end, was a matter for my own conscience. Who was to say I wasn't being guided by my own inner teacher? That thought would have come to him very quickly. Nor did he complain, as he might justly have done, about my keeping him in the dark. He understood it, I think. He had the imagination for that.

What did your mum say when you announced you were joining the RAF? Did you get your three seconds? Evie was no friend of the military, or wasn't in the time I knew her. Did she try to talk you out of it? Was she disappointed? But I'm remembering her as a twenty-three-year-old! Ridiculous to think her ideas might not have changed by the time you were leaving school, that by then it would be anything other than your happiness that counted with her, not some old objection to uniforms and marching.

I kept out of Dad's way until dinner time. The evening meal was one we always sat down to together. Other meals could be missed or taken on the hoof but he liked us to eat dinner at the table in the kitchen (the same old table!). Sometimes he'd have a glass of cider with his food, and when I was of an age I joined him, a bottle of Sheppy's or Rich's split between the two of us. More often it was just water, poured from a jug. He wasn't a bad cook – not that I really knew the difference. We had a lot of sausages, a lot of mince, a lot of potatoes, plenty of green veg from the garden, cabbage mostly. There was always bread on the table, thick slices buttered and cut in half and laid on a white plate set between us. It may have been just as well he had a son rather than a daughter. I once watched you and Lorna eat a salad of flowers followed by slices of chocolate cake. No liver and mash for you two, no slabs of boiled gammon, though in the RAF your food must have been a bit plainer.

I've no idea what he cooked for us that night. He asked more questions. He'd had time to think about it and once or twice a kind of exasperation came through in his voice. He wanted me – as fathers do with sons – to be clear. At one point he said I was joining on a whim. There was some truth to that. It *was* a sort of whim. Why the army? I certainly hadn't been the sort of boy who longs to be a soldier. Like anyone else my age I'd watched a lot of war films and read a lot of comics where British soldiers knocked German heads together or rushed machine-gun nests. In Britain the Second World War didn't end until the 1970s. And I'd seen the recruiting films at the cinema between the trailers and the ads for local curry houses. 'Join the Professionals! If you've got it in you we'll bring it out.' They might have had some effect, I suppose.

But more important than any of that was a restlessness I knew I needed to do something with before it did something with me. I was a little afraid of myself. All through my teens I'd been carried along by moods I didn't have much control of. I did a lot of brooding. I had – no getting away from it – quite a lot of aggression in me. I was suspended from school at fifteen for taking one of those playground fights too far. I wasn't particularly big for my age but I was solidly built and I learnt quickly enough the way a fight goes. I wanted to leave school at sixteen. I asked Dad. He was very against it. I think later on he believed he'd made the wrong choice. I went back to do my A levels, switched schools halfway through the sixth form. My last year, I spent a lot of my time out in the fields. I'd walk for hours, never got tired. Sometimes I'd sit and read something. I might see a farmer, a fisherman, a dog-walker. Mostly I saw nobody. Nobody at the school seemed to notice I wasn't there. Needless to say I failed my exams. At the time I couldn't have cared less.

If I'd been brought up in a harbour town I might have gone to sea. I can even imagine, in a different time, shaving the top of my head and entering a monastery, getting up in the middle of the night to say my prayers. It's the appeal of handing over your life to strangers, doing something high-stakes, something you can't easily come back from. I wanted to throw my life in the air like a deck of cards! That's not the kind of thing you can say to your father or I didn't, at nineteen, think I could. I wouldn't have known how to have that conversation. And I was afraid that if I spoke too much, too openly, he would realise part of the reason for joining was to get away from the house and from him. I didn't want him to see that. I didn't in any way wish to hurt him. He had raised me, and mostly on his own, and whatever tensions had grown between us – inevitable tensions – I never forgot that or forgot to respect it. I had what you have not had: a father who took on without complaint the day-to-day business of tending a child. Later, when he was dying here at the house and my life had unravelled, I had the chance to do some tending of my own and perhaps to show that his example wasn't entirely wasted. It might have been too late by then. I don't know. It might have come too late.

The next day, or the one after, I gave in my notice at the place where I worked – a chicken 'processing plant' tucked away down a green lane, somewhere you could always get a job because nobody stayed for long. A coach used to collect us from the town centre. Nearly everybody I knew, boys and girls, worked there at some time or another.

In the killing rooms we dressed like trawler men expecting foul weather – boots, waterproofs, sou'westers. Water or blood or both ran off every surface. The management peered in at us through glass panels in the wall. The chickens entered the building upside down, their legs trapped in steel frames that moved along a rail suspended from the ceiling. A rotating blade cut their throats, though some of the birds, seeing what was coming, lifted their heads clear at the last moment. These were taken care of by a woman who stood all day with a knife in her hand, a rubber apron down to her boots. After they had bled out they were passed through a machine like one of those automatic shoe shiners they used to have in fancy hotels. That got rid of most of their feathers. Another machine, another blade, cut through their legs, dropping them from the metal frame onto a conveyor-belt that carried them into the gutting room. All this was done to the sound of Radio 1 – the monkey-chatter of the DJs, the jingles, the charts.

I worked my week's notice, then hung up my oilskins and went to see the pay clerk. He was about Dad's age, a stout, plain-looking man of the kind there seemed to be more of then than now. When I told him what I was going to do he shook my hand and said it was good to see a young man making something of himself. I was surprised at that! I liked it. And I liked even more the smiles of the typists (yes, all pay clerks were men, all typists women).

With my last wage packet in my pocket – twenty-seven quid – I walked out of the car park onto the lane and, though I had no hurry, I ran up it, the best part of a mile, to the bus stop on the main road. No one else was there. The trees were in their first green, the hedges full of blackthorn. I had to wait an hour for the bus but would cheerfully have waited half a day. And when it did come, a double-decker, the upper deck warm as a greenhouse, I leant into a corner and fell asleep, and in that way, swaying on an empty bus through the lanes, I finished a whole phase of my life.

In the town there were four or five to say goodbye to, boys and girls who, like me, had left school but not moved on to much. I don't recall many from our year going to university. A handful. Of the rest, one became articled to a local solicitor, one a plumber's apprentice, one went to work on his family farm. Tess did home economics at the college in Salisbury or Bath. One girl married within a week of leaving school and was pregnant by the autumn. No one joined the forces.

On my last night I gathered the old gang – Alfie Nichols, Tim and Debbie Levett, Colin Douel (who later married Tess), his brother Reg – and we sat on stools along the bar of the Crown, small-town boys and girls nicking each other's fags, flicking peanuts. Tess wasn't there. I can't remember why. It was a long time since we'd been together but we were good friends and I must have wished she'd been there too.

The idea, of course, was to get off our faces and we had a go but the mood wasn't quite right, as if it was all of us on the cusp of a journey, not just me, everyone's thoughts tugged back to the morning and the setting out. When the pub closed we went to the fields. We had some carry-outs and Alfie had some dope. He could be relied on for that. We sat on the bank above the weir where men and boys from the town have swum for generations (the women have their own place). We smoked, drank, talked of going into the water but didn't. At some point I sloped off with Debbie and there was some kissing at the side of a rhyne. It's not that we fancied each other so much but boys on their way to being soldiers must be kissed, and girls being left behind likewise. There was no harm in it. It was as if we'd sat and sung some old folk song.

Back at the house, a bit drunk, a bit stoned, but also, as I remember it, clear-headed from all that chill night air, I soft-footed through to the kitchen and saw, under a single light, a plate left out for me with a sandwich covered by a sheet of grease-proof paper. It was only then I felt what I'd been looking for all night, the full weight of what I was doing, what I was leaving. Who would do *that* for me again? Who would care if I came in hungry? Who would I be important to now? I was a bit shaken by it but it was too late for changes. Early the next morning Dad drove me in the old Citroën to the station at Bath. He came to the barrier with me and shook my hand. I forget what he said. What does anyone say at such a moment? Good luck, take care. I think now of how hard it was for him. These days, a parent might say something about love but not then, though love was as common and as rare as it is today when people end phone calls with a casual 'love you!' I don't know which way is better.

It was a long journey, or felt so to a boy who wasn't used to going far. London first, then across the city with my suitcase, one of those old cases heavy even when it's empty. Then a second train, north, out of King's Cross. At each station we stopped at, places I had never seen before, I would look out and wonder what would become of me if I got off *here*. Could a life be made anywhere? A place to sleep, then a job, a friend. Any of these unknown cities might do. And then, with a shock of nervous energy that must have rocked me in my seat, I realised we were on a slow curve of rail into the place where I was expected.

Maggie – writing is no cure for insomnia, though it is, I suppose, a use for it. When I started all this, still reeling from the letter, threads of panic in my chest, I wanted . . . what? To get in my side of the story before they got in theirs? One more, one last go at making sense of it all? I think for the last couple of years I'd almost given up on that, making sense of it, and was having a go at living. The letter changed all that. It was like hearing in the middle of the night some small sound – a shifting, a cracking – and knowing at once it's the noise of the house about to collapse. So I'm trying to get things down before the chimney comes through the ceiling, though I notice now how hard it is to say anything without saying everything. Words have shadowy roots tangled around the roots of other words. Pull up one and you pull up twenty more. It may be why I'm eight months late with my *Mill on the Floss* essay.

Goes without saying Carville and Co will want none of this. The roots of words! All that will just be seen as buying time, which it probably is. Unless it's a symptom and I'm losing it, going round the twist, gaga. My last HE attack was four years ago. I don't know exactly what I did but when I woke to myself I was sitting at the kitchen table naked as the day I was born, bruises on both knees and ash on my hands from the ash bin by the stove. Later, I found my clothes carefully folded on a shelf in the fridge. I can't say how likely another attack is. When it starts I won't know because the part that knows such things will be the part that's changing. I could be having an attack right now and this, these pages, just a record of madness.

Are you waiting for it? You've read some of the bumph. God knows I've piles of it here. I use it sometimes to light a fire. You'll have discussed it with Lorna. What to do, who does what. The numbers are on the whiteboard. You wrote them there. The unit in Bristol, my GP (not very sympathetic), Sarah Waterfall's number, Plant World.

Sickness would get me off the hook, of course. A man on a ventilator can't be expected to account for himself. He can't be shamed. In the meantime, for lack of a better plan, I'll go on as if I'm sane, as if with enough late nights I may stumble across the right arrangement of words. As if you'll care one way or the other. As if.

Four a.m.!

Around the lamp, two moths small as sand flies have been playing for hours.

I was feverish when I first woke and I almost called you. One thing being brave and nobly resigned when you feel well, quite another when you surface with your heart racing, pin-pricks of unidentified trouble in your guts. I went downstairs, drank a glass of water and came back to bed, watched the rain ploughing the window, dozed, and woke a second time with the sense that whatever it was had passed, for today at least.

In that second sleep I dreamt I had replied to Ambrose Carville's letter. I had the envelope in my hands, sealed, my writing on it, a stamp. What had I said? Even in the dream I didn't know and was mystified to have done it – replied – without having a clue what I had written. I even thought of trying to sleep again, find the envelope and steam it open with a dream kettle, discover my own mind. Because certainly I'm no closer to knowing what to do. I swing fifty times a day between all possible options, all wordings. I speak to him in my head, Ambrose Carville, and he speaks back in an accent like one of those Royal Ulster Constabulary characters I used to patrol with, men – the women too – sounding like they might be lay ministers accustomed to rolling out God's commandments to congregations who believed in the reality of Hell. They were not people to argue the toss with. I felt boyish in their company, though one time, sitting with an RUC sergeant in an RUC Land Rover (quite nice, as theirs had better armour than ours) I found myself talking about the Quakers and had the feeling, as the two of us looked down the length of some sad little Belfast street, he was adjusting his opinion of me. People often say religion had nothing to do with it, the Troubles, that it was all tribal – 'ethnic' we might call it now. I don't think that's quite right. There *was* religion, and deeply felt. The power of the priests on one side, and on the other, that stern, bare-hilltop facing into God the old settlers brought with them, people who were never sure that what they had they could hang on to, or that it was theirs at all.

In real life, rather than just the inside of my head, Carville might have a cheerful southern accent, so that everything he says could be taken as the beginning of a good story and a funny one. Or he may even be an Englishman and sound like one of those rosy-cheeked Etonians who run our country now. When, by the way, will we get over wanting to tug our forelocks for those people? Is there something wrong with us?

Last night, writing into the small hours (I heard the first bird, that brave first singer), I left myself on a train pulling into a small station in a town where my army life would begin. In that last minute before the train stopped I had some sharp worry I would get off and wait in the wrong place and be left behind, stranded, the boy who couldn't *quite* join the army, but I saw them all immediately, two men in uniform and a group in civvies a little further down the platform. The two in uniform were Wright and Darling. They ticked my name off the list and told me to wait with the others. There were about fifteen of us, some smoking, some talking, most just standing there, visibly on edge. We waited for another train to come in, another clutch of boys stepping off with their bags. Then we were walked across the car park to the coach. There was a roll call. As you answered your name, you boarded the coach. When we were all on, Wright and Darling stood at the front and introduced themselves. They were not fierce. There were no jokes about lambs to the slaughter. I remember being impressed at the way the sleeves of their shirts were rolled. Was there a regulation way of doing it? They were young men – I'd certainly call them young now – and it was hard to believe they'd ever had any life outside the army. They were upright, square-shouldered. They missed nothing. And if they were a little like robots they were also like dancers, men who had given themselves to a discipline that had made them exact and confident. They were what we hoped to be and I think we all had an instant crush on them. I may never have got over mine.

The camp was only a short drive away, a road between big flat fields, one of England's empty pockets, a landscape that was mostly sky. There was just enough time to smoke a cigarette and start on a second before we saw the signs, then the fence, then the barrier. We wiped portholes in the steamy windows and peered out. The barrier rose, the barrier fell. The coach drove on through a setting I would come to understand as typically military – everything nailed down, everything in good order, functional, slightly bleak, and all of it looking as though it could be dismantled tomorrow and moved somewhere else.

We swung to a stop between the flat horizon and a bunch of prefabs. Wright and Darling were on their feet at the front of the coach. We looked at them with terrible interest. They knew all, we knew nothing. When Darling spoke he seemed to wake us from our childhoods. We got out, dragged our luggage from the belly of the coach and did our best to form up in a straight line. That was when I really noticed who I was with. My intake. All physical types, including those you might think not much fitted to soldiering. Some were dressed in 'best' – cheap suits and kipper ties. Some in denim. Some in what looked like school uniform. There was a pair of skinheads in white shirts and DMs. There was a Pakistani lad with a smudge of moustache. One boy, ginger hair and freckles, looked on the point of tears. He disappeared a week after we started. I don't think I ever learnt his name. They came in one evening and cleared out his locker. No explanation given, none asked for.

There were eight in my room. Three from London, two of us from the West Country, a big fellow from Leeds, a Geordie called Bradley. The Asian lad was from somewhere in the Midlands. We called him Faz, though whether that was his name or just some version of it we could get our tongues around, I'm not sure. He was, by us and by the NCOs, routinely referred to as a Paki. If anyone had suggested there was anything racist about it we would have been surprised. We were part of Training Company A. Our room was in a hut opposite the guardhouse.

They cut our hair. Four chairs, four barbers with electric clippers. When it was my turn the barber asked how I'd like it and wheezed with laughter when I started to reply. He may have used that joke on everyone. It may never have got less funny. When we were done we went back to our rooms, sat on our beds and touched our scalps. We touched each other's scalps. I remember thinking how, without hair, people's eyes looked bigger. Now we were all skinheads, even Faz.

Our first lesson was on how to recognise and address NCOs and officers. Who was 'Sir' and who wasn't. How to salute, how to stand to attention. The second lesson, much harder, was how to organise our lockers. Corporal Darling used my kit and my locker for the demo, patting, doubling, piling, all the while accompanying himself with a monotone commentary on angles and creases. I was smug with the idea I wouldn't have to do it, he'd done it for me, but when he finished he picked everything up and scattered it on the bed and floor, treated me to one of those dead-eyed stares he used when he knew exactly what we were hoping to get away with.

They showed us how to bull our boots, how to use an iron, how to sew on a button. They soon picked out the weaker boys and stood over them, chivvying, mocking, though with a patience those boys might never have come across before. Beasting was certainly part of army life but I heard about it more than I saw it for myself. Perhaps I was just lucky.

Room cleaning, block duties, how to operate the washing-machines. Lectures on discipline, pay, care of equipment. We recited the oath of loyalty to the Queen, were fed it a sentence at a time. I, Stephen Rose, swear I will be loyal and bear true allegiance to Her Majesty Queen Elizabeth II, her heirs and successors.

What did it mean to us, loyalty to this woman on the postage stamps? Did I really think I was going to fight and die for Elizabeth II, her heirs and successors? But I liked the sound of us all making the same grand promise, chanting the same solemn words, crop-haired boys in a gym hall. It's something we've both done, Maggie! And perhaps it's for life, I don't know, they didn't say. We might still have to come if they call us. It will be announced over the radio perhaps. All those who took the oath of loyalty are to report immediately . . .

* * *

Our days were very simple, very full. Up at what we called stupid o'clock, tasks all day, always at least two hours of physical, plenty of food, and in the evening, when we weren't out in a field somewhere, an hour in the NAAFI watching telly, playing table football, drinking a can of beer (strict limits on how much you could have – there was no drunkenness on camp).

We learnt to use a compass, we learnt to judge distances. We did, of course, a lot of drill. We started to get fit. The chubby boys lost their softness, the skinny ones filled out. We used army slang – jankers, scoff, stag, tab – and all those acronyms the military is so fond of. We began to feel ourselves different from and better than those on the other side of the wire. And it suited me! I felt I'd made a good choice, that I'd been clever or lucky. I had no problem with the discipline. I liked how clear it made things. Play by the rules and you'll do well, break them and you'll be made to suffer. I must have wanted that for a long time – needed it without knowing. As for the other lads, I got along with them well enough. We laughed at each other's jokes. There were no fights, or no proper ones. Was I the same as them? Yes and no. Some came from places of real poverty and hardship. I'm not sure that sort of poverty even exists in this country any more. I hope not. They were marked by it – you could see it in their skin, their teeth. The education system had had nothing to do with them. Others, like me, were from middling families, boys who hadn't done well at school, who had lost their way a little. Several had had run-ins with the law, nothing serious, but they were in need of some straightening out and the army's a good place for that. In Spain one time, years after all of this (when I was on the far side of anybody's straightening out), I was sleeping off a bottle of wine in an olive grove somewhere south of Granada and woke to hear bells and saw the goatherd coming up the valley with his goats and dogs. One of the dogs was frisky, not doing its job, so the herdsman took hold of its ear and twisted. The dog didn't yelp, it screamed. I don't know how that ear didn't get torn right off its head, but the moment the man let go the dog jumped up to lick his hand. Well, the army wasn't quite like that but neither was it entirely different. We worked hard and tried not to get our ears twisted. At night we slept like the dead, dreamlessly.

The first shooting we did was with .22 rifles. I'd shot .22s before, out on the Levels, trying to get a rabbit or bring down a magpie. I'd never hit anything. Next, we had proper rifles, .303s, and picked off targets at the range while the weapons instructor, another corporal, a regimental shooting champion, the son, I think, of a Norfolk gamekeeper, walked behind us with a pool cue, correcting our posture with little touches and prods.

I'm not sure when we were introduced to the SLR. In memory it feels like we'd already been there several weeks but it must have been sooner than that. The whole training company was squeezed into a classroom one morning. The gun was on the table. Corporal Darling stood behind the table wearing his most serious face. This, he said, when we reached that pitch of silence he thought appropriate, is the British Army infantry soldier's principal weapon. You will, all of you, become expert in its use.

He gave us the weapon's history. I thought there was real emotion in his voice. The L1A1 self-loading rifle had been tested in combat in Korea, Borneo, Aden. In Vietnam it was used by Australian forces. It had, of course, been carried for years in Ireland (and was – though this wasn't mentioned – the weapon carried by the Paras in Derry on Bloody Sunday). A gas-operated semi-automatic with a magazine holding twenty rounds, accurate up to six hundred yards. He broke it open, field-dressed it and laid the parts along the table, pointing to them with the tip of a pencil. Magazine, bolt, bolt carrier, gas plug, gas piston, spring. We leant forward, craning our necks, mouthing the words. The SLR he was using was one of the old type with a wooden stock. It made it look more like a proper rifle. All the others I ever saw were manufactured with a type of black fibreglass or plastic, indestructible.

At the end of the talk – a kind of climax to it – he held up a single round between thumb and finger. This, he said (and how many times he must have said it) is a NATO 7.62 round. Steel jacket, lead core. A big round. A heavy round. A stopping round. The target, when hit, *will* fall. The target will not get up again . . .

We left that classroom jostling and swaggering, boys who believed themselves men because they had seen what they might do, the power they might have. I wish I could tell you I was the exception, less interested, more thoughtful, but it wouldn't be true. Depressing how strong it is, the pull of a weapon. It must always have been so. The flint knife, the bronze sword. In Belfast, patrolling day after day, a lot of that excitement wore off. All of it, really. The SLR is not a heavy rifle but anything you carry for hours becomes heavy. It was a tool, and one we had always to tend and keep with us. Even when we slept it was in a rack within hand's reach. As the gardener his rake, the plasterer his trowel. You must have done some shooting as part of your basic. I wonder what you made of it. Did you like it? The first time I fired an SLR on the range I got a black eye from the recoil. Another lad shattered one of the lenses in his glasses. I'd be happy never to see another gun in my life, of any sort. Even the sound of them puts me on edge. There's a farm not far from here where they shoot clays on Wednesday afternoons. I'm always glad when it's over.

Around the middle of our training we had three days' leave. I could have come home and I can't remember now why I didn't. Perhaps I felt the transformation wasn't complete. Instead, I went with the Geordie, Bradley, to some rundown little town on the coast near Middlesbrough. He had a big, cheerful family and they made no fuss about squeezing in another chair around the table. We went fishing off the docks, drank in a club where a drag queen was belting out 'We'll Meet Again' and all the old folk with their fags and industrial skin sang along. And Bradley had a sister, a green-eyed girl who liked my West Country voice as I liked her Geordie one. When it was time to leave she came along to the station with us. Bradley's dad gave us each a pound note to buy some beer and sandwiches on the train. I don't think he had money to spare. He shook hands with us and I made the girl laugh by shaking hands with her too. I wish I could remember her name. I hope things worked out for her.

Back at camp it was Bash week – day after day of runs, sometimes in full kit, sometimes with a medicine ball in our packs. We threw grenades. We charged with bayonets, *Dad's Army* style. We went up in a helicopter, a Wessex. They're astonishing machines.

Battle Camp was in Cumbria. I wouldn't want to do it in the depths of winter but we were there in good weather. MoD land, free of the plough, free of pesticides and the rest of it, is basically a nature reserve. Other than shelling and a lot of tanks and whatnot spilling around, the place had been left to itself for decades. A big area, perhaps twenty-five thousand acres. I saw kestrels, red squirrels, red deer. And I swear, one night while crouched in a fighting trench waiting to set out on one of those advance-to-contact exercises, I heard a wolf. Most likely, of course, the sort of wolf who joins the British Army and fancies himself a comedian, but out there, a place like that, you never know.

We were fitted with our No. 2 uniforms for passing out. (You told me your parade uniforms were called 'Best Blues'. I like that.) Drill intensified. Drill is the heart of it, isn't it? Hour upon hour on the square ('Turning, by numbers, about turn . . . one!'). It was the dog days of summer. The combines were at work in the big fields. The air was dusty. I had written to Dad giving him the date but saying I would understand if he couldn't make it, that it was a long way to travel and was, after all, just a parade. I wanted to make it easy for him not to come. I assumed the day would be awkward for him, offensive even, all that military pomp. I wrote late and didn't hear back, but when the day came and we marched out and swung round onto the square I saw him immediately. Taller than most, hatless, unmistakable. I felt such a rush of love for him I almost missed my step. We formed up, stood to attention, rigid, that transformed gaggle of boys from the railway station. There'd been a storm the day before, but the afternoon of the parade was faultless – or so I remember it. The full light of the parade ground, the slack flags, the swept blue stillness of the shadows around the buildings. The national anthem was played over the speakers, then the CO and some local lady dignitary with a hat like a liquorice allsort inspected us. I got a friendly nod from the CO, a motherly smile from the lady. Then a speech, partly for us, mostly for the families. Tradition, service, honour – not words I'm inclined to laugh at, then or now. Various awards were given out (not to me, I'm afraid, or my section). Then it was done. The RSM dismissed us, and the families, all those mums and dads and brothers and sisters we'd hardly known ourselves to be longing for, came forward in a colourful line and joined us. Dad shook my hand. You look very smart Stephen. Then, after a pause – I'm sure your mother would have thought so too.

Later on the CO stopped by. Comical to watch Dad in conversation with him, though they seemed to get on well enough, men of a similar age. The CO said I'd made a good impression. Something like that. Thought I'd make a good soldier. Of course, he must have said the same to everyone.

Maggie, I know I'm labouring this but I want you to know I was once someone others could speak well of. That I could do things without making a mess of them, and if you, through some play of time, could have been there, you too might have clapped and smiled and thought well of me.

But you were not at my passing-out parade, I was at yours, and made a very different sort of impression. Where was it? Buckinghamshire? As luck would have it the date fell bang in the middle of my living rough in the orchard, that time – about six months all told – when Tess came up with the tea and the socks. I'd lost my job repping for the agri company, going round the farms trying to sell fancy cattle feed. I'd put the company car into a ditch, twice. In fact, the second time I put it through a stout hedge, knocked myself senseless and came-to apparently floating over a silver field on a flight to the rising moon. The farmer pulled me out with his tractor. He wasn't very pleased about his hedge. They fired me the next Monday. It wasn't much of a job and I don't know how bothered I was to lose it. I had other worries, bigger ones, above all Dad, who was in the early stages of the cancer that killed him the following year. I can't remember if he'd had a diagnosis by then but he was losing weight, throwing up after meals, in pain. I was scared witless by the thought he would die before I was able to make myself decent in his eyes, that he would take his last breath knowing his son was living in a field and drinking himself into a stupor every day. (And if you're thinking how selfish that sounds, how my worry was what his illness meant for *me* rather than what he would have to suffer, then you're right, and this is exactly what makes drunks unbearable, first to others, then to themselves.)

Evie's letter was a bolt from the blue. I hadn't heard from her in years. I must have collected it from the house on one of those trips I made, usually in the dark, to get food or a change of clothes. Even in Somerset letters are not delivered to orchards. It was short, to the point, but not unfriendly. It explained where you were and what you were doing. It invited me to the parade. There was, at the end, a line or two of warning. I don't remember how she put it but the gist was that if I came I had to behave myself, that I must do nothing, absolutely nothing, to spoil the day.

At the time, I assumed the idea was all hers. Her idea, her gesture. You were more or less invisible to me. But tonight, writing this, it occurs to me that *you* might have said something, that perhaps the two of you sat down and thrashed it out, the pros and cons, and in the end settled on the letter, the invitation, the warning.

It felt, at first, impossible. How could I go and be among people, decent people, sober people? The risk was huge. But I understood that Evie was giving me a chance, probably the last, to be, as a parent, a degree or two above absolute zero. Not to go – I think in the end that scared me even more than going. It would have meant closing something off for ever. It would, I think, have meant despair, and what that leads to.

I should have told Dad, of course. He was still well enough to travel and I think he would have made the effort. No, I'm certain of it. But all I could think of was the two of us side by side on a long cross-country journey, a trip I knew I couldn't possibly make without alcohol. I regret it now more than I can tell you, that missed chance. I did you both a great disservice.

The day came. I put on the suit I'd worn as a rep, a cheap brown suit. I cleaned the mud off my boots with handfuls of grass. On the train I measured out my drinking with great care. A couple of bottles of wine – oh, the looks you get starting that second bottle at ten thirty in the morning! – then scalding coffee in the buffet car and ten minutes in the carriage toilets horrified by what I saw in the mirror, the clumsy shaving job, the wildness of my hair that no amount of damping down with the water that dribbled from the tap could put in order.

When I finally found the camp – I seemed to have crossed acres of bare countryside to get there – I was late and the sentry couldn't find my name on any lists. In my nervousness I said I was Maggie Rose's father. He scrolled down his screen, shook his head. It was the year after the Twin Towers in New York, and though I could hardly have fitted anyone's idea of an Islamic terrorist, security had become more than a formality, a return to those jittery days when the IRA were running campaigns on the mainland and bins disappeared from public places in case somebody left a bomb in one. I told him I was ex-services, gave my regiment, my service number. A call was made (Wait there, he said, pointing to where I was and meaning it). A woman arrived. I didn't recognise her rank, an officer certainly. I got your name right this time, and after several seconds of hesitation, of weighing me up, she escorted me onto the base, led me towards the music, left me at the back of the crowd. It wasn't a hot day but I was sweating heavily, deeply uncomfortable to find myself on military ground again. Actually, uncomfortable doesn't really do it justice. I was paranoid, close to losing control. On the train I had made a solemn vow to bring no alcohol to the parade but when I reached into a pocket of my raincoat I found two miniatures of Beefeater gin and I turned at once to where the world seemed emptiest and drained them both. It helped. That's one of the problems with drinking. Sometimes it works. The need is supplied. The confidence, the calm, the sense of having renewed your grip on things.

I tucked away the empties and moved around the edge of the crowd until I found a place for myself where I could see. You had a real band to march to, and not a bad one. I tried to find you but all those young faces looked the same, and the last time I'd seen you was when Evie brought you to the hospital in Yeovil. You were thirteen years old then. I'd been rushed in after collapsing in the foyer of quite a smart old pub in Wells, pretty much in the shadow of the cathedral. When they'd been able to get an address out of me I'd miraculously recalled your grandmother's house in Preston and gave that rather than the address here. God knows what they told Evie when they got hold of her. Did they say I was dying? Did she bring you because there wouldn't be another chance? Or was it simply there was no one to look after you that day? In fact, I wasn't dying, and by the time the two of you arrived I was on a general ward, rehydrated, flushed out, and feeling better than I had in a long while. A bit shaky but no tubes, no delirium. I got out of bed and put on a dressing-gown, perhaps just to demonstrate that I could. You stood very close to your mum the whole time. You looked and looked and looked, swallowing me with your eyes, the beast who bred you.

We went down to the hospital café. I hoped there'd be something nice for you, a delicious cake, but all the food in the cabinet looked like it had been nailed to a cross. You had a hot chocolate, Evie had tea. And she was heroic, keeping the chat going, lots of inconsequential stuff, snippets about your school, about some play you'd been in, the weather, the drive down. She wanted, I suppose, in some way to make it feel normal. She wanted you not to be frightened. She must have been exhausted. You spoke about ten words. I managed a few more. I found it hard to meet Evie's eyes. I thought she looked beautiful. I thought you looked beautiful. You wore something far more conventional than you wear now. I can remember a charm bracelet around one thin wrist. Your hair – undyed then! – was the colour of my own, not as curly as mine but with little waves and flicks, strong-looking, thick. I was, I understood perfectly, being visited by life. Life had descended to the underworld of the hospital café. And even though I couldn't follow you into the light that day – it wasn't that kind of story, it wasn't a TV show – and seeing you did not cure me, did not even keep me out of hospital, *something* shifted. And for you? What did you say to Evie on the long drive back north? Were you full of questions? Or did you pass the drive in silence, turning it over? Your interest, your disappointment, your anger. And did you then try to forget me? No one would blame you.

But how to pick out – seven, eight years later – that girl's face among the ranks of blue thirty yards away? I shaded my eyes, scanned faces. The band played 'The Dam Busters'. A lady NCO shouted commands. Starting to feel desperate – wrong base? wrong day? – I looked round at the crowd and almost immediately saw Evie in one of the temporary stands they'd put up. I followed her gaze, drew a line straight from her to you. I laughed out loud! Be grateful I didn't shout your name. You were standing at ease, your eyes shaded by the not very flattering headgear the girls had on. The band fell silent. The padre led us all in a prayer for Queen and country. Why is that nonsense so touching? Were my tears just gin? Then you were marching again, your white-gloved hands swinging. I could see they'd done a fine job with you. I know good marching from bad. The band followed you off the square and everybody starting clapping. For a minute – it may have been as long as two – I clapped like crazy and felt part of something normal and decent. I think it shocked me a little, how much I wanted it.

Evie came over. Even at a distance her expression might be described as mixed. There was a man with her. That was Ray, of course. They had the look of a well-worn couple. You've told me bits and pieces about him. He saw you grow up and to some extent you must have looked to him for fathering. I haven't asked you about that and I probably won't.

I shook hands with him when we were introduced. His accent, his brogue, took me aback, startled me. I was so used to the obsessive circling of the past that their being together, Evie and an Irishman, seemed somehow aimed at me. Then he said something sweet about you, something carefully pitched, not parental, not possessive, something meant to reassure me, and I liked him very much for that.

And suddenly you were with us. The sky had darkened and the shoulders of your uniform were dotted with rain. Ray had one of those golfing umbrellas and the three of you stood beneath it. You were high still from the parade. You hugged your mother. Gorgeous to see how it was between you, the deep back-country of love. And you looked at me then, cautious, but choosing to be kind. Perhaps, on such an occasion, nothing else is really possible. I wanted to tell you about my own parade, to make everyone laugh at the story of Dad, the great conchie, chatting politely with the CO, as if army life was entirely familiar to him, entirely agreeable. But I said nothing. The gin had worn off, the rain was getting heavier. I peered down at my boots, struck dumb by the enormity of my failures, the apparent impossibility of recovering any of what had been lost, principally, of course, you, my daughter. I left shortly afterwards, said I had to make the train. For a moment I thought you might hold out your white-gloved hand. I'm glad you didn't. It would have been lovely to touch you – even now we rarely touch and each time we do I take nothing for granted – but the formality of a handshake would have burnt me. Instead I shook Ray's hand again and he played along with it. Us as old mates. And Evie – Evie at the end said simply, Go safely, Stephen. For which now, in thought, I thank her.

You drove me to Bath today, roof down and faster than felt entirely wise. You were showing off! I loved it. I wanted to roar things into the wind-stream but I was afraid of what might come out. Afraid, too, of any suggestion of intoxication. Wind-drunk is still, in some way, drunk.

When you picked me up from the house you were annoyed about something. It might just have been the chore of driving your father to a hospital appointment. But the morning was so lovely, and the driving so enjoyable – whole stretches of road free from tractors or those squat lorries loaded with quarry stone that seem to travel in convoys, unpassable – you forgot yourself, whatever had bothered you, and we sped on like characters in a picture book, not talking much – too noisy for that – but revelling in it, our flight past fields of rape seed and almost-ripe wheat.

You dropped me at the hospital and headed into the city. I went in by the new entrance, a big well-lit area with a pharmacy, a newsagent, somewhere to get coffee. Today there was an art exhibition, paintings of nature, quite a lot of sunsets. A strong belief now in the power of art to heal. Does it? And there were men and women, just a little older than myself with bright sashes on, holding collecting tins a little shyly. I took the lift to the third floor, then down broad corridors to the swing doors of the Liver Unit where Dr Rauch, like a small business on the up, has opened a new clinic. It's slightly quicker to get to than the infirmary in Bristol and I prefer to come to Bath. I have no real history in Bath. That's not true of Bristol.

There were four others in the waiting area, all versions of myself – men in their fifties or sixties, blotchy faces, fidgety hands. They glanced at me, then sank back into the old problem of trying to work out how they had come to be there at all, this place that the nurses must call the boozers' clinic, the drunks' clinic.

As a child I must have had some days off school. I remember chickenpox, measles. I remember on one or two occasions having special sickroom food – Bovril tea and toast. But I don't recall ever seeing the doctor or taking any kind of medicine beyond aspirin or the blackcurrant syrup Granny Rose made for coughs and colds. If you were ill you waited it out. Doctors might make things worse. As for hospitals, they were for operations or for the very old who would die soon. The first time I ever went inside a hospital I was in Ireland and even then it wasn't for me. I was escorting a soldier who'd been hit in the face by a half-brick during a riot. A good shot by someone or a lucky one. I couldn't tell you what the riot was about, what specifically. The year before had been the year of the hunger strikes when ten Republican prisoners starved themselves to death over a demand for political status, a demand our prime minister, rightly or wrongly, refused. There were riots every day then and a lot of people got into the habit. For some of the youngsters who took part there was, without a doubt, an element of fun in lobbing things at the British Army. Tie a scarf around your face, let rip, perhaps see yourself on the evening news.

As it happens, I saw that soldier get hit. The brick dropped him but a moment later he was on his feet again. In shock the body runs itself, and for a few seconds he was hollow, all his me-and-mine shattered by the impact. Then he was back and it was the insult more than the pain he seemed to feel most. He tore off his helmet and flung it to the ground in a rage. By the time we reached him he was ready to keel over again. The side of his face was swelling, he was spitting blood, eyes starting to roll. There was an ambulance on stand-by and we loaded him into the back of it. I was told to go with him – I think I was just the nearest available squaddie – and swapped my SLR for a Browning pistol, glad to be getting out of the way of bricks and bottles but hoping very much we didn't get stopped at an IRA checkpoint, have some kind of stand-off at the ambulance door. I didn't know how well I'd manage that. What I'd be ready to do.

At the hospital I handed him over to an RAMC medic. He was OK in the end. His nose was never going to be quite straight again and he had fewer teeth but he was back on patrol in a week. Soldiers were expected to put up with that kind of thing. You didn't get a medal for it. You didn't get counselling. You got the minimum medical attention necessary and were passed fit the moment you looked even vaguely capable of performing your duties. I hung around at the hospital, scrounged some tea, and got a lift back to the riot in the same ambulance. It was raining by then and people were going home. It's less fun rioting in the rain.

Not that it was just bored boys and young men having a party. I wouldn't want you to get that idea. There was real anger too, and more than that, a passionate hating I'd never come across before. One figure, one memory, holds all of that for me. A woman – were we on the Falls? – wanting to bring the sky down on our heads. Her crow voice, the fluency of her insults. Her invention! Had she been offered a cup of our hearts' blood she would have drunk it gladly. Other women, neighbours I suppose, were holding her back. She was a great thrashing fish in their arms. She wanted to get at us – soldiers armed with rifles and clubs! She spat at us. It fell short, but something reached us. And though later we said things about her, called her the usual names, laughed, she had rattled us. It was like her body was the break in something, a tear in the fabric, and through it poured the whole force of a river. Every time her friends slackened their grip she came at us again, this roaring woman. I'll tell you, twenty more like her deployed in line might have driven the whole British Army into the sea.

I sometimes think of telling Dr Rauch this stuff. Is it not relevant? I haven't even spoken to her about how it ended, my time in Ireland, in the army. It's not like I wasn't drinking before. It's just that after Ireland it was completely different. I was different. The purpose was different. But Emilia Rauch has strict limits to her interest. That might be part of her training. Stay with the body and leave the rest alone. Or it may be that as a canny woman she knows it anyway. Not the details but the gist of it, the broad pattern. It may be that all our stories – the stories of the men in the waiting area – are essentially the same.

When my turn came I followed her into the consulting room and took my place on the chair. It was still warm from her last patient, a magnificent-looking disaster of a man, big and craggy, who I'd imagined as some old sea captain, a man who even in the centre of Bath would be lashed by the waves. She sat at the side of the desk – doctors don't sit behind desks any more. She looked tired.

We went through the usual list of questions. Symptoms, appetite, bowels, sleep patterns etc. She asked me to undo the top of my trousers then palpated my liver and abdomen. She washed her hands and tapped away at the computer while I looked at the odd collection of things on the wall – some postcards that came perhaps from grateful patients, a poster in which the liver was a cartoon character finding out what was good for it and what was not. Another poster – very uncomfortable to look at – showed a child watching a man, her father presumably, pouring himself a drink. The caption below asked who pays the price.

I did the flicker test. Have I explained that one to you? It's new or quite new. I think I started doing it about a year ago. There's a machine that sits on the desk. I peer into it as if I was going to look at slides or watch a little film. What I see is a flickering light. When the light becomes steady, when I judge it has, I push a button. This is to help predict the likelihood of another hepatic encephalopathy attack. Today she made me do it twice. I asked her how I'd done and she said the second time I was within the normal range. I should, of course, before the session finished, have told her I was coming off my medication, weaning myself off it, but I didn't feel ready to have her look at me in that deep way she has when she's concerned, have those pale eyes settle on mine until I started spouting justifications, jabbering. All that really needs to be said is that I've had enough of the stuff, and I want to find out where I am without it, what the baseline is. I'll tell her next time.

From the consulting room I went to the nurses' station to have blood taken. I hadn't seen this nurse before. She asked if I thought I might faint from the needle. I promised I wouldn't, though as usual I kept my eyes away from what she was doing. She sent me off with a bent arm and a plaster. The joy of stepping outside again! The relief! One day – and this is just realism, I'm not wallowing – I'll go in and stay in, my mortal remains trolleyed off to the part of the hospital that has no art on the walls. But not today. And isn't that the point? Not today.

I set off for town, past the golf course, then through the Circus where the foreign students from the language schools were sitting under the trees, and the open-top tourist buses followed each other around. I had something in mind, part of your birthday present, and I worked my way over to Walcot Street and a shop I thought might have what I was looking for. It did. An old wooden frame, lacquered and much polished by time. Because this was Bath – and even Walcot Street is a smart street now – it cost twice what it should have done, but I was just happy to have found it. In fact, I must have been a little high from the walk, the sunshine, my escape from the hospital. I started telling the man who worked there what I was going to put in the frame. I was babbling. Perhaps he thought I'd had a drink. Bath is full of drunks. It's probably why Dr Rauch chose it for her new clinic.

When I reached our meeting place, the café in the bookshop, you were already there and had, I think, been there some time. You were reading, lost in it, an empty coffee cup on the table in front of you. I stood by the door a moment to watch you turn a page, then – some snagging of gazes – I noticed the young man two tables down also busy watching you, though more secretly. I suppose I could have told him not to waste his time but maybe he wasn't. Looking can be its own reward. It doesn't have to lead anywhere.

When I sat with you, you showed me the things in your bags, the cardigan and dress from Oxfam, the vintage buttons from the Heart Foundation, a summer scarf from the hospice shop. You showed me the label in the dress, and when I didn't understand you explained it was a top-end brand for which people buying new pay foolish money. You asked what I had in my bag and I touched my nose and said you'd have to be patient. I caught the young man looking at *me* then. He didn't want me there. I wasn't part of the daydream he'd been enjoying. I grinned at him and he looked down at his tray, frowning. I felt nothing but tenderness for him.

The day is behind us now. The night is clear but still has some warmth. I have the window open and the usual collection of small visitors around the lamp, fellow life forms. There's a group in India – or so the radio told me the other week – the Jains, who try to keep themselves from harming any living thing. They will not swat a mosquito. Imagine it! And imagine the whole world like that – as John Lennon invited us to in that song, which for some reason I've never much liked. Lennon was murdered during my first winter in the army. I was stationed in Aldershot, December 1980.

Maggie, the letter remains unanswered. That's been my response. Silence. Four and a half weeks now. And it feels like the silence is a thread becoming taut. I thought I could just keep it unwinding until October. Then the moment would come and pass and they would move on to something else. There's no shortage of something else. My part would not be forgotten, of course, I'm not pretending that. There are people who could never forget it. But the moment for *speaking* would pass. Their lives would go on as before. Mine too. Is that so bad? Nothing would get any worse. The worst has already happened.

In some weird way the letter in the bookshelf has become the centre of the house. Staying silent, doing nothing, gets harder every day, and we're still a week from the beginning of August.

There's not enough thread for two more months of silence. There's not nearly enough. Nor do I believe they will simply leave me alone. The phone rang in the early morning a few days back, somewhere around seven. I lay in bed listening to it and wondering, Do they have my number? Any half-competent investigator could find it. I'm not ex-directory. They could just look it up on the internet, the web.

Should I take the letter out of the house? Would that help? Take it out to the shed and let the mice have a go at it? I'll do it in the morning, perhaps. I can't bring myself to do it now, creep across the sleeping garden with a letter I'm going to hide. I don't think I want to witness myself doing that. It's the kind of thing I might have done with a skinful of booze in me. If I start doing stuff like that when I'm sober . . .

But today was a glory, wasn't it? For an hour or two we were as close as we've ever been. And I don't believe that's just me, my wanting it so much. I think you might have said something like that to Lorna when you got home. Is the bridge between us a little stronger tonight? Did we make progress? Let's say that we did. Let's say that today we won. Anyway, it's what I'm going to take into sleep with me. The hour, the bridge, the possibility. I'm going to put down my pen, switch off the lamp and be hopeful.

I found the picture in the back of an exercise book. I think, some years ago now, I intended to keep a diary. It might have been something suggested by an alcohol counsellor. I've seen several. Keep track of life, moments of weakness, of temptation. Well, nothing came of it. All the pages are blank, apart from three addresses, two in Bristol, one in London, that mean nothing to me now. But in the back of it, floating free as I fanned the pages, the unlooked-for treasure. A photograph – colour! – of Evie and me standing together on Clifton suspension bridge. There's no date but I'd guess it was a short while before you appeared in the world. It may be – it's just possible – that Evie was already pregnant and it's a picture of all of us. All three.

We have our faces towards the city. The background, Leigh Woods, looks quite rural. Hard to say what time of year exactly. Both of us in dark coats, mine a donkey jacket, your mother's a longer coat that ends at the narrow white border of the photograph. The colours are soft, either because that's how the day was, one of those fogs over the river that never quite clears, or because time has done something to the dyes in the paper, a fade, a leaching. If she *is* pregnant, newly pregnant, then it could be January or February 1984. Her coat is buttoned but unbelted. Hard to know what it might have been hiding, how much of you.

My hair is almost down to my shoulders! Thick hair, Jim Morrison style. Put the photo beside the two or three I have of myself in the army and it's hard to make the connection, to see the soldier and the young man on the bridge as the same person. That, of course, was the point. The squaddie hidden from sight, buried in a new identity. New clothes, new hair, new life.

Our expressions? I've studied them through a magnifying glass. But what a tease photography is! It has no depths. Through the glass I saw us less and the photograph more. I learnt nothing.

I didn't immediately think of giving the picture to you. I'm still far from sure it's the right thing to do, that it will please you. What will I seem to be saying? I was going to ask Lorna's advice – she would know – but I haven't had the chance and now I'm almost out of time. I suppose I'd been hoping the picture would be the beginning of a conversation, the two of us sitting down with a big pot of tea, you asking questions, me giving back long, looping answers, the full nine yards. A creation story, though not one they'd want to teach in Sunday school. Will it ever happen? This pretty scene, father and daughter side by side, our mugs steaming? I don't think I can depend on it, not now. So I'll put some of it down here, add a little to this pile of paper I meant to be no more than a few pages.

When I met Evie I'd only been back from Belfast a couple of months. I'd moved in with Dad again. I can only guess at how that was for him, his son back home but changed into a kind of stranger. He fed me, gave me money when I was skint, did not disturb me if I stayed in bed all day or scold me when I came home drunk. He made gentle investigations about Ireland. He knew the outline of the story, had been given that by my commanding officer in Belfast but he never pressed me for a first-hand account, nor did I ever offer one.

The only thing he got wrong – and it hardly ranks as a mistake – was to persuade me one Sunday to go to the meeting with him. We went. I found the silence there close to unbearable. Out on the Levels, that was one thing – and even there it threatened in its own way – but the silence of a roomful of men and women, a weighted silence, purposeful, I wasn't ready for that. Did I tremble? If so, there might have been some who imagined I was about to stand and break into tongues, though the voices in my head belonged firmly to this world and nowhere else. Some I could identify. Most seemed simply to live in the air and be pulled in by my breathing. Shouts, gibberish, obscenities. The voice I was most afraid to hear was my own – or that version of it, very calm, very mad, which had all the secrets, or would pretend to. I knew that voice was the most dangerous.

I didn't go again and Dad didn't suggest it. We muddled along for another couple of weeks. Then one morning in early November I couldn't do it any more. I packed a rucksack, propped a note on the kitchen table, stole some money from the housekeeping tin and walked away. I went through the town but if anyone saw me with my boots and pack they thought better of stopping me and asking questions. I dare say I had a certain look that discouraged it.

As I came past Glastonbury I climbed the Tor. It had fewer of the dreadlocks-and-pendulum brigade on it in those days but we all knew it was an important place, a place of power. At the top I looked out over miles of small fields and orchards, glints of water, ramshackle farms. The Mendips one way, the Quantocks the other. A sea light in the west over Burnham. The loveliness of it almost took the legs from under me. This was what I was taking leave of – I had no thought of ever returning. My life, at twenty-two, was spoilt. I could see no prospect of happiness or even peace of mind. I did not believe there was anyone or anything that could help me. Had there been some quick way to bring things to a close up there I might, in that moment, have taken it. But you cannot throw yourself off the Tor. You would roll like an egg. So I trudged down again, like the soldiers in the song, and took the road out, lost myself in walking, threaded the heart of the old apple country all the way to Shepton.

At the edge of Shepton there's a lay-by near a roundabout. It's still there. I stood at one end of it and stuck out a thumb. Most of what passed was no use to me – local farmers peering out of ancient Defenders wondering if they knew my face, women in little cars with children and shopping – but after an hour and a couple of sharp rain showers a van pulled in, an old ambulance. You could still read the word along the side where the lettering had been peeled off. It had a mushroom-top stove pipe through the roof as if it ran on steam. The driver was a young man, one of those rare types you would have to call beautiful. His name was Marcus and he wore a hat with a pheasant's tail-feather in it. He said they were going to Bristol, and though I had not thought of going there, had not been in the city since my visit to the recruiting office, I pulled open the rear doors and climbed in. Three boys and a girl back there, sitting in air as heavy and scented as someone's dream of Arabian nights. The boy opposite passed me the bottle of Natch he'd been drinking from. The boy next to him was rolling one of those joints you need half a packet of Rizlas to make, a skill I never really mastered. The girl looked about fourteen but was nearer seventeen. Not, in case you're wondering, your mother, but she knew Evie and later claimed that the moment she saw me she thought of her. Perhaps she did, though she was a sweet, slightly addled girl, who liked to say what she imagined people wanted to hear. Her name was Jenna.

By the time we reached Bristol, the city under a cold, clear sky, that last hour before the streetlights come on, a day that had begun with so little hope of anything good was ending quite differently. That's how it is, isn't it? This strange walking into the unknown. It's certainly how it is when we're young. On the drive they had learnt enough about me to realise I was a stranger to the city. Marcus, the least stoned, listening from up front, had probably worked out quite a lot more. I was invited back. There was going to be a party. I could doss the night. There was plenty of room.

Their house – not theirs at all of course – was on a hill near the gorge and the suspension bridge, part of a terrace of tall Georgian or Regency buildings that looked over the city and the river and breathed a cleaner air. It had been a squat for years. No one seemed sure of when that had started or who had been the first there. I got the notion the original tribe had moved on and I was with those who had come later, had come, perhaps, exactly as I had, to stay for a night that became two that became many.

Into the big bare rooms they had brought what they needed. Mattresses on the floor, a scatter of oil heaters, furniture scavenged from skips. The area, the city, was being smartened up.

Despite – or because of – three million unemployed and the shutting down of industry after industry, the country was starting to make money for the first time in years. For those who understood the character of the time it was the start of a heady period in which the world we'd grown up in faded from sight, like a tramp steamer into the fog. People – some – started going to wine bars rather than pubs. They holidayed in Greece, skied in winter, drove German sports cars. Above all, they invested in property – old houses in a doze for fifty years were gutted and fitted out with fancy kitchens and walk-in wardrobes. Rich pickings for skip divers! In the hall of the squat was a grandfather clock that a bunch of them had carried off one night from under the builders' rubble. It didn't work, was riddled with worm, but it was impressive, a treasure. There was a claw-foot bath in the astonishingly cold bathroom, and in the drawing room a leather sofa that looked like it had once been in a gentlemen's club. None of this made the house comfortable or in any way smart, but it made it possible. It was a firetrap and a health hazard, particularly the kitchen, but I had spent months in a converted factory in Belfast where conditions were equally bare and a great deal more crowded. And in Bristol, no one was going to rouse me out of bed and send me onto streets where some of the houses had their lower storeys painted white, the better to show us up to a sniper.

I signed on, collected the dole, went with Marcus and his equally beautiful black girlfriend, Nina, to buy sacks of rice from the Asian supermarket, or paraffin from the garage or great bags of knobbly veg from the hippie co-op at the bottom of the hill. There was always music, reggae or punk, depending on the mood of the house, what people had been taking. When you came down to the kitchen in the morning – or whatever time it was you came down, midday, mid-afternoon – there might be someone making pancakes while someone else sorted psilocybin mushrooms on the kitchen table and a third was busy trying to fix a toaster or a portable TV they'd found. There was no trouble in those first months, though later things started to go wrong, people using harder drugs, people whose lives were genuinely chaotic or who had the kind of problems that needed more shape and order than the squat could provide.

At the weekends there were parties that began on Friday afternoon and might still be going on Monday morning. Some invention went into these. Flags, banners, Chinese lanterns. One thing we never seemed short of was candles, so that the house, even without a party, was lit as it would have been when it was new, though what the first inhabitants would have made of us, whether on stormy nights they ever dreamt of us, boys with Mohican haircuts, girls with pink hair, Heaven knows. We would have seemed like sprites, members of a barbarian tribe from AD 40. But maybe I'm underestimating them. Not far from where we were, a short walk, Romantic poets and their friends had sucked nitrous oxide out of silk bags and got as high as we ever did. Did more with it too.

For the weekend before Christmas we decided to put on something special. A tree had been foraged from somewhere – Leigh Woods? – and brought back in the ambulance. We put it up in the hall. I doubt there was a tree in Bristol decorated with more excitement or care. Dope fiends, cider heads, people who, like me, had walked out, runaways, none of us had left our childhoods far behind. We lit fires in the rooms and rigged up speakers, and after dark we spilt out into the garden, with its sundial, its glassless greenhouse and exploded armchairs. Snow had been forecast and, sure enough, an hour or two after dark, it started. It fell orange through the light of the streetlamps and settled blue in the garden. We danced in it, flung it at each other, lay down blinking and stuck out our tongues to taste it. As the pubs closed more people showed up. You never had to worry about that. The parties at the house were known across the city. No one waited for an invitation, they just came trudging up the hill with their baccy, their pills, their bottles of carry-out, their new friend. And suddenly, in the midst of it there was a pale girl with a fringe of dark hair and big loop earrings, holding out her hands to the snow, laughing, but steadier than most of us, more contained, more watchful. Maybe just more sober.

I saw her through veils of snow and the light of lanterns and then she was gone. Was she inside? Had she left? I searched for her in rooms jammed with dancing bodies, went up and down staircases that had so many people on them it was like wading a river. I gave up – you were *that* close to not existing! – but at some hour of the night or early morning I went into the garden again. The snow had stopped. Half a dozen people were standing out there, probably passing round a joint or just cooling off. Marcus, Nina, Jenna, a couple of others I didn't know. And Evie, in her black coat and scarf. We didn't speak – I'm sure we didn't speak at all that night – but we had noticed each other and that was enough. You wake to somebody. You feel them wake to you. The first movement is so small.

The next day when I went down to the kitchen she was sitting at the table rolling a cigarette. The kitchen, the whole house, was in that state of advanced chaos only human beings can create. Everything had become an ashtray, every glass with a couple of dog-ends floating in the dregs. I was still enough of a soldier to be slightly scandalised by such scenes, could never quite get used to them, could all too easily imagine the arrival of Wright and Darling.

The house was quiet. People were in their cider dreams or had gone home or followed the party – imagine it like a ball rolled by dung beetles – to another squat across the city. I sat at the table, facing her. She asked my name, I asked hers. I was troubled at first by the thought she had stayed the night *with* someone. Had she come with a boyfriend? Had she found one? Then I felt sure she had not. Some instinct, something in the way she had been sitting alone in the kitchen, poised and complete. She smoked her cigarette. We spoke in low voices, watched each other slyly. By the time we got up to take a walk, had found our coats and stepped out into the trodden snow, everything important had been decided. Stephen was with Evie and Evie was with Stephen. Or that's how I remember it. At the time it might have felt a good deal more uncertain than that. I expect it did.

We slipped and slithered our way down the hill, reached the docks, the river, the grey water. In our walking, the glitter of snow light, I was freer to notice things about her. The seriousness and steadiness of her gaze, her talent for frowns, the way laughter seemed to surprise her and leave her thoughtful for a moment, pleased. And I noticed other things too. Don't worry, I won't labour them! The scatter of freckles over her nose, the velvet of her eyebrows, her legs, strong-looking and shapely in winter tights below the little denim skirt. Her voice, of course! That almost more than anything. The north-country vowels, whole words flattened like nail heads. Did it put me in mind of Bradley's green-eyed sister, that first leave from camp? It wasn't quite the same accent but it might have worked the same charm. Anyway, it's a voice that won't have changed much. It will be much clearer in your head than mine.

She told me about her parents, their harsh religion, the way it shaped everything. A whole community that seemed to be spying on each other. No alcohol in the house, no coffee, no make-up, the flesh distrusted. I told her about the Quakers. I expect I tried to make it sound the same. Luckily, she didn't seem to know much about the Quakers, how little they give to kick against. She told me that at sixteen she broke free, played truant from school for two years, took up smoking, took up drinking – took up boys too, I think, though she didn't mention that. But the real rebellion lay in thinking the forbidden things. She became a reader – a proper one – something, if I've managed it at all, I only learnt to do later, in prison first of all, and then again after Dad died when I read for hours every day the books up here in the study as a way of keeping some sort of conversation going with him. But your mother was in a different league. She read the municipal library dry and at eighteen strolled back into school to take her A levels, passed them and went to Oxford . . .

Oxford *University*?

Yeah, she said. It's full of working-class northern girls. Didn't you know?

She asked if I'd been to uni. I said I'd been in the army. I said it as casually as I could, as if the army was my excuse for not going to Oxford. But Evie was the first person in Bristol I'd told about it, the other life, and it came out with a weight that disturbed us both.

We went on in silence, past old cranes that had not worked in years and warehouses that were either empty or being turned into something else, restaurants, offices, an arts centre. I could feel her thinking about it, turning it over. I had enough sense or good instinct to let her do so. A rooted dislike of all things military was pretty standard then among the young, particularly the kind you'd find partying in the house on the hill. The military was nuclear weapons and mindless square-bashing. It was old colonels telling you to get your hair cut. It was reactionary and deeply uncool. Also, to many educated and left-leaning people, people like Evie, it was a repressive colonial presence in Northern Ireland. There were no Troops Out posters in the squat but I'd seen them around the city. There was one in the wholefood store, a cartoon showing Great Britain with a truncheon raised over the head of Ireland.

In the end she might have decided to see my joining the army as a version of her rejection of a religious upbringing. Or she simply decided I was worth taking a chance on, despite my unfortunate history. She didn't say anything. She glanced up at me, unreadably, then took my hand, just reached for it as if a moment earlier she had let it drop. What could be simpler? But to me it was like some thrilling trick of the high trapeze, in which, with a puff of chalk dust, she caught me at the very last instant before I fell to where no safety net was strung. And that sense of being saved lasted a surprisingly long time – months rather than weeks. I don't know who else could have done it or done it so well. She took my hand and held it as we walked. Many grander things since have counted for far less.

There was some kissing that night (the shadows outside a pub), but it was another two or three weeks before we became lovers in the sense most people use the word. Logistical problems mostly. The squat offered no real privacy and Evie was sharing a place off the Gloucester Road with three other girls. In the end she must have persuaded them all to go out and stay out for a while. I remember the two of us sitting in her bedroom and having an attack of shyness. The more clothes we took off the more formal we became. We might have ended up sitting naked on the bed and shaking hands but a bottle was found and we took it under the covers with us, dived under them laughing like children.

I heard on the radio the other day someone reading excerpts from Richard Burton's diaries. He – you may or may not know – was an actor who married, twice, the film star Elizabeth Taylor. One thing he wrote that made me grin was that her beauty was beyond the dreams of pornography. Your mother certainly seemed that way to me, and at the risk of making you wince I think it's worth your knowing that we were a good match, a good fit, and when you were made, whatever night or lazy afternoon that was, you were made in the heart of a fire and no cooler place.

When we met, she was writing things, had ambitions in that direction, though it was always very private. I once saw a pile of notebooks on the bedroom floor but it would have been more than my life was worth to peep into them. To make money she drove for an all-female taxi company called Cagney and Lacey, named after a pair of women detectives in an American TV show. I made money selling dope. Not a charming thing to hear about your father, though it seems a trivial enough matter now. Everything, as they say, is relative. I worked with Marcus, not that much actual work was involved. Blocks of resin arrived, sometimes off ships in Avonmouth. We cut it up with heated craft knives, weighed it out on kitchen scales and bagged it up in polythene. We sold mostly to regular customers. We weren't standing around on street corners. We weren't 'pushing'. On a good week we could bring in a hundred quid, sometimes more. Smart money for the time (in the army I'd got about forty pounds a week after deductions, plus a pound a day danger money while serving in Northern Ireland). Evie and I started looking for our own place, and at the beginning of the summer, sometime between the arrest of the serial killer Dennis Nilsen and the Tory election landslide, we moved into a one-bedroom flat in a little crescent of eighteenth-century houses not far from the house on the hill, quite a smart area, high up on the side of the gorge, but also bedsit land, lots of students, and behind fancy front doors a lot of genteel single ladies living off cobwebs and fresh air.

The flat was furnished but we got rid of the bed and splashed out on a new one from Habitat. We put up red velvet curtains, big paper and wire lampshades, laid Afghan rugs over the mushroom-coloured carpets. Evie filled all the shelves with her books, and when she ran out of space she built more shelves with planks and house bricks. She put her Georgia O'Keeffe posters on the wall, put on the mantelpiece a framed photograph of someone I thought must be a grandfather or great-grandfather but who turned out to be the Irish poet W. B. Yeats. When she saw how little I had, not much more than the rucksack I'd arrived with, she laughed, then hugged me as if I was some poor orphan child.

My experience of living with people was my life with Dad, my life in the army, my life in the squat. None of these prepared me for life with Evie. In the squat I'd picked up some bad habits, and when I saw how these wound her up I dropped back a level to what I'd been taught as a soldier, everything buffed and scrubbed to within an inch of its life. This at least she found funny. Not that Evie was always easy to share with. Who is? She'd leave a glass or mug exactly where she'd finished with it and that was where it stayed until I picked it up. She'd go out to buy food and come back with books. She'd spend half a day and all the hot water washing her hair, leave the bathroom light on and the taps dribbling. And she had her black moods, which she might or might not have left behind her by the time you were growing up. I worried at first they were to do with me but later decided they were a staring back into the past, at the difficulty of finding herself the child of crazy parents, though it was about this time that her parents came to their senses. Religion can be a sort of drunkenness. Her mother sent her a long letter, apologising. Evie read it out to me one morning and I wish now I could remember what her mother wrote, the words she found.

She once threw a glass at me! It missed and smashed on the wall behind, left a dent in the plaster. We were probably off our faces when that happened, or on our way to it. The local pub was two minutes' walk and there was always plenty of drink in the house, small brown bottles of barley wine for Evie, anything for me. But if I'm making it sound like our time together was just a muddle, and a bad-tempered one at that, then I'm giving you the wrong impression. For most of it we were very loving, children who have built a den in the woods and sit in it holding hands determined not to go home until the whole village is out searching.

Sometimes she did twelve-hour shifts in the taxis, night shifts, coming home in the morning and flopping onto the bed, just lying there in her clothes, too tired to undress. More than once I put her to bed when she was in that state. Marcus and I quietly expanded our business. We no longer dealt only in dope. We had other things, lighter and more profitable. Not heroin. You have my word on that. Or if Marcus did he kept it away from me. Like Evie he was university-educated, knew I wasn't and was kind enough never to point it out. Unlike Evie he was officer class – his father had actually been one, some smart cavalry regiment – and in the background there was a big house and family money, none of which he wanted much to do with. We drove around the city in his white Datsun Cherry, listening to Weather Report and Keith Jarrett. We made stops, deliveries. It occurs to me now that I was, among other things, the muscle. Security. By the time we were dealing he knew I'd been in the army and he might have believed I'd be useful in a fight. Certainly I'd had unarmed combat training, both as part of basic and later at Tin City when we were preparing for Ireland. And the drinking hadn't yet made much of an impact, not physically. Incredible what you can do to a young body and still expect it to get out of bed in the morning. If we were less robust we might learn caution sooner.

When the warm weather came we hauled up the old sash windows in the flat. There was a green in front of the house, a communal space, raggedy and nicely hidden from the main road, the big world. Neighbours came out, spread rugs. Someone built a barbecue. Someone strung a cable of lights between the trees. On the longest day a celebration began, a rolling festival of summer, not as drug-fuelled as things used to be at the squat but equally improvised, equally free of any formal organisation, equally unmilitary.

Among our neighbours I don't remember anyone who worked regular hours in an office. I remember herbalists, sculptors, makers of bespoke furniture. The man who lived below us built instruments out of what he salvaged around the city. The girls upstairs said they were beauty therapists but Evie was convinced they were on the game. There was a scatter of young children, a big grey wolfhound called Gandalf. There was always music, and most of it played rather than coming out of a machine.

We made friends. We fitted in. We were liked! The whole summer was one long dusk at the side of a fire, talking and drinking. More than once we woke up in the dew, our heads pillowed on unmown grass. Nobody thought about the future – or that was my impression. It's probably wrong. Other stuff creeps in, you can't help it. And there's rent to be paid to people who haven't sat up all night holding an impromptu moon-viewing party, who don't much care for those who have.

It teased me. Perhaps I was OK after all. Perhaps I was going to be OK. You press your face to another's skin and for a moment that's all there is, the comfort of it. This was what I'd left home for, stolen housekeeping in my pocket. To be comforted, to find some version of myself I could live with. But, of course, nothing had gone away – where would it go? – and as if to balance things out, the pleasures of the new life, I began to dream again of Belfast. In the dreams I patrolled up Ross Street, Albert Street, Milford Street, through the Divis flats (where once a crisps packet full of human shit was dropped on me from a gangway). These dreams were exhausting. They were very physical. One thing that I've noticed about dreams is the way you have to stay with whatever strange task they set you. You have to keep trying to close the drawer that will not close. You have to keep looking for the missing part of your weapon, the part without which it cannot be used, is useless. You have to keep doing these things until you wake and lie there, strung between worlds, your jaw aching, your T-shirt stuck to your chest with sweat.

Then there was the drip-drip of news from Ireland. In August that year a young man called Thomas Reilly was shot by an army patrol. There had been what the news report called an altercation. Reilly ran and was shot in the back. His death had more coverage than most because he was a roadie for an all-girl band well known at the time, regularly on *Top of the Pops*. Later, the girls went to his funeral in Belfast and that brought the cameras out. The soldier was charged with murder and convicted. It's only quite recently I found out he was released after serving a couple of years and went back into the army. I believe that happened more than once.

Because of the dreams I drank more. Because of the drinking my mental state deteriorated. Evie was worried. She saw it, but at twenty-three or -four she had her hands full trying to make sense of her own life. I have never, then or now, thought she in any way let me down. She asked – asked many times – what it was, this thing that would not let me be, that in different ways frightened us both. She asked very kindly, holding my hand, and once or twice she asked in a mood of pure frustration. Just *tell* me! But I could not speak about it. There was a stone in my mouth.

I set the bed on fire! Our expensive Habitat bed. Fell asleep, or passed out, a lit cigarette between my fingers. Oh, I got the full northern wrath then. You must have had it once or twice. Impressive, isn't it? God knows she had cause. Anyway, I knew I had to do better or risk losing her, and about a week after the fire I took the stone from my mouth and spoke.

We had been in the pub since it opened in the evening and had got ourselves an armful of carry-outs before the last bell. In the flat we sat on the floor, rolled cigarettes, opened cans. I'm pretty sure there was a little bottle of gin there too. We were, as they say, on a mission. I don't remember how it started, whether she asked again or I just set off, moved, in all senses, by the spirit. I became aware of myself speaking, heard the names – certain people, certain streets. Was this 'full disclosure'? I think I intended it to be. And how close it still was then! I was talking about the events of the previous summer. I spoke, I drank. I wanted her to understand the thousand things that had surrounded the moment. To understand the army, to understand Ireland, to understand me – none of which I understood much about myself.

In truth, I don't know to this day how far I got with it. I remember the litter of tins on the floor, my mouth burnt from gin and tobacco. I was trying to show her my shame. Hard enough to show your love. To show your shame? And if I did say it, the point of the story, that part they'll want in BT2, the only part they'll want, Evie was in no condition to make sense of it. Drunk for a penny, dead drunk for tuppence. She was sick as a dog that night and swore off the booze for two or three weeks afterwards. I waited a few days for her to say something. When she didn't I took it as a sign. I made no second attempt. Whatever was going on with me I would manage it privately. There was no need to burden anyone else. I would attend to it in the dark, my secret illness. I stopped looking at newspapers. We didn't have a television. And I was more careful with my drinking, more private, more cunning. Things got better for a while.

The summer ended and the sash windows came down. The string of lights was unhooked and coiled. Next summer – so we told each other, neighbour meeting neighbour on the stairs – it would all happen again. Even better! The leaves slid off the trees and lay shining on the green. We had Calor Gas heaters in the flat. It gave the place a gassy smell we covered up with joss sticks.

And then, on a winter's night, icy air in crowns around the street lamps, you enter the story. Or that's the first I knew of you. Evie had known for a while but had kept it to herself. I should have noticed things. My mind was elsewhere. When she did tell me, there was no build-up, nothing to warn me. We were in the kitchen, and once again either side of a table from each other as we were at the beginning. She said everything plainly. No drama and no tears. For her, of course, it was a truth without limits. She had crossed the threshold. She watched me – watched rather than listened – and I gave myself away in the very first moment, betrayed myself with a hesitation that reassurances later in bed could not repair. But it wasn't just selfishness. It wasn't even not wanting a child with her. It was just so far off my radar! Anyone less ready for fatherhood than that young man, that ex-squaddie and small-time dealer who answered to my name, would be hard to imagine. A father was a man like my own. Steady, predictable, living a principled life. Someone with dignity. I could see so little good in myself, almost nothing apart from whatever it was Evie still loved.

From that night on – or this is how I remember it – a gap opened between us. She changed. How could it be otherwise? You, her unborn, must at all costs and at all times be protected. I think she reverted to some old battle-mode, something that had worked in her guerrilla war with her parents. As for me, I would have to earn my place, and with deeds rather than words. She stopped smoking, she drank very little (the occasional bottle of Guinness she thought of as a medicine). She spent more time in the company of women, particularly the older women at the taxi company, Cagney and Lacey. They guarded her. They gave her advice. Some of the advice must have been about me and I suspect it had the character of a warning.

The first person I told about it was Marcus. He laughed, shook his head, bought me a drink. He teased me a little. I'm sure he could see what a mess it was. I didn't tell Dad. I could guess pretty much what he would say. I didn't want advice. I didn't believe advice would help, and I was probably right about that.

Well, life has a way of offering its own solutions. Three days after speaking to Marcus we were coming out of a club called the Mandrake when half a dozen plain-clothes police surrounded us, handcuffed us and put us in the back of a car. They had been watching us for months. They had photographs. The Datsun was full of not very well hidden gear including, under the spare tyre, a half-kilo bag of heroin. I still don't know if the police put it there. Police in the 1980s were very capable of such a move. I never got the chance to speak to Marcus about it. They kept us apart from the beginning. At my interviews I was impressed by how much they knew about me. They knew I'd been a soldier, knew the regiment. They knew about the squat. They knew about Evie (though not that she was pregnant). I waited for them to mention Belfast, to drop onto the table the statements I'd made to the Military Police and the RUC. When they didn't I wondered if the army was protecting me. Later, thinking it over – I had a lot of time to do that – I decided it was a case of not finding what you had no reason to look for. Would it have made any difference at the trial? And if so, in what direction?

I was refused bail and kept on remand at Horfield in north Bristol. After the trial and the sentencing I was sent to Shepton Mallet, the old prison down by the cider factory. A certain symmetry in being sent there, the town where the old ambulance had stopped for me. I saw Evie every week when I was in Horfield but it was harder for her to get to Shepton. She used to drive herself out in the taxi, and on visiting days I'd look out through the mesh of the big window on the upper floor of the wing, hoping to see a car with the Cagney and Lacey logo on the door (I never did). The three-year sentence had shocked her. I, on the other hand, was almost calm. Prison was not so different from the army. More dead time, a slightly higher proportion of nut-jobs for company, but ex-squaddies – there were several of us in there – probably do better than most.

The last time she came was in late July. I think that's right. She was so heavy with you that you might have been born on the floor of the visiting room. She wore no make-up and had the look of someone who has cried all the tears they have in them. She said she was going back north. She would stay with her mother (they'd become friends again). It was all arranged, it was all for the best. She needed to be practical, to think of the child. To think of you.

Does love always die publicly? Or not love – I still loved her – but the hope love brings? The visiting room of an old HM Prison is an unforgiving place to let go of someone. Notices and warnings on the wall, the reek of disinfectant, the constant presence of the officers. I think we were brave that day, Evie especially. I think the last thing we did was smile at each other. I felt, as she left, I would never see her again, which was almost true.

After visits, prisoners are supposed to be watched more closely. It's the classic time people try to harm themselves. I don't know if I was watched. I remember sitting out the night on my bunk, though whatever I experienced then I can no longer find it. Perhaps I told myself I was better off alone. Less to worry about, less to be disappointed by. Just do your time, put life on hold. Stuff like that. The little lies.

I had regular visits from Dad. These were not as difficult as you might imagine. His own father had been in prison! And he himself had worked in labour gangs during the war where he was treated in much the same way as a prisoner. He encouraged me to read, and though the library at Shepton was not one of the greats it had a few treasures. I read *Robinson Crusoe.* I read *Far from the Madding Crowd.* I started to write poetry! I wrote it on little squares of paper that later I either burnt or tore into pieces small enough to flush. I didn't want there to be a cell search and some screw to find poetry under the mattress. In half an hour the whole wing would have known about it.

I was released at the end of February 1986 having served twenty-two months of my sentence. I was given my clothes back. I was given some money (fifteen quid?). Among my very few possessions when I passed through the gate was a photograph of you that Evie had sent. That picture, I'm afraid, has fallen through some crack in the universe and is lost. It showed you as a baby on a bed, an adult bed. You were wearing one of those all-in-one baby suits. Evie herself was not in the picture, which I thought told its own story, though a simpler explanation is that she was the one taking the photograph. No selfies in 1986.

Dad would have collected me and taken me home but I kept the date of my release from him. I misled him. I didn't want to go to the house. Other than Dad himself there was nothing there for me. I walked into Shepton town centre and went into the nearest pub. I think they were used to it, men in their first hour of freedom. We must have had a certain look, all of us drawing the money to pay for a drink from a brown HM Government envelope. I didn't follow your mother up north. You know that, of course. I could have made other arrangements, ways to stay in touch, to show some interest, give some support. Again, you know I did not and it's nothing I can change now. All I'll say in my defence is that I knew my downward flight was far from over. It may not be over yet. None of this is what the poet called recollections in tranquillity.

I'll go down and wrap your present now, give the frame and the glass a last polish. If it turns out to be a mistake, something clumsy, you can just set it aside and we need never mention it again. But everyone, I think, needs to know something about their beginnings, and that picture, Maggie, that boy and girl on the bridge, that's yours.

When I got down to Plant World today only Debbie was in the office. She was sitting there without her wig. What's left of her hair is cut short, about half an inch. The bald patches are oddly shaped. One swirl of hairless skin on the back of her head looks like a question mark. I don't know why she chose to go wigless today. Perhaps because Tim was away, or because the day was close, and to wear a wig – basically a hat made from a stranger's hair – was more trouble than it was worth. I would have walked past but she called me in. She had the computer open at one of the orchid chat-room sites, one her brother uses, and she pointed out his moniker – Brutal Dreamer. How's that for a name? And who would have guessed it of Tim Levett? What did he mean by such a name? For surely he meant something.

The exchanges on the site are slightly comical if you're not part of that world. 'Nice dendrobe!' etc. We sat together and chuckled subversively. She knew where all the most absurd postings were. By the time we were interrupted by Radko asking if a customer could have a tray of pink pelargoniums for a fiver she was wiping away tears of laughter. I hope it did her some good. I'm fond of her.

Tim had left a list of jobs for me. Some maintenance on the trolleys, some pricing (we have cheap gumboots at the moment if you fancy a pair), some dead-heading of the tea roses. Summer darkens, fills in. That's how it feels to me. A blue sky in August is not like a blue sky in May or June.

Then into the orchid house to do some repotting. I have to trim the roots. As much below as above, says Tim, which sounds like something the old alchemists might have come out with. And he insists I use sharp, clean secateurs. I had the good pair today, made in Japan, where they know a thing or two about sharp blades.

I have decided, with my not-very-generous five-per-cent staff discount, to get an orchid for you. I think you're more of a girl for cornflowers but I have my eye on one of the slipper orchids. They have striped or mottled petals, often flower in winter, need a little extra care but are worth it. If nothing else, it will take some of the weight off the photograph. I was in the process of choosing one when Annie Fuller showed up again. I had the unkind thought that she sits over in Shrubs where you can see who comes and goes in the hothouse. I fear I might have bared my teeth a little at her Hello Stephen, the trouble she took to sound surprised at finding me there. As I'm guessing you've never been into Fuller's Funerals, let me tell you that Annie is a well-built woman. Can the word 'buxom' be used without sounding ridiculous? Well, that's what she is and she was making the most of it today with a close-fitting short-sleeved blouse. She said she wanted to brighten up her office, by which she means, of course, the funeral parlour. I showed her things. We discussed colour and from colour went on to the language of flowers. In her line of work it must be no trivial matter. Chrysanthemums versus lilies, roses versus carnations. In the end I sold her a purple moth and a white one and she thanked me for my help. The number of an undertaker is not one of those we have on the board in the kitchen but I'd prefer, when the time comes, if you'd use the Co-op people. It's not that I think she's a necrophiliac but I can't help feeling choosy about who sees me after I'm dead, who stands over me. And the Co-op did a good job with Dad. They're probably cheaper too.

Home at teatime, I padded around in my overalls, moving without much purpose from one sun-warmed room to another. The radio was on in the kitchen. Lots of chatter about the London riots, Broken Britain etc. Predictable responses from the usual suspects. I turned it off and let the house fill with silence, my own head likewise, at least for a few moments. Then I realised I had not thought of what to wear tomorrow for your party. I know you and Lorna will be dressed to the nines, and suddenly I wanted something decent to wear, smart, and I went upstairs and started rummaging through drawers, inspecting shirts, sniffing them. I put a couple out on the bed, then went on to the landing and opened the big wardrobe looking for a jacket. The soft breath of that old wardrobe! It's a piece of not very fancy Victorian furniture that was once in the house at Langport and may have absorbed the waterlogged air of that place. But what it really smells of is time. To breathe it in – a sweet feeling, but also vastly sad. Life as a kind of cloud, an afternoon shadow on the wall. It rocked me for a moment. I forgot what I was about and seemed to travel somewhere before waking to myself again, an old ape peering into a box. The best of Dad's jackets are in there still, but from about the age of eighteen or nineteen my back and shoulders were broader than his. I don't know why I keep them. Among my own stuff was only one I thought would stand up to close inspection. The others, despite the cedar moth balls, have been nibbled at. That made the choosing easier.

The photograph is wrapped in green crêpe paper and waiting on the hall table in a bag. The orchid – *Paphiopedilum Maudiae*, a beauty – has a ribbon round the pot that Debbie tied for me. I also bought a card at Plant World (apple trees in blossom) and have signed it 'Much love, Stephen'. It took me half an hour to come up with that. I considered many small variations. Saying more, saying less. It's hard all this. If I had married, perhaps my wife would advise me. If I'd married Evie, or Tess, or one of the other two or three I became close to over the years. Or Annie Fuller? I can imagine her becoming intensely interested in you. And if I had a wife you would have someone to ask about *me*, what I'm thinking, what I'm up to, if I'm taking my meds. But the chances of my marrying now are about the same as my becoming a member of the British National Party. So we must deal with each other directly, without intermediaries, without anyone to translate us. Easier said than done, eh?

The last party I went to was three, maybe four years ago. It was a Quaker thing, Sarah Waterfall's seventy-fifth birthday, so not a wild affair. It was in the big garden of her very nice house and I was sitting on a bench under a walnut tree, sipping a glass of home-made lemonade. My hands were shaking badly and at some point it occurred to me I might be about to collapse, that what I saw and heard might be the very last things I would see and hear. I don't think I was particularly frightened but I couldn't make up my mind whether I should try to get someone's attention or just slump over on the bench and let them deal with it later, couldn't decide what would be easier or more correct. In the end it began to rain – a cloudburst – and in the shifting about, the carrying in of chairs and plates of sandwiches, I managed to slip away, get home in time to have my crisis in private.

I like to think I've come a long way since then, that there's no need to fear a replay. Let's hope I'm right. I have a jacket, a shirt. I have ironed a crease into my trousers and will, before bed, clean my shoes. A tie? There's a couple of Dad's in the wardrobe and you never need to worry about another man's tie fitting. There's a dark red one with WEA in gold thread, and one with little elephants on it that must have been given to him by someone who didn't know him at all. But wearing a tie I think I'd look like a committee member of the local bowls club – or someone trying to pass for that, a roguish antiques dealer type making a lunge for respectability. So, no tie. I'll wash my hair in the morning, try to tame it a little. And I'll brave the shaving mirror (the regular side rather than the one that magnifies), get to work with the little scissors and snip away at the hairs that grow where I think no hair should. My practice trimming the orchid roots should help. Let's see if I can do it without spilling blood.

Things certainly started out well. Night rain gave way to a morning of streaky sunlight. By ten it was warm and we strolled together, you, me and Lorna, to the meeting house. When I was a boy, Sundays in this town were dead. Now they're quite busy. People on the move, lots of the shops open, cafés doing brunch.

It was a good turn-out for the meeting. The weather helped with that. Ronald Hamm, the Durbyfields, Sarah Waterfall, Ned Clarke, Tess, the Carters, and a couple up from the Exeter meeting. The building, full, could hold a hundred of us. Were there ever so many? Now, double figures are good. I've never seen more than twenty, other than at a funeral.

It was warm in there, wasn't it? A couple of flies buzzing round the windows. A wood pigeon cooing on the roof. Some meetings – you've been to enough now to know this – are restless. Shuffling backsides and shuffling feet, half the folk there with a cough or some crimp in themselves they need to keep stretching out. But today there was a sense of our listening together. You could imagine an antenna, a dowsing rod, rising through the roof and up, up, up into the belly of space. At one point I fancied I could feel your heart, the rhythm of it like a wingbeat travelling through your shoulder into mine. And later I raised my eyes and met Tess's gaze, held it very easily, was held by it, no self-consciousness on either side. That's what happens at the best meetings. A shrugging-off of the social weight. I'm not saying we quite manage to become naked souls but we move a little in that direction.

No one stood to speak, nobody picked up the radio burst of the divine, but it didn't feel like failure, and when Sarah brought things to a close and we all shook hands, people looked satisfied, as if they had found today what they came for, more or less.

Then into your car and off to Glastonbury. I had your presents in a big bag from the Spar. I was unsure of the correct time to give them to you – I didn't want to just thrust a bag at you – and at the Silk Shed, while you were in the Ladies, I asked Lorna and she said there was going to be a present table and I should put them there once the party started. Yes. Good. I was glad of it. You would look at the presents in your own time and not have to be watched while doing so.

The two of you tied on aprons and set to, laying the tables with crockery you've picked up in auctions and car-boot sales. I asked if I could help and you said, very honestly, that it was easier for the two of you to do it. You knew where everything was and what needed to be done. I was sent to sit at a table by the window, given tea, then left alone to watch you both, you with your new haircut, short as a boy's, and Lorna with hair the kind of red that never appeared in nature, each of you sporting a pink triangle tattoo on the underside of your right forearm, there – so you explained when I first saw it – in honour of the gay men and women (mostly men?) in the Nazi camps who were marked out by the wearing of a piece of pink cloth. That, surely, is a victory of sorts. Old symbols of oppression worn with defiance while those who oppressed are dust and yellow bones. Is your generation going to be the one that gets this right? Who takes people for who they are rather than what they do in bed or how they speak to God or the colour of their skin? Unlikely, I suppose, and you and Lorna can no more stand in for an entire generation than the kids who tore up part of London last week and ran through the streets with looted TVs. But I don't hear the kind of stuff I would have heard once (and heard from 'respectable' people). The casual racism, the sexism, the Irish jokes. Things I might have come out with myself – things I *did* come out with. It hasn't all gone away, I know that. It hasn't even all gone away from me, from my thinking, but there's less of it, a lot less, and that feels like progress.

Your friends started to arrive, coming through the door in ones or twos, sounding the little shop bell. Some of the women looked as though they had just come off the stage of an opera. For all I know some of them had. The men seemed gentle and well groomed. People smiled at me, though might have wondered how I fitted into the picture. One girl, with an accent that suggested she was one of your home-town friends, strolled over and asked if I was your dad. When I said I was, she stayed for a while to chat. Had I grown up in Glastonbury? No, not quite. A town nearby. I wondered how well she knew you, how much of your history. Tempting to ask her things, ordinary stuff about you as a girl, but I was stupidly reluctant to make my ignorance so obvious. What could it have mattered? If she *did* grow up with you she knows the score. My absence would be no news to her. Well, I missed my chance. We chatted about the Silk Shed, we talked about the legend of King Arthur. She said she thought you were very happy down here. Even smiled at me as if I might have had something to do with that. A nice girl. Big, amused eyes. Chocolate-coloured nails. You'll know who I'm talking about.

Tea was served. Also cocktails. I read their names from the blackboard over the bar. The Somerset Leveller, Kiss of the Spider Woman, the Alibi (crushed raspberries stirred through a vodka martini). I've said before that it doesn't bother me to see people drink. The desire for it still lives in me. That won't change. But it's in an isolation cell, a poor goatish thing that withers but cannot quite die. And the drinking in the Silk Shed was a very playful variety. Serious drinkers don't trouble themselves with raspberries, crushed or otherwise. I noticed the volume in the room getting louder. I noticed faces, the women's particularly, getting a little redder. Nothing more than that.

The present table was heaped! Looks like you'll be unwrapping for a week at least. I took my bag over and found a little space for my gifts. (Fabulous orchid, said one of the gayest of the gay young men, who I'd seen arrive with his boyfriend, the boyfriend carrying a handsome cockerel in a cage, the bird seemingly quite used to it, happy to play his part. This is well out of my range.)

Then the little incident, the one I suppose I have to think of as unfortunate because of the impression it must have created, the possible embarrassment to you. There was something in the inside pocket of my jacket. I had been vaguely aware of it all day. Now, sitting back at my window table I reached in and took it out, a scratched blue plastic case about the size of my palm. I knew immediately what it was. Dad's dentures case. But what was it doing in the pocket of my jacket? When had I last worn the jacket? Dad's funeral? Was that possible? I was, of course, drunk at the funeral, was seen drunk by the mourners and handled as people handle a drunk, one who's out in public, who must be contained. But why would I have taken his dentures with me? The only other person who could have put them in the jacket is Gracie Passmore, the hospice nurse who, a few days before Dad died, persuaded him to let his teeth come out and stay out. Poor Dad! Without his teeth his face was like a tent missing its ridge pole. She might have slipped them into the pocket to get them out of his sight but it's far more likely that I took them with me as a kind of charm, a splinter of the True Cross. If I think about it hard enough I can picture myself doing it, though that's not quite the same as remembering.

I opened the case. By then, two or three of your guests were looking on. They might have imagined you'd arranged a magic show and this was its strange beginning. The dentures, off-pink, off-white, seemed unharmed by their years out of the light, still serviceable, still with some bite left in them. They're made of something indestructible, a sort of acrylic. Grandpa Rose had a set he showed me when I was a little boy, the plates made of a material called vulcanite, a hardened rubber with a deep red colour, like uncooked beef. Anyway, aware of some stirring of interest around me, I held the teeth out for people to see. My father's teeth, I said. I just found them in my pocket. Wow, said the girl with the ring through her eyebrow. The young man beside her looked as if I was showing him the freshly severed head of something. He might never have seen dentures before. I started to tell them about dentistry in the 1950s (and 60s?). How common it was to have all your teeth out, the trouble it saved, the money. And no one thought it ugly or freakish. Teeth were for film stars. Everyone else kept them in a glass by the bed. Some wit among my audience suggested we should feed them. Someone else – that lad with the bleached hair – said they could be recycled, which I believe they can. One girl asked where Dad was and if he wouldn't be missing his teeth.

I was trying to decide whether to push on with my explanations or snap the case shut – show's over, folks – when Lorna appeared. I saw her eyes flicker towards the glass on the table, half full of Somerset Leveller. Hers, I said, smiling at the girl with the eyebrow ring. I know, said Lorna, and put an arm round my shoulders. I think Lorna likes me. Does she? For your sake, perhaps. I also think she would be very fierce if she reckoned I was any threat to you, your happiness.

I put the teeth away. My audience drifted off. The cock crowed! People went over to see what it was up to. I think it had been let out of its cage and was free-ranging around the Silk Shed feeding on cake crumbs. Ten minutes later your Buddhist friend, Nagamudra, came up, squatted by the side of the table and said if I'd had enough he had his van outside and was at my disposal. He put it like that. Did Lorna send him? If so, he was a good choice. I remembered him helping with the renovations when you were setting the place up, someone who could do a bit of wiring, a bit of plastering, knew where to find old tiles, a sheet of zinc for the bar top. How old is he? (And why am I so interested in people's ages?) My guess is we're about the same, though he looks at least ten years younger. I was glad to see him. A likeable man, clear-eyed. A good advert for Buddhism.

I went to find you to say goodbye. You were standing with a gang in the middle of the room, laughing fit to burst. I've no idea what the story was, but your face, the unguardedness of that laughter, made me want to laugh too. I wished you a happy birthday again. You thanked me for coming, thanked me for the presents, though I knew you hadn't opened them yet. Then you went on tiptoe to kiss my cheek. I never know when you're going to do that so am never quite ready for it. Sometimes at the end of a visit, sometimes not. Sometimes it's Lorna who kisses me and you take your cue from her. The first time – do you remember it too? – was a couple of months after you moved down, your first winter here. You and Lorna came for supper. I had spent the entire day preparing a perfectly simple meal. I baked bread. I lit two fires. An hour before you arrived I was cleaning the windows with newspaper and vinegar even though it was too dark to see if I was doing a decent job. I had not written out a list of things to talk about but I had considered it. No need, of course, for a list of things we shouldn't talk about. I remember how good Lorna was, playing for us the part Evie had played in the hospital that day, keeping the chat going, telling stories about her old job at the Gatwick immigration centre. It was good material. I was full of admiration for her. She'd been through something hard and come out, as far as I could see, intact. Later on – you were both high on love and the excitement of a new life – I was given a little insight into the online dating world. And didn't Lorna hint I might try it? I don't know how serious she was. Then, when you were leaving – it wasn't late, not much after ten – the three of us in the hall, you two buttoning your coats and nothing left to say or do, you put your hand on my arm and kissed me. It was all very swift and with no meaningful glance to follow, everything hidden in the bustle of leaving. A couple of seconds later I was alone in the hall and am not ashamed to say I wept. In the days that followed I was careful to instruct myself that your kiss was not forgiveness. Well, that was fine. I wasn't asking for that. But it said *something*. It said, at the very least, I don't despise you. It said, We can have something between us. It was, I think, permission, which is better than forgiveness, more practical, more interested in the future than the past.

*   *   *

Nagamudra brought his van round to the front of the Silk Shed – does he think there's something wrong with my legs? – and we set off. The van smelt of paint and timber and, I don't know, something like grout. I liked it. It was like being in someone's workshop, which I suppose, in a way, I was. On the drive I started quizzing him about Buddhism. We compared silences. I described what we do at meetings. He talked about the silence of meditation. It turns out that the difference is they're not waiting for anyone or anything to speak. But if it did? I asked.

He said it could only be his own voice.

I said that we imagine God can get inside a voice.

I like that, he said.

Might Buddha speak to you? I asked.

He laughed and shook his head.

So you're on your own?

Yes, he said. But also, no.

I wanted to know if he believed in karma. In some form, he said, yes. Don't you? I said I believed in consequences, if that was the same thing. He thought it was. And intention, he said, is important. What you were trying to do. What you *meant* to do.

And if you don't know? I asked.

He said he didn't think that ever happened. Not really. That when we're honest with ourselves we always know.

I shook my head. I didn't care for his certainty. I thought it had more to do with some Buddhist rulebook than the way things are in truth. I wanted to knock him back a little, disturb him, but when I looked out in search of inspiration all I found was the road and the people in the cars around us, sunk in their own lives, sealed off.

He parked outside the house, switched off the engine. He had, of course, noticed my moment of confusion, and now, as if he'd been thinking it over more carefully, he said, Sometimes it *is* hard to know. About intentions. Sometimes impossible.

I felt the kindness of that, though I don't believe he'd changed his mind. I'm not even sure I wanted him to.

You all right? he asked, as I started to get out. From somewhere I found a grin and said I was, thanks, right as rain. We nodded to each other and left it there.

My first overseas posting was to Germany, the British Army of the Rhine. There were a lot of British troops out there. Dozens of bases. Some soldiers spent their entire service in Germany. My barracks were an old Luftwaffe base. There was a concrete eagle – about fifteen feet from wing tip to wing tip – that had been removed from its plinth above the gates and dumped in one of the old air-raid shelters. The place was a good deal grander than any of the barracks I'd seen in this country (with the exception of the old Peninsula Barracks at Winchester). Blue-painted corridors wide enough for four men to walk down, shoulder to shoulder. A parade ground surrounded by chestnut trees. And nice touches of Teutonic attention to detail. The attics of the main buildings had been filled with sand. In the event of a fire and the ceiling giving way the sand would pour down on the flames and stifle them. That was the theory. It made us feel quite snug, quite grateful to the Luftwaffe.

The point of our being in Germany was to hold up a Soviet invasion. This – the Red Hordes pouring westwards – sounds fanciful now, part of Cold War paranoia, but a lot of sensible people believed it might happen. Our particular job (as I understood it – the view from the bottom) was to soak up the first wave of Soviet shock troops and buy perhaps a week of time during which reinforcements (Americans) would arrive, or the political leaders would have come to their senses, or the war would have shifted from conventional to nuclear and we'd all be dead anyway. Because this war, our bit of it, was imagined as fast-moving and mechanised, we spent a lot of time training how to knock out tanks. I remember a week up by the Baltic coast firing the new MILAN anti-tank weapon at German seagulls. There was also something called Blowpipe that British soldiers called by a slightly different name. It was a fairly useless weapon that failed to hit much during the Falklands War and was quietly withdrawn from service. Apparently, quite a few were shipped off to the mujahideen in Afghanistan to use on the Russians. Maybe they had better luck with them.

From time to time we joined up with the British Frontier Service to patrol the border. The Iron Curtain was mostly just an idea when Churchill first spoke of it but real enough by the time I arrived. We would drive down roads that ran parallel to mile upon mile of mesh fencing, past concrete towers, arc lights, minefields. I remember the signs: *Halt! Hier Grenze.* This is the border. We often saw our opposite numbers in their greatcoats. We took pictures of them, they took pictures of us. Sometimes we were close enough to see their breath in the air. When the Wall came down and the border collapsed in 1989, I was in the Netherlands working in a canning factory. I watched the Berlin crowds on a television in the hostel where I lived with fifty men from Anatolia, migrant workers like me (though also not like me – they were all teetotal). The excitement of '89 didn't last very long but it was the end of one particular chapter of human idiocy, and there was something very cheering in those processions of overloaded Trabants and Wartburgs coming through crossings where, a week earlier, they would have been shot at. (What happened to all that wire? There was well over a thousand kilometres of it. Somebody made money.)

I won't say I was a model soldier in Germany but I wasn't a bad one. My boots were as boots should be, my locker likewise, and when there were call-outs, usually at three in the morning, I was on the square in good time and in good order. I was proud to be a soldier, proud of the regiment, of my uniform. I wasn't alone in this. I'd say most of the young soldiers, new to the army, new to Germany, had the same idea, but among the older men, those with five or ten years' service, some had a very different attitude. More than once I heard soldiers and NCOs back-chatting junior officers and not much done about it. And one of the things many of these older men had in common was Northern Ireland. Some had done multiple tours there. They talked about the place a lot. Ireland was proper soldiering. In Ireland they had done their job. I heard names I knew from the newspapers. Armagh, Crossmaglen, Andersonstown, the Bogside. They spoke in mixed ways about the Irish. They were all right, they were not all bad. They – the IRA – were an enemy you had to respect. They were also Fenian bastards, and the Irish in general more trouble than they were worth. If we had a free hand for a week the whole thing could be sorted. Certain people just had to be taken out. Everyone knew who they were. Bang! Job done. In these conversations – and I was never a part of them because they made a point of ignoring the existence of new recruits – there was the whiff of something, a bigger and more dangerous world. I listened. I don't know what kind of appetite I had for it but I was interested.

* * *

Off duty meant going to bars. God knows we were not well paid but we had little else to spend our money on, very few needs beyond those the army took care of. We wore white shirts and denim jackets, desert boots, football scarves. One lad, Gosling, had a pair of bright orange platform boots. He was an Elton John fan. This was before people understood Elton John might not be completely heterosexual. Or before soldiers in the British Army understood. Or it might just have been before Gosling understood. In the army, of course, there were no gays, which is to say nobody would have been insane enough to admit to it.

We wore a lot of aftershave. Brut, Old Spice, Hai Karate. Blue Stratos! Some squaddies swilled out their mouths with the stuff. We were always in a gang, always loud, always looking for a laugh. We leant over bars and held up our fingers. *Fünf bier, bitte. Acht bier, bitte.* We were not unpleasant, not exactly. We had been given a lecture on how to behave with the locals. Some of them – certainly those selling alcohol – did pretty well out of the British bases. The rest put up with us, though might privately have looked forward to the day we would disappear. They might have felt the same about the Luftwaffe.

There were girls, a few, not as many as we would have liked and certainly not enough to go round. I have a fuzzy image of someone called Astrid who taught me to say *Ich leibe dich*, though I didn't and neither did she. The stink of beer that must have come from our bodies on certain morning parades, the great yeasty stink of it, would have turned your stomach. It turns mine a little to remember it.

I wasn't there long – nine months, something like that – and I don't know how much I can claim to know about that young soldier, what I could tell you about him that would set him apart from the others. He must have had his worries but I'd have to guess at what they were. Am I measuring up? Do I look the part? Do people like me? The usual things. I may also have worried about Dad, for although his letters – one every fortnight – gave no hint of disapproval, I was nagged by the idea that he was, in his heart, disappointed. I don't believe that now, by the way. If he had concerns about what I was doing he would also have trusted in the working out of a greater scheme, have been more interested in how clear my conscience was, questions of character, rather than whether or not I wore a uniform. And I think – or came to think years later when I paid him the overdue respect of giving his life some proper consideration – that he was, after Mum died, always a little afraid one or both of us would not survive the loss of her, and it was this, over the years, that shaped his attitude towards me. The army is not what he would have chosen for me, far from it, but it was, at least, evidence of some kind that I *had* survived, and that we were both, in our own ways, keeping going.

German winters! *Sehr kalt*. In our rooms – ten beds – there were big iron radiators but the Nazis had apparently taken with them the secret of how they operated, and in the morning we often had ice on the inside of the windows. I remember shovelling snow off the parade ground, sometimes while it was still snowing, which is an effective way to use up the energy of young men. Quite a lot of what we did seemed to have that as its main aim.

Then came the thaw, the sudden spring, the chestnut trees in bud, the sound of songbirds behind the revving of diesel engines. Rumours began. There's nowhere like the army for rumours. New kit showed up. A pair of security cameras was installed on the gates. The rhythm at the barracks was subtly altered. Even the German barmen in town seemed to know we'd be off soon, which doesn't say much for the military's ability to keep secrets.

The CO disappeared, then turned up again. He looked different too. Perhaps he had new red tabs on his shoulders. We were mustered in the camp cinema. The CO stood on the stage and wished us a good morning. He beamed at us, looked down at our young faces with real affection. He had some news he thought most of us would be jolly glad to hear, though even before he'd come out with it I heard someone along the line mutter 'Ireland'. He was right. We would deploy in June – West Belfast. There would be a forward party of officers and NCOs, and two weeks later the rest of us. It would, said the colonel, rubbing his hands, be a chance to show our stuff, what we were capable of. Ireland, of course, sometimes a pretty thankless task, but important to understand that we *do* make a difference. Anyway, he knew we would put on a first-rate show. He knew he'd be proud of us. He wished us the very best of luck.

From then on it was full preparation mode. PTIs bawling at us in the gym as we squatted and vaulted and shimmied up ropes. Longer and longer runs, all ending with a scramble over the seven-foot wall of the vehicle-wash bay. Morale was high. If there was anyone with misgivings he kept them to himself. Nobody signs up to be a peace-time soldier. Certainly nobody would admit to it.

For the final phase they sent us to a place called Tin City. This was a training camp intended to simulate the conditions we'd find in Ireland, a mock town in the middle of empty German countryside. When it first went up the streets were just props like a film set, mostly corrugated iron, hence the name. By the time we were there the houses were built of breeze blocks. There were 'shops', a pub called Murphy's, even a church (though no meeting house). In Tin City we learnt the system of patrolling in a four-man team called a 'brick'. We learnt how to set up a vehicle checkpoint, how to pat down a suspect. There was much laughter and some squeamishness when it came to touching other men's crotches. One instructor, after being searched by a squaddie who didn't want to go there, fished a hand grenade from his Y-fronts. This isn't my f**cking d*ck. We got the point.

We rehearsed riots, a line of us shuffling behind six-foot Makrolon shields while a team of soldiers known as 'civpop' pelted us with stones and bottles.

We studied their weapons. Armalites, AK-47s, M60s. There was even an old Tommy gun. I'd never seen one of those before. They fired the guns into a wall on the live range, partly to teach us the different sounds each made, partly so we would understand a wall was no guarantee of safety. To reassure us, they did the same with the SLR and we were reminded, if we needed it, of the power of that weapon. It was at Tin City that I first heard the SLR referred to as a 'paddywhacker'. When did that start? Before or after Bloody Sunday?

There were talks on the different paramilitary groups. Official IRA, Provisionals, Irish National Liberation Army, Ulster Defence Association, Ulster Volunteer Force, Red Hand Commando, and so on. Most of them still exist. It was the Republican groups – IRA and INLA – who did most of the damage. They were better organised, better armed and better at it. The Loyalists practised a more chaotic brand of violence, shooting up a pub or snatching someone off the street at night in a Catholic district, taking them on a ride they wouldn't come back from.

We were shown maps of the Province. We might, as a kind of footnote, have been told why there was a Province at all, but if so I don't remember that. Most of what I know of Irish history I learnt long after I left the place, and that may be a common theme of British involvement there. At Tin City the emphasis was on the practical – 'absence of the normal, presence of the abnormal' – and not making stupid mistakes, like going on patrol with your rear rifle sights folded down, something I did in my first week (they filmed us) and was bollocked for.

Back at the battalion barracks we had a few days more or less free, time we dedicated to drinking. We mothballed the kit we weren't taking, packed it in cardboard boxes, wrote our names and numbers on the side. We were advised to take out army life insurance and most of us did. Dad was my beneficiary. I don't know if that would have amused him. Probably not.

The day before we flew out there was a drumhead service. The wind was blowing in the padre's face. It sent most of what he said swirling over the roof of the barracks but we felt it, the moment's weight, our part in the long pageant of men being blessed before battle. You didn't need much imagination for that.

The next morning, before it was fully light, we boarded coaches and were driven to the airfield. A DC-10 was waiting on the apron. Someone asked where first class was. That got a laugh. Then the doors were shut, the engines picked up. Flying was still a novelty for most of us. I'd only ever flown with the army. I remember the excitement of breaking through clouds into that pure blue above that seems untouched by weather, a child's idea of Heaven. We should have raised our arms and shouted hallelujahs. Instead we grinned at each other, said things that were lost in the roar of the engines. Mid-morning, I looked down and saw the sea, two or three lonely ships, then the coast, a lighthouse, the grey scatter of a town, and after that nothing but little moss-green fields. Bandit country? It couldn't have looked more peaceful. And much more like home – my home – than the plains of

Germany, those tank lands where, if your boots were good enough, you could walk all the way to the Arctic Circle.

We landed at an RAF base near the border, lugged our kit into a transit area, sat on orange plastic chairs. There was a vending machine but long since overwhelmed by soldiers sticking German coins into it. On one wall there was a picture of the Queen that might have dated from the time of her Coronation. She seemed not much older than us. Quite pretty. Anyway, she was the only woman there so we looked at her.

Late afternoon the transport arrived. Coaches again, a local company of the kind that sometimes paid a heavy price for working with the army. At the edge of Belfast we were squeezed into a convoy of Saracen armoured cars. The Saracens were 'locked down', which meant in the back we could see nothing at all. It was rush-hour in the city and we stopped and started like anything else on the road. I didn't find the normality of that reassuring. In Tin City we'd been taught to equate stillness with danger. Even behind armour it put us on edge. A rifle bullet might not penetrate but M60 machine guns had armour-piercing rounds, and we'd been told they had rocket launchers too, RPGs, courtesy of Colonel Gaddafi of Libya. You sense the thinness of your own skin. How, once whatever's around you is opened, you could be torn like paper.

We were replacing a company of Welch Fusiliers and from the cab came a nice Welsh voice welcoming us to our new home, a security forces base nicknamed the Factory. We accelerated, swung hard through gates that closed swiftly behind us. The relief of it! Inside and with our own! Night had fallen. We gathered in the yard in the bluish light of arc lamps while NCOs with clipboards made sure no one had been left behind. Low sheds, the struts of a watchtower, a whiff of coal smoke – peat smoke too, I think – from the terraced houses we could not see now but which were only yards away. The building we were going to live in for the next four and a half months was a piece of the city's Victorian industry, six (seven?) storeys of brick, with sangars on the roof. By the time we arrived it had been an SF base for ten years. Nothing about it was lovely. It gave shelter to near enough five hundred men at a time. It was, essentially, uncleanable.

We followed one of the forward party inside, climbed the stairs, our guide's voice echoing from the walls. Laundry room, shower room, support platoon this floor, the rest of you keep climbing . . .

My room – our room – had yellow walls and a carpet it was best not to look at closely. Bunk beds, plastic chairs, one armchair, a rifle rack, a TV. There was no window. Gosling of the platform boots was in the bunk above me. Across from me was our corporal – new to us though not to Northern Ireland. This was John France. He was mixed race, or however you're supposed to say that. A handsome man with a sort of suaveness about him. He had one of the very few moustaches in the British Army *circa* 1982, which actually suited him and looked good. And he had a Walkman portable cassette player! Cutting-edge technology at the time. It certainly impressed us. We liked him immediately. More importantly, we trusted him.

That first night, a room lit by the light of a television screen. I believe the television was on when we first came in and I don't recall it ever being switched off. Poor Gosling ground his teeth. Someone moaned in a dream. I heard a patrol coming in or going out. I heard sirens, though maybe no more than I would have heard in Bristol. But what kept sleep away for an hour or so wasn't the noises – I was used to that, could tell in my sleep, like any soldier, the noises I needed to pay attention to and those I could ignore – it was the thought that out there in the city were people who would not be sorry to see me face down in a pool of my own blood. And they were not the Eastern Bloc hordes, the Grepos and Vopos we'd seen through the wire mesh, but people who spoke the same language, ate the same food, watched the same TV programmes, probably supported the same football teams. Were we not alike then? Why was this old factory rammed with young men sleeping next to their weapons? Where had it all started? What necessity drove it forwards? I'd like to be able to say I had such thoughts regularly while I was in Ireland but that first time might also have been the last. It wasn't encouraged and it's not like we sat around talking about it, six hundred years of history so tortuous you could spend your whole life trying to untangle it. We didn't do that. Some will have thought about it privately – squaddies are not stupid – but the first time you're spat at or bricked, the first time you hear of a fellow soldier maimed or killed, the first time you're really afraid, then you think differently. Which is to say you don't really think at all any more.

Morning in a room with no windows is a fairly meaningless event. I saw Corporal France slide from his bunk, lie on the floor and do press-ups. When he finished he sat on his bed, lit the day's first smoke, caught my eye and nodded. Rise, Rose.

We were lucky. We didn't have to go out at all that first day. Induction, briefings, orientation. We got some kit, including seventy-five rounds of ammunition, a mess tray and a flak jacket. The flak jackets had been bought in large numbers from the Americans at the start of the Troubles. On the tour that followed us they were issued with proper body armour, a thick ceramic plate over the heart. I don't know how much a flak jacket was ever expected to stop. Nothing serious. The one I was given was damp and smelt clearly of a man's sweat, as if he'd taken it off just a few minutes earlier, which might have been the case. Whoever it was, he'd biroed his blood group on the collar. It wasn't the same as mine (cue jokes about Welsh blood, Taffy blood) and I made sure to block it out. We queued for our issue of black Northern Ireland gloves but they ran out long before I got to the front of the queue. What they didn't run out of were yellow cards. These, which we had to carry with us at all times, stated the rules of engagement. In what circumstances you could and could not open fire, the warnings you were supposed to give (Army! Stop or I fire!). Depending on the side you were on, the card was either a licence to kill or it was a legal trap, a hobble to keep us from doing our job properly. Unsurprisingly, these cards are mentioned many times in the report of the Saville Inquiry.

In the briefing room there was a map of the city that took up half a wall. Our company commander used his fly-fishing rod to point out our position, the main streets either side of us, the location of other SF bases, RUC stations, the sites of recent incidents. We were shown photographs of known or suspected terrorists. These people were called players. They were mostly young. They did not, for the most part, look sinister. And there were women too. It was strange to think they were part of it. What does it mean when even the women are against you? The Factory, of course, was full of pictures of women, hundreds of them Sellotaped to the walls of our rooms, and every sangar had its semi-secret stash of 'mags', but the women whose faces we studied in the briefing room – pictures taken at police stations or by a covert camera – stared out at us very differently. They would not be dancing with us. They were not offering themselves as the raw material of our fantasies.

And then, next morning, somewhere around five a.m., we began in earnest. You think you won't sleep but you do. A quick wash, a scrape with a plastic razor, finish dressing, then down to the canteen. Another briefing, another look at the pictures, the arranging of call signs etc, and finally out into the air, the first hour of a summer's day, lovely even in an SF base. We loaded our weapons. Those with sights zeroed them in at the pipe-range. John France was waiting by the iron door. He checked us over and looked at his watch. There were no last-minute instructions. We either knew or we didn't. With ten seconds to go he counted down in a soft voice. We were tight as drums. Then, with a nod to the soldier acting as doorman, the door was unbolted and dragged wide.

When we left the base we always ran. A twenty-yard sprint, everything on you jangling, shifting, chafing, your breath coming hard, and all you can see somehow a source of confusion. I was the last one out. Tail-end Charlie. I stumbled as I went down the big step but did not, thank God, fall.

At the main road we slowed, checked our distances, caught our breath. A red and cream bus full of sleepy faces went by. Those who bothered to look at us did so with no obvious interest. Four more soldiers on the street, a cool morning, a scrape of moon still up. I walked, sometimes turning to walk backwards for a few paces. It did not look like Tin City and the few people who were out were not squaddies playing civpop. Yet we seemed to understand what to do, that curious dance, slow, slow, quick-quick slow, along our route. Another bus rolled past. A man in shirtsleeves took in his milk. I was only a few feet from him but we didn't wish each other a good morning. Some philosopher whose name I have forgotten, someone who, I think, spent time in a concentration camp, said that when you look at another person their face is saying silently, 'Please don't kill me.' I'm not sure what that man's face was saying. Quite a lot of people dealt with us by pretending we weren't there. They blanked us, and after a while that becomes quite powerful, wears away at some simple human need to be seen. But in those first minutes I wasn't bothered with any of that. I wasn't thinking about the man, his life, the life in that house. I was scanning ahead for the others, that little boat I must never get too far from, and when I saw them I pushed on, twenty-one years old, a gun in my hands, the low sun throwing my shadow ahead of me on the pavement.

That first patrol passed without incident. We saw no players. No one took a shot at us or lobbed a brick or even told us to eff off. Our route took us in a big loop towards the city centre. The worst place, the place even John France seemed nervous of, was an area of high-rises and courtyards where people lived as tightly packed as bees. A poor place even in a poor city. On the central tower there was an army observation post they resupplied by helicopter to avoid having people ambushed going up the stairs. A solid Republican area and a place we never passed through without some expectation of harm. Where we felt most exposed we ran – 'hard-targeted' – regrouping in an underpass or anywhere sheltered, anywhere it would be difficult for a gunman in one of those countless windows to settle his sights on the back of your head.

From the flats we crossed the new ring road and came to where things looked almost normal and felt safer. It wasn't, in truth, that safe. People had been killed there and the IRA regularly bombed the place as part of its economic war. But there were shops and restaurants and cafés, and while some of the names were unfamiliar, others – Boots, Woolworths, Wimpy – were not, and to see them was comforting.

For a few streets we were followed by a boy who should have been in school, a crop-haired middle-aged ten-year-old sauntering five yards behind us, hands in his pockets. Eventually, while I was hunkered down at the corner of a junction and about the same height as him, he came up and asked if I was new. He said he hadn't seen me before. How's that for cool? I think I fobbed him off with something. I probably believed my newness was a military secret, a weakness to be exploited by the boy's uncle or even by the boy himself. He stood beside me until we moved on. Having a child next to you was often thought of as a good thing, and I saw soldiers sometimes encourage their presence. Let them try on your beret, let them look through your sights. The hand holding the end of a command wire might hesitate to flick the switch if a child was there. A dead child hardly furthered the cause. In those flats we had run through, in the autumn of the year I'm talking about, INLA set off a drainpipe bomb that killed a soldier but also killed two children. The bombers were hounded out. People knew who they were, where they were hiding. They might have been lucky to get away with their lives.

We finished the patrol at an RUC station. The desk sergeant greeted us with some remark so thickly accented I couldn't understand him. We hung around in the yard of the station, glad to be hidden, then returned to the base in the back of a Humber 1 Ton truck, a vehicle known to everybody as a Pig. A quick debrief – we had nothing of official interest to report – then off to the canteen to cram our faces with the food in the trays under the heat lamps. Our first patrol! Done. Survived. Everybody had seen something strange or funny, or just *something* – the old fellow in his dressing-gown, the good-looking bird, the morning drunk singing his heart out in the underpass. We had shown our faces to the enemy. No one had messed up. Northern Ireland?

No sweat. We chattered like schoolboys. Only John France was quiet and perhaps we understood that one day we would be quiet too. We smoked, tipping our ash onto the edges of the metal plates. We drank mug after mug of over-sweetened tea. Then everyone, as if touched by the same hand, was suddenly randy for sleep and we trudged up to our room, our narrow beds with their black, wipe-down mattresses. We were QRF (quick reaction force) so we weren't allowed to take off our boots and we certainly weren't supposed to sleep but we lay down anyway, watched cartoons on the television, programmes intended for pre-school children – Rolf's Cartoon club! – then drifted and drowsed, lost ourselves in that half-world where you hear the voice of someone who's not there, a friend from boyhood, or your mum or dad calling your name. Most of my dreams in Belfast were just about Belfast. Sometimes I walked the patrol again in what felt like real time, and what I saw in the dreams was what I had seen on the streets.

Three hours after that first patrol I woke to see the others pulling on flak jackets, taking their rifles from the rack. And suddenly I understood it. This was what it would be. This was the tour. An exercise in repetition. How many times you went up and down the stone steps, how many times you loaded your weapon, how many times you stood by the iron gate watching Corporal France count the seconds down.

On his next tour John France was hit in the leg by a ricocheting bullet from an M60. It was an ambush on a street near the same SF base. The bullet had already passed through someone else, another soldier. That soldier didn't survive. John France lost the lower part of one leg. I read about it while I was in prison in Shepton, a newspaper already weeks old that I found while working in the kitchens. It had been put down to soak up the water from a dripping pipe. The dead soldier's name – I didn't know him – then Corporal John France from Didcot, his name swollen on the grey paper, the page so wet I could have held it in my fist and squeezed the water from it.

This morning your card arrived. You thanked me for your gifts though made no comment on them. Well, it was a card. There wasn't space. You told me that you and Lorna were going away for a week to Madrid. Madrid! This was Lorna's present. Just the two of you, flying out of Bristol. A late-summer break.

I spent three months in Madrid during my drunk's tour of Europe, most of it in a doss house off the Plaza de España that I shared with some of the great world's human refuse (who I bow to now in thought), all of us cock-a-hoop to be living in a country where a litre of red wine cost pennies. We found work when we needed it, on building sites, in tourist hotels. We were afraid of the police. They didn't like us. Occasionally someone was badly beaten. I at least had the advantage of a white face and a British passport. Others had it much harder.

Our landlord was a gypsy called Chano. He looked as scruffy as the rest of us during the day but in the middle of the night he would appear in a long black coat, his hair shining with almond oil, and go out to gypsy shindigs. I forget what he charged us to sleep in the house but it couldn't have been much. On some days in Spain I drank seven litres of wine, the kind sold in plastic bottles and so rough it might not even have been intended for drinking. It coloured our teeth and you would have known us all immediately by our smiles.

The picture on your card puzzled me. Two big buttons on the front of an old machine, something industrial. A green button marked START and a red button marked STOP. It made me scratch my head. It seemed pointed and I began to feel you meant me to choose one – stop or start, the green or the red. Stop what? Start what? More likely, of course, you meant nothing at all and the card was simply one you picked out of a drawer, the first that came to hand. It's become a bad habit of mine, this constant imagining that the world is signalling to me, every bush a burning bush. Is it self-importance? A sort of vanity? Or just the hope of some guidance? The need of it.

Yesterday – Friday – I went up to the meeting house to mow the grass in the burying ground. We don't mind it getting a little ragged – in fact I prefer it like that – but once or twice a month throughout the summer I give it a trim. At this stage in the season the grass isn't growing fast. I quite fancy scything it but we haven't got a scythe and if we did I would probably end up cutting off one of my feet. And to be seen scything between gravestones might not help my general reputation in the town. People would pass the front of the house here with their fingers crossed.

Anyway, I was in the shed pouring two-stroke into the mower when Tess came by. I knew she was likely to be up there. She often goes in on a Friday to do an hour or two in the office. We hire out the meeting house for suitable events, and there's some property in town owned by the meeting that brings in a small income. All that needs dealing with, plus a surprising amount of paperwork that comes from Friends House in London, forms to fill in about modern slavery or the safeguarding of children, though we have neither. I'm not sure if she's our official clerk but she's the nearest we have to one. One day they'll ask her to become an elder and I hope very much she says yes.

I stepped outside to speak to her, though behind her the sky was darkening and I was worried I'd only get half the grass done before the rain arrived. She asked about your birthday party at the Silk Shed. I told her the story of the teeth and after a moment, during which she might have wondered if she was meant to take it seriously, she began to laugh and I joined her. She said I'd looked very happy at the meeting, sitting with you. She'd even wondered if I might get up and say something. This – the business of saying something – is a long-time tease between us. Neither of us has ever, at a meeting, said anything (unless she did while I was away, which I doubt). I asked her what she thought I would say. Oh, something surprising, something she could not have guessed. We were quiet then for a few seconds, took breath. There were smells from the shed of old grass and petrol. Smells outside of the sea, the front edge of the coming rain. I said I was afraid of losing you. It came out quite suddenly – came out as things are supposed to in a meeting. It rocked me a little. The truth and the bluntness of it.

But why should you? said Tess. You won't lose her.

I tried to answer but my throat was tight. She said it again. You won't lose her, Stephen.

I don't know, I said. I think I could. It wouldn't take much.

She's your daughter.

I said that was true in one sense. In another, perhaps not.

She made a face at that. She thought it was dancing on the head of a pin. She pointed out you could have opened a tea room anywhere but did it five miles from where I live. This I had to accept. You're here for a reason and I am clearly part of it.

You know what I am, I said.

She said she thought I was many things.

I said that you were wary of me, that when you got a clearer view, when you knew more . . .

What she will know, said Tess, is that you love her. The rest is old history. It's not part of her life.

I shrugged. It's not that I thought she was wrong, not entirely, just that it wasn't enough. The scales didn't balance. I told her about your card. I don't think it made much sense.

Talk to her, said Tess. Trust her with it.

I nodded. I should have left it there but I went on. I said things were getting out of hand. I meant the letter, was hinting at it, but as Tess knows nothing about it she must have thought I meant my health, physical or mental or both. She put a hand on my arm and asked if I was taking my meds. I said I was, which is, of course, not quite accurate. It's an odd thing, but somehow, through her touch, I had this sharp memory, a mental snap-shot of her parents' front room as it was when we were both sixteen. The gas fire, the china animals. The swirly Artex ceiling. And the carpet, a sort of cream colour, where once, the house ours for an hour, we made love on the floor and left behind a little spot right in the middle of the carpet, a spot no amount of scrubbing could get out, and the first thing I noticed every time I stepped into the room. (Sorry if that's too much information.)

Then Ned came round the side of the building – Ned Clarke – looking like a man having rich and godly thoughts but also trying to remember where he'd left his glasses. He greeted us and wondered aloud if I would beat the rain. That was his way of saying get on with it, Stephen. Unlike Tess who volunteers I am paid a little for the work I do. Tess asked if I felt up to it and I said I did. I felt embarrassed at bending her ear like that. My troubles are my own! I seem to have difficulty learning that lesson. She smiled and left with Ned, the two of them in conversation about the meeting-house roof, which we all know will have to come off in the next couple of years. The slates up there were hung by men who later went to fight at Passchendaele and the Somme. They've lasted pretty well.

I rolled the mower out, primed it, and after half a dozen big hauls on the cord, got it going. The work was welcome. You know the old painting of the man screaming on the bridge, holding the sides of his head as if his skull was crumbling? That man needs a lawn mower or a spade. I cut the grass path first then changed the setting to cut a little higher and moved in among the graves. A young blackbird watched me with great intensity and seemed to dare himself to come closer and closer. In the oak tree a wood pigeon cooed. I like their steadfastness. They keep going hour after hour.

When you work among headstones you start to talk to them, the people who owned those names and who, fifty years ago, a hundred years ago, would, at the sound of that name, have turned with eyebrows raised. There are two or three out there among the newer graves I knew and can remember. There's Dad, of course. The rest are just what I make of them, dream bodies fitted to stone names. Hard not to do it, though, not to feel you're in company. Stepping back onto the soft hump of a grave I apologised, out loud. The glorious dead. The dear departed. Do you have views on the afterlife? I expect you do. Most people do. There isn't really an official Quaker line. The more traditional friends just follow the traditional Christian teachings

– judgement, Heaven and Hell, the resurrection of the body. The rest will have their private theories. I had an aunt (so you had a great-aunt) over in Pawlett with an unshakeable belief in the dead. She thought of them as constantly surrounding us. She had a habit of suddenly staring in the way cats do at something others can't see. I always wanted to ask her what they do all day, what the point was of all the hanging around. Weren't they bored? Or were they skittish with the pleasure of not having bodies any more, of being able to blow around like dandelion seeds?

On that drunk's tour I mentioned I was also for a while in Italy, the northern city of Milan, and one winter's day I went into the cemetery there. I forget its name. It's quite famous. I went there to have somewhere safe and private to drink. On a bench in the city there was always the possibility of being moved on or finding yourself on the wrong side of a civic law and having to pay a fine or even spend the night in a cell. The day was cold – very – but I had on this big overcoat, a coat I thought of as most of a bear, and which I'd bought for not much from a young Greek dope fiend who had gone home in search of a beach to sleep on. The coat had deep pockets perfect for keeping bottles in. I strolled into the cemetery with a party of older women. The warden at the gate might have thought I belonged to one of them, the embarrassing nephew, the one who won't get a job, or can't.

Inside the cemetery, in air that glittered, I lost myself along avenues and pathways lined with graves and mausoleums. Some of the mausoleums were unlike anything I'd seen in this country, anything you *could* see. About as far removed as it's possible to imagine from what we have around the meeting house. I remember one that looked like a scaled-down model of a prize-winning office block. Sleek marble, tinted glass. A spiral staircase inside! And there were lots of statues, also of a very high standard. Most were religious or classical, the kind of thing you'd expect, but some showed the dead person doing what they had enjoyed in life. There was, for example, a man in hiking gear – back-pack, Tyrolean hat, stick, a small dog at his heels. Others were just standing there like people who had come to a party and found they couldn't leave, who had to stay until wind and rain and the smoke from the car factories dissolved them. I found a place to sit among all this and have my bottle. A pair of bronze children dressed for the 1950s watched me steadily. It might have unnerved me, should have done perhaps. Instead, what I felt – what arrived in me with the force of revelation – was not a sense of presence but of *absence*. Complete absence. All the stuff there, the flummery – the very expensive flummery – was simply the anxiety of the living, their grief. Spend a million lire on marble, hire that architect everyone's talking about. By the end of the bottle, or halfway down the next, I knew the dead did not exist. Life existed. Death existed. But not the dead. The whole cemetery was a kind of mad ash heap of love. Those metal children, the hiker with his stone hat gazing at mountains that were just snow clouds above the cemetery wall, these were offerings to the silence that stands at the beginning and end of everything and is, I suppose, the one thing we might call eternal. Don't get me wrong, I'm not mocking it. I didn't think the people who had put those things up were idiots. Grief is real and it makes people desperate. They tear at themselves. It can be a frightening thing to see.

I left the cemetery with a sense that I'd understood something important. I can't say it gave me much comfort. What it did was to make the living more unmissable. It brought them closer, their scarves and wintry breath, as if I'd shaken them free of something that had blurred their outlines. All this, I know, could be put down to the products of a European Union wine lake. It could be put down to the budget grappa I bought in the little stores, a drink I revered for its taste of grape stems and chemistry sets, the way it turned my head into a helium balloon floating over the city. Are a drunkard's thoughts less? Less reliable than those of the sober? Eventually, yes. But on the way there's a handful of understandings only available to the serious barfly. My moment in the cemetery was one of these. I thought it true then and think it true now. So it's very strange that without giving up on this – the dead do not exist – I have, like my aunt in Pawlett, spent so much of my life in their company. Or the company of one.

I did beat the rain. It started as I shook the final bin of grass onto the compost. The first drops were big as berries. One broke on my hand, a slap of water. Then another on my shoulder, one on my face. Everything the drops hit sounded. The leaves, the grass, the path. Then it changed gear and came down with a lovely weight. Nothing was held back. The gravestones darkened. The oak and the plane tree rattled. The last birds made a dash for shelter. By the time I'd got the mower back to the shed I was wet enough not to worry about getting any wetter. I locked up and walked home. People were looking out of shop windows waiting for it to pass. They watched me. Who knows what they thought? An old sailor, shipwrecked in a burying ground in the middle of town. At home, when I stepped into the hall and shut the front door, the house felt hollow, and as if, somehow, it hadn't really been expecting me back. I peeled off, dumped everything in a sopping pile on the boards and walked up the stairs leaving footprints on the carpet.

When I'd dressed and towelled my hair I didn't know what to do with myself. The rain was lighter but it had settled in. I thought of baking bread, took out the flour and the scales but got no further. I put on the radio. It was music but the wrong sort and I turned it off. I was thinking of Dad as bones. Did the mower make them vibrate? Does the rain? Very fine vibrations. Tibula, fibula. The plates of the skull. The hips like antlers. And then I thought again of those days – days and nights – when he was here in the house and dying.

I had come back from the orchard. I had shaved off my beard and cut my hair with kitchen scissors over an open newspaper. I set strict limits on my drinking, and though I did not keep to them, broke them almost immediately, I managed to keep some order, some discipline. By this point, the autumn of 2002, there was no pretending Dad was going to get better. He was jaundiced and in some pain. There was morphine. He told me once that morphine doesn't take the pain away but it stops you caring about it. The hospice nurse, Gracie Passmore, came in twice a week, then every other day, then every day. I was grateful to her, but couldn't help seeing her as bringing death into the house, a kind of midwife. Also, from the beginning, I knew she was a drinker. Not heavy, and certainly much more careful about it than I was, but a drinker nonetheless. I think we saw it in each other the first time we met. So we were a strange household. The drunken son, the tipsy nurse, the dying man spaced on opiates. But in its own way it worked, if that's the right word. Sometimes I read to him. When he was still well enough he'd been reading a biography of the country poet John Clare who he liked and admired, and I went on with it, sitting on a chair by the bed. We didn't quite finish it. The copy is here in the study, a WEA flyer as a bookmark. In that sense, John Clare outlived him.

There were visitors, people from the meeting, Somerset relatives, a few from work. Sarah Waterfall was often here and she would sit with one of his hands between her own while he slept.

I saw that several times and finally wondered if there was more between them, or had been once, than friendship and Friendship. I could ask her now and she might tell me though it's none of my business. It would be nice to think there *was* something. There were a lot of years for Dad after Mum died and nobody with blood in his veins lives on books alone, even very good books.

During the last few days he was unconscious, or mostly so. Sometimes he opened his eyes and slowly focused on me. I would smile and hold my breath so as not to breathe fumes on him. The morphine now came from an electric pump, a black box about the size of a pack of butter that hummed quietly on the floor by the bed. Gracie Passmore showed me how to use cotton buds to moisten his mouth. I was glad to have a job. There was no more reading aloud, though when it was just the two of us I talked to him, mostly, I'm afraid, about me. I don't believe he heard much of it. He was concentrating, but not on me or anything in the room or the house. The last night of his life I slept across the bottom of his bed like a dog. His wrists, his jaw, his brow, were so frail and beautiful. He died in the late afternoon while I was out of the room and Gracie Passmore out of the house. I, of course, was fixing myself a drink. I was only away for ten or fifteen minutes. When I came back upstairs I stood in the doorway and knew. It wasn't just the silence. The room had changed. In those minutes I'd stood at the kitchen window sinking a tumbler of gin the universe was at work upstairs sealing over the place a man had been, smoothing out the fold in the cloth. I'd known death as something chaotic and public, everyone yelling and running, adrenalin pumping so hard you think you're going to throw up, go mad. This was different.

In the kitchen I made calls. I left a message with the receptionist at the surgery. I left a message for Sarah Waterfall. A man's voice answered the phone, her son I think. Please tell Sarah that James died today.

It was November and already dark. I poured myself another drink, a big one. Who could I shame now? There was no one left to shame. I shook coal into the Rayburn, then went outside to the garden, walked down towards the shed, turned and looked back at the house. Every night in the cold months Dad used to go out before bed to check the chimney wasn't on fire. I have a theory it started after Mum died, that he couldn't trust the world any more and was on the look-out for the next disaster. I would hear him from my room, the opening of the back door to go out, the opening as he came back in, and more or less knew the time from it. As a boy I found it comforting. Last ceremony of the day. As a teenager I thought it was daft, one of those things a parent does you know you'll never do yourself. I mean, did he really expect to find the chimney spewing sparks, a sinister orange glow above the house? Just go to bed! But outside that evening, standing there cold in shirtsleeves, a glass in my hand, it seemed to me the house had indeed burnt down, and that all his caution, far from being excessive, was just a kind of prophecy, one (as is the nature of these things) he had been powerless to prevent.

I spent today in bed. I wasn't unwell, I just felt completely unable to face anything or anyone. I called in sick to Plant World. Luckily it was Debbie who answered so I was spared the heavy sarcasm. In the afternoon I forced myself to go down for food, ate out of the fridge, then went back to bed. Fitful sleep and a knot of fear in my guts. I worried that this writing was unwise, that I was stirring things up I wouldn't be able to control. I decided to stop it, and immediately I felt much better. I slept for hours, deeply and dreamlessly. Today, however, I'm at it again. The study, the pad, a pencil from an old box of them I found at the back of one of the desk drawers. And I hardly understand any more why I'm doing it. For you? For him? For me? Anyway, it's too late now. I think so. That's how it feels. These words are a river and they cannot be turned back.

The Falklands War finished just as we were going out to Ireland. Did you hear things about that war (though neither side actually declared war) when you were in the RAF? It came out of nowhere, or that was the impression we had. People had never heard of the Falkland Islands. I, like a good few others, thought they might be off the coast of Scotland. It turned out they were so remote as hardly to be in the world at all, the world most people in Britain had any experience of. Of course that didn't stop us feeling very strongly that the islands were ours and nobody else's.

Two hundred and fifty-five British military personnel were killed, about three times that number on the Argentinian side. The British task force was carried in whatever serviceable ships they could get hold of. Some of these were civilian liners, one of them an old cruise ship called *Canberra*, built, as it happens, at the Harland & Wolff yard in Belfast. *Canberra* arrived back in Southampton in July, a month after the fighting stopped. We watched it on the television between patrols. A white ship streaked with rust, scores of small boats escorting her into port. Soldiers were lined up along the side of the ship, every spare inch of rail. On the dockside the families were gathered in a great crowd, many with banners showing the names of the men they were waiting for. One just said, 'WE'RE OVER HERE!' There was a band playing 'Land Of Hope And Glory' and everybody sang along, or at least the chorus. As the distance between ship and shore grew smaller so the emotion of the crowd grew more intense. Anyone who thought the British a stiff-lipped people would have been surprised. Not a dry eye out there. One girlfriend or young wife lifted her top to show her breasts. That wasn't on TV but it was in the papers the next day. She was standing next to a big Union Jack and the tabloids loved her for it. Now that I think of it they may have set it up themselves. That's not unlikely. The whole Falklands War was a gift to them.

How we envied those men their heroes' welcome! Oh, we knew they'd worked for it, knew the IRA was unlikely to fire an Exocet missile at us (though they would have loved to try). We understood all that. We were respectful. We also knew there would be no victory parades for us, no adoring crowd. We got medals, of course. A Northern Ireland edition of the General Service Medal. It has a green and purple ribbon. Anyone who served more than thirty days in the Province was eligible. And, yes, believe it or not, I have one too. It's in its cardboard box in the bottom drawer of the chest in the bedroom. Feel free to do as you like with it.

Here are some of the other things that happened in that Summer of 1982.

In South Belfast a sixteen-year-old Catholic boy was killed by an INLA booby-trap bomb that had been attached to a stolen motorcycle. The bike had been left leaning against a hedge and one of the boys decided to check it out. He was, apparently, trying to mount the bike when the bomb went off. Two other boys were injured.

In Derry, a policeman was blown up while inspecting a cache of stolen televisions. The bomb had been hidden among them. Two others were injured, I don't know how seriously. Being injured was not a light thing. Being injured might mean spending your life disabled and traumatised, never really making it back.

In County Tyrone, a town called Strabane, a part-time member of the Ulster Defence Regiment was shot by the IRA as he got into his car outside the menswear shop where he worked. Three masked men walked up to the car and opened fire. He was hit in the chest and neck. An off-duty nurse gave him first aid but he was pronounced dead on arrival at hospital. His family refused to accept a letter of sympathy from the British Government and sent a letter back saying the hands of the security forces 'should be freed'.

In Newry, a sixty-year-old man, a former member of the RUC, was shot dead in his car. His wife was with him and she struggled with one of the gunmen but to no avail. It was the third time the IRA had made an attempt on the man's life.

In Derry, a young man died after an IRA punishment squad shot him in the legs. Because they didn't have a handgun they used a rifle. The rifle was so powerful it blew off one of his legs completely. His attackers ran off in a panic and the young man bled to death. As far as I know nobody was ever arrested for that.

In another incident in Derry, an IRA volunteer was shot by soldiers outside a pub. He was unarmed and was shot in the back. Two young soldiers were charged with his killing and both were acquitted. The judge who acquitted them was killed by an IRA landmine in 1987. Also his wife.

In a village near the town of Armagh, a former member of the Ulster Defence Regiment died when a bomb exploded under his car. He was thirty-seven and had four children. His fourteen-year-old daughter asked that there should be no retaliation. God, she said, would deal with those responsible when the time came. The dead man's brother, a part-time policeman, had been shot by the IRA ten years earlier.

In Belfast, a homeless man, a drifter, was kicked to death in the back yard of a club on the Shankill Road. One of those who assaulted him was Lenny Murphy, ringleader of the Shankill Butchers, a gang that lifted Catholics off the street at night, tortured them, then murdered them with butcher's knives. Later in the year Murphy himself was shot by the IRA as he got out of his car. As revenge for this, the Ulster Volunteer Force kidnapped a twenty-five-year-old Catholic man, drove him to a garage in East Belfast and shot him in the head. One of the UVF convicted of the murder gave an interview from prison in which he said, 'You hear a bang and it's too late . . . You've went somewhere you've never been before and it's not a very nice place and you can't stop it, it's too late then.' In 1998 he hanged himself, leaving behind a note saying he was tired and that he hoped the next generation would be able to live normal lives.

But the 'incident' of that summer that went in deepest – to me, to British soldiers, British people – was not in Belfast or Derry or Crossmaglen, not in the South Atlantic either. It was in London. A bomb with twenty-five pounds of gelignite and thirty pounds of four- and six-inch nails was left in the boot of a parked car in Hyde Park and detonated as a troop of Household Cavalry came past on their horses. A second bomb in Regent's Park was hidden in a bandstand where musicians from the Royal Green Jackets were playing hits from the musical *Oliver!* An eyewitness in the audience said, 'Suddenly there was a tremendous whoosh and I saw a leg fly past me.' In the two explosions eleven soldiers were killed and one horse. Six more horses had to be shot because of their injuries. Behind all this was Drogheda, the Easter Rising, the death of the hunger strikers, but we didn't care about any of that. All through the Factory there was the same mix of terror and fury. White faces, tight mouths. Among other things we discovered in ourselves a deep love of horses. At the briefing before our next patrol the CO appeared. We were warned to be professional. To do our job and nothing but. Were we listening? I'd say we were half listening.

Back at the garden centre today. Very quiet. People are on holiday and, anyway, they don't want to plant much in August. Summer's playing out. Most gardens just go their own way. Some roses bloom a second time. The unpicked courgettes turn into marrows. I arrived late and Tim said he needed to be able to depend on me and at the moment he couldn't. He had a piece of paper on which, in tiny handwriting, he had noted my times of arrival since the spring. He said he didn't want to start docking my pay but I was making things very difficult for him. Then, perhaps because he thought he'd gone too far, he said he knew there were problems and he didn't want to be unkind. All this might have made sense if there'd been a queue at the till or a heap of boxes to unpack but there was nothing.

At home again the study was so full of the heat of the day's sun I sat in my boxers and for an hour had a go at that *Mill on the Floss* essay for the OU. You know, it was your mother, one day in Bristol, who told me about the Open University. She encouraged me, and when I said it was above my head she said it wasn't. It took me a long while to believe that! When I did start I was angry with myself for not getting going sooner. It had a greater effect on my self-esteem, my self-respect, than anything I'd done since the day of my passing-out parade. I got a decent mark for my first essay, a nice letter to go with it. It was a revelation. And I kept it up for a while, but bit by bit fell back into old ways and bad habits, the thought that perhaps after all it wasn't for me. Not too difficult, that wasn't it. Hard to say what it was. Some fear of doing well, of having success. Of who might be deserving of that and who not.

Lord knows if anyone's still waiting for this essay. I studied my notes, hoping to catch my thread again. At the bottom of the last page I had written down a quote, 'The great thing is to last and get your work done and see and hear and learn and understand; and write when there is something that you know; and not before and not too damn much after.' Nothing to say where it's from or who it's by. Not George Eliot, I think. Anyway, I made no progress with the essay, unless opening the folder counts as progress.

I had a kip on the floor, just curled up on the rug, my folded T-shirt for a pillow. When I woke I went downstairs, drank water and ate a pot of strawberry yoghurt that was about to go past its best-before date. My head is so crammed with the past I sometimes have to hang on to things – the rumble of a tractor going past, the ache in my knees – to stop myself sliding down into it. If I don't, you'll come looking for me one day and I'll be hidden behind a wall thirty years thick. Or else you'll come in to find a young man sitting at the kitchen table in DPMs and webbing, his beret in his hands, his rifle sloped against the edge of the table.

Don't expect to get much sense out of him.

So, today I had to sign for a letter. Cheryl held out the box with the little glass screen and said I could just write with my fingernail, which I did, a signature that was no more than a spider scrawl, a signature – should it matter one day – I could say was not mine at all, nothing like it. She gave me the letter. She knew where it was from. It's where they built the *Titanic*, she said. She wondered if I'd seen the film. She loved it even though it starred Leonardo DiCaprio who usually she doesn't like at all. Something about his face. She smiled, watching me closely. She gave me some other mail, said I seemed popular today, then moved on to my neighbours.

There were no breathing exercises this time. What could they tell me I had not already imagined? I opened the letter in the hall, but because it was dark there I took it into the kitchen and read it by the window. 'Dear Mr Rose, as we have received no reply to our last . . .'

Once again he sets out the terms. It is not a court of law. Nothing I say as a witness can be used as the basis of a prosecution. This was guaranteed by the police and by the prosecution service of Northern Ireland. Because of this there was no need for me to arrange legal representation, though of course if I wished to . . .

I was urged to attend. Strongly urged. The value of my testimony, the information I was in a position to give. The Commission recognised that the event in question was long ago. It recognised that I could not be expected to recall every detail. All that was asked for was the fullest account I was able to offer, nothing else. It was anticipated that the hearing would last approximately a week but my part was unlikely to take longer than a single day. I would then, of course, be at liberty to return home.

And there were practical touches. A fund – small – that could, in certain cases, be used to assist in the matter of expenses, and a photocopied sheet giving the names of budget hotels and the numbers of taxi companies.

In the last paragraph he hopes that he will hear from me in the very near future. It was his experience that all who engage with the Commission in its work are glad to have done so. And he quotes the line that became the motto for the Saville Inquiry families, their rallying cry: Set the Truth Free. In setting the truth free we can, he says, set ourselves free. This is the kind of thing I used to hear at AA meetings. What if Carville turns out to be a fellow drunk? Would he go easy on me? And is that what I want? Someone to go easy on me?

I still have time to think about it, or that's what I've been telling myself. No need to say anything yet. No need to send anything. Behind such thoughts I try to glimpse the decisions of my heart. We play games with ourselves, don't we? Pretend to be weighing it up, this against that, on the one hand and on the other, when the decision is already made, there like the moon at the bottom of a well.

Maggie, I'd hoped Cheryl would give me a card from Spain. Instead, the other letters – more mail than I usually get in an entire week – seem the work of some imp who thought it might be fun to give Carville's letter a not-so-subtle background of farce. One is from Somerset libraries, a brochure with the title *Somerset Alive*, and a picture of a couple out walking with a small excited dog. The couple, who I think are meant to be retirement age, look to me about forty-five at most. Good teeth, plenty of hair. It's like the stair-lift ads I occasionally get where the models gaze gratefully at the hardware strapped to their banisters but give the impression they could race each other up the stairs and arrive laughing. The brochure has a list of classes I might like to attend. Old-time dancing. Something called Zumba for Seniors. And Memory Lane, a 'class' for people suffering with dementia and Alzheimer's, also their carers.

The other envelope was from Annie Fuller, a note on headed paper – Fuller's Funerals – asking if I fancied coming to see a folk band called Dragonsfly at Wedmore village hall next Saturday. A BNP fundraiser? For a while I was very angry with her. I have done nothing to court her interest. I think she's a very stubborn woman. I may have to be a lot blunter with her.

In the afternoon I went into town for groceries, and before turning into the Spar I gave a hard glance towards the door of her office. I scowled! Can you think of anything more cretinous? But there was more. I went to the library and asked in an offended voice why I had received information about dementia classes. She was a young librarian I hadn't seen before and she looked flustered. For all I know she's a volunteer helping to keep the place going in Austerity Britain. Finally, I sat down at the computer and went through my usual list of searches – the Commission, Ambrose Carville, me. I learnt nothing new, saw nothing I hadn't seen a dozen times. My last search was Dragonsfly. I imagined I'd find a video of them singing the Horst Wessel anthem but it wasn't like that. Their lead singer is called Maya Love. The mandolin player is a gentle Liverpudlian who talks about the little folk. There were no George crosses in the background. As far as you can tell good people just by looking at them, these were good people. I think I was slightly disappointed.

I have, since getting back, spent hours in the house I could hardly begin to tell you anything about, anything sensible. I could not find a place to rest, could not stop the noise in my head. Tried reading, tried not reading. At one point I got into a state thinking I couldn't think, that I'd been plunged into dark water. An HE attack? Some days now since I came off all medication. I made myself do sums. I wrote a list of everyone I know, full names. The panic ended, though in the calm that followed I had the very clear and mad thought that I might pop out to the pub, have a couple of beers, perhaps a beer and a chaser. I could taste the stuff. And the voice that spoke to me seemed like the voice of a friend. It seemed like the voice of life. Well, that passed too. I shut myself in the study and started scratching away on the paper again, writing this. The second letter has been filed with the first, between poetry and history. They have time for three or four more. At some point – a week or two to go – I imagine the tone of the letters undergoing a change.

I have no idea what's going to happen, Maggie, only that something is. I thought I'd faced it, gone down with my bottles to the deepest part of it. I thought I was somewhere else. But tonight it feels untouched, the whole thing, just as it was, all its old power. So – start again? I don't have the strength for it. I don't even know what that would mean. And suddenly I think of your card downstairs in the kitchen, the red button and the green. Start. Stop. Start. Stop. Start. Stop.

No sleep last night. It's a long while since I had a night like that, without edges, without a shore. Seven a.m. now and I feel about as solid as the dead moth I found on the windowsill in the front room the other day. I hardly use that room in summer. It smells of the fireplace, of dust, of old things.

What kind of event is the death of a moth on a windowsill?

And why are we trying to sort things out *now*, after thirty years? In South Africa after apartheid they got on with it straight away, or as soon as practically possible. In Rwanda, after an attempt at genocide, the machete the weapon of choice, they set up communal courts and those courts got on with it. They knew it was urgent. Memories were fresh. Wounds in the flesh and in the mind still healing. They went in while it was all still hot, bubbling. It's risky – must be – but what you face is what happened, the thing itself, and not what thirty years has made of it. Set the truth free? After thirty years the truth is either free already or lying on its back with its feet in the air. And why has no government minister – those same people who like nothing better than being photographed next to a tank, who cannot get through a speech without some tribute to the heroism and professionalism of our armed forces – why have they not put a stop to it? Why have they not just said that no soldier can be tried or even *questioned* about what happened during Operation Banner? I'll tell you why. They're embarrassed. That whole period embarrasses them. The British government using troops against its own people? That's what they used to do in the old Soviet bloc. They don't want to be reminded. It makes them squirm. They look away and fiddle with their shirt cuffs while British soldiers, men who put their bodies on the line as soldiers have always done, there to soak it up, whether it's bricks or bullets, those men are treated like they have the mark of Cain on them. I'll tell you this, our smooth-cheeked prime minister would not have lasted a week on the streets of West Belfast. He would not have lasted a week in Crossmaglen or South Armagh. And meanwhile, over there, the men who *really* got stuck into the killing game, they rise and rise and nobody dares whisper car-bomb or knee-capping or sectarian murder to them. They're groomed now and smile like babies. They're sitting in clean rooms. Every day they're quietly rewriting history. What are we supposed to feel about that? What are the veterans supposed to feel, with their mass-produced medals in a box in a drawer? Maybe Annie Fuller and her friends have an answer. I should talk to her about it, membership subs etc. Ask what would be required of me.

This morning, for the first time in three days, I got out of the house. It was cool outside. Scents of dry grass, and ten gardens away, a bonfire. One day it's high summer and the next we look out and see a red-brown flare in the chestnut tree, blackberries ripening in the hedgerow. I caught myself tilting up my face, turning my head side to side, not very different from what I see the rooks and jackdaws do, the way they balance on a chimney stack, shape themselves to the wind and read not just the weather but the weather behind it, the one that's being cooked up in some system still a hundred miles out at sea.

Where are you, Maggie? Are you back? You should be, by my count. I want to call you! I make plans to, I get close to it, stand right in front of the phone, but I'm afraid of what you might hear in my voice. You're not slow to pick things up and I may be losing my talent for bluffing. I want to sound easy. A fond father asking, as a fond father should, how you are, how it's going. Was Madrid a blast? (And no Madrid stories about doss houses and cheap wine. I haven't forgotten what Tess said about 'old history'.) I want you to hear a voice that weighs nothing, asks for nothing, but I'm scared I'll say your name and sound desperate. You'll ask what's wrong and I won't have a clue how to go on. Either silence or something obviously untrue. And then what?

When you first moved down here – that shock of good luck – I swore to myself I would never become a burden to you. Better to go out to the orchard with a blade or a bottle of pills than have you stuck with an old fool and his wheedling. I was serious. I meant it. That hasn't changed. So I will not call you. Not yet. In the state I'm in now I'm not sure I should even answer the phone, let alone make a call. If I could get some sleep. Five hours would do it, I think. Four good hours. Four hours and maybe I can see my way again.

In the middle of making breakfast today I imagined meeting him, Ambrose Carville. He appeared in my head without any warning. I don't know who he looked like other than himself, which is not possible as I have never seen a picture of him. Red-cheeked and sandy-haired. A tweed jacket. Younger than me but not by much. I let him have it. I crushed him with my arguments. He couldn't get a word in! And the more I defeated him, the more I wanted to go on. I taunted him. You call this justice? And what's this famous impartiality you boast of? In Belfast? Don't make me laugh. And I slapped him. One clean, hard slap. He staggered. He did not complain. He had the lost and slightly stupid look of someone coming to understand what he should have understood years ago. There were tears in his eyes!

Meanwhile my eggs hard-boiled in the pan. The tea grew tepid.

An hour later I was in the library looking up flight times Bristol to Belfast. The tenth of October is a Monday. Nine a.m. start? Quick confession and we can all go for lunch in the Commission canteen, corned beef and cabbage. There's only one flight on a

Sunday, a couple more on Saturday. I wrote the times down on a piece of paper given to me by the same young librarian I made a clown of myself with asking about the *Somerset Alive* brochure, the dementia classes. On the way home I took the paper out of my pocket, tore it into small pieces and put them in the bin outside the Indian restaurant.

In the afternoon I went to the meeting house to fix one of the toilets. Ned's been on about it for weeks. We're wasting water, Stephen! The toilets were put in just before I went away to the army. 1970s plumbing. As far as I can remember, putting them in at all was a bit controversial. An unspoken fear of certain odours seeping into where we sat, open before God. Now, of course, most of the Friends are of an age where the thought of a nearby toilet is a comforting one. The toilet acting up is the one the women use. The tank keeps filling and the water pours away down the overflow pipe. I took my shoes off and got up on the seat. It's a high cistern and even on the seat it was awkward to work with. I don't know who put it in. I messed around with the float arm but that didn't do it. I groped blindly, hands in the water, trying to feel if there was something wrong with the flapper seal or the chain. In the end I decided to replace the fill valve. I turned off the water supply, emptied the tank, unscrewed the locking nut, got a cupful of water down my shirt as I lifted the valve clear. I took it to the hardware store where Grahame who runs it said it was a museum piece and I'd have to find one online. I went back, sat in the cubicle, stared at the valve. What I could take apart I took apart. I cleaned it, then stood on the seat again to put it back, turned on the water, flushed and waited. The water came up, came up too far and began to trickle down the overflow. I have a small torch. All handymen have a small torch. I stood on tiptoe and tried to see exactly what was going on, more or less wedged my head between the tank and the ceiling. Nothing was going on, nothing visible, except the water coming up too high and going down the overflow pipe. And then I heard Ned. I know the sounds he makes. Very few people are completely silent and almost no older people. I know the creak of his sandals, the clicking of the little bones in his ankles. I thought, If he comes in here and says something like Getting it done, or Good man, I'm going to tell him to fuck off. Fuck off, Ned. Pardon? Then roar it – *Fuck off!* I heard him pause in the cloakroom. Was he listening? Then the door to the yard opened and he went out. I felt cheated. I wasn't going to get my moment. No sound of the pretty vase being dropped. My heart was racketing. It was hard to draw breath. I was still standing on the seat. I could feel tears at the back of my eyes. I wanted Ned to come back and hear my confession. A broken toilet as good a place as any. But more than that I longed for Dad to rise from his freshly mown grave and come in dusting the earth from the shoulders of the blue suit we buried him in. Let's go home, Stephen. And I would step down off the seat like one not already ruined and we would set off together, silently through clean woodland, every bough repeating the slowworm's song . . .

I'm in the study now, one minute past midnight, the day's fever already remote, already hard to explain or understand. I track this man, his comings and goings. I have some record of his thoughts and a kind of grainy film of what he's done all day, where he's been. I'm very suspicious of him. Is it time to hide the matches? Too late to hide the matches?

Woke up at midday to hear the phone ringing. It rings eight times before the answer machine kicks in. When it stopped I shut my eyes again and slept. I had a morning dream. Corporals Wright and Darling had a walk-on part, or I was, at least, expecting them. In the dream the house was empty. No bed, no desk, no books, no mirror in the hall. Perhaps Wright and Darling were coming to make sure nothing was left behind, to check the empty rooms and collect me. Certainly it was a departure dream. I knew that about it straight away.

And somehow the dream buried the memory of the ringing phone. Dusk before I remembered. The last few weeks I've been getting calls from a female robot that tells me there has been suspicious activity in my bank account. She gives me a number to call and I've wondered who would answer if I rang it. Who and where. The only suspicious activity in my bank account is that no money goes in, or so little I should really keep it all in a teapot on the mantelpiece. But it wasn't the robot, it was you. You were back. You liked Madrid. You'd put on a half-kilo of weight that was mostly Estrella beer and *patatas bravas*. And you had caught a summer cold, on the plane you thought. You would come and see me next Sunday. You would probably be all right by then. We could go to the meeting together. You hoped I was well. In the background I heard the bell on the Silk Shed door, heard Lorna calling a welcome to someone, and you rang off.

After playing a message the machine asks if I want to hear it again. I did. I pressed the button and out you came. I played it four or five times, while in the kitchen the light drained out of the window. Are your northern vowels starting to soften, or was that just your cold? I love to hear the north in you. Reminds me of Evie, I suppose, but mostly it's just because it's so much a part of who you are, my northerner, my northern daughter. If you'd grown up down here not only would you sound different I think you would be different. Not better or worse, but different. I never thought I had an accent at all until I went into the army and on day two or three some lad, at the mention of my name, said oooh-aargh. It was one of the London lads with a voice like a dog you don't want to get too close to.

So, I have until Sunday. And this helps. It sharpens the picture. Three days. I have three days to finish this and take the consequences. In three days you will find or you will not find. I'm tired, Maggie. It's time to bring this to an end.

On 4 August 1982 we went out with the RUC to search a house in the Ardoyne. The Ardoyne is a working-class Catholic area in North Belfast. In 1969 nearly two hundred houses there were burnt down by Loyalists, and the Loyalists have a song about it called 'The Night We Burnt Ardoyne'. It takes its tune from a Johnny Cash song and contains the line 'The next time you start trouble Ardoyne will be no more'.

When British troops first arrived, the wives in the Ardoyne competed with each other to see who could provide the most cups of tea, the most slices of home-baked bread and cakes. The army was there to protect them from Loyalist mobs who were, in fact, their neighbours. Then came internment, the imprisonment without trial of anyone thought to be a troublemaker. Nearly all of those rounded up were Catholics. None of it was done tenderly. Some of the interned were subjected to 'deep interrogation' – sleep deprivation, white noise, hooding etc. Before internment it was said that there was only one gun in the Ardoyne. Well, that changed. By the time we arrived, and long before it, the whole area was an IRA fortress awash with weapons and volunteers. If the IRA couldn't recruit in the Ardoyne they couldn't recruit anywhere. An off-duty soldier wandering around on his own would have been lucky to see the end of the day.

It was not a beautiful place. There was nothing quaint about it. Rows of little houses, bare red brick or pebbledash. A few small shops, pubs with Gaelic names we could not have begun to pronounce, tricolour flags in people's windows, washing in the yards, dogs, dog shit. But at the end of dull streets you could see green hills that in some lights looked so close you might imagine a short stroll taking you into the midst of them, giving you larks for company. I don't know what the locals thought about those hills. Much of the top was MoD land, observation posts, radio masts and the like, so they probably had mixed feelings.

It was mid-morning when we set out and I remember thinking it was a strange time to go. A Saturday morning, lots of people around. All the searches I'd been on before had been early, between four and five o'clock, so the man or woman answering the door was half dressed and half asleep. Usually the RUC did the searching and we were just there to set up a security cordon, but sometimes we did it ourselves. Can you imagine? You open the door in your dressing-gown and half a dozen squaddies pour through. We usually left a mess behind. It's hard to search and not make a mess but some of it was certainly deliberate. Drawers emptied onto the floor, curtains pulled down, floorboards levered up with a crowbar. Petty destruction as payback. Even when we found nothing, which was almost always, we assumed the people in the house were our enemies, and if they weren't before, they were afterwards. You may think this sounds bad enough (I think so too) but listening to older soldiers I got the impression that things had improved. By the time I was in Ireland it was no longer the norm to put a front door in with the boot of the largest soldier then treat some of the male members of the household to a bit of shoving. The shoving now, if there was any to be done, was left to the civil authorities while we, the military, played a secondary role. The idea was to make life in the Province more normal.

It was the third month of our tour and we felt like veterans. Soldiers in their third month were, I'd say, at their most effective. We knew our way around the city, or those parts of it that mattered to the army. We knew what to look for. We knew the other members of the brick like family. And we hadn't started to think too much of home yet, to count the days. We were sailors on a long voyage, out of sight of land and just going through the routines of the voyage. A letter might unsettle somebody for a morning, or a phone call with a girlfriend who didn't sound as fond as you'd hoped, but I didn't have a girlfriend and the only letters I got were from Dad and they were not unsettling. News that was no news, small stuff about the comings and goings in the town, how the garden fared. I loved them.

We patrolled up to four times every twenty-four hours. It doesn't leave you a lot of time for brooding. That's intentional, of course. You don't want five hundred fit young men sitting around with nothing to do. You certainly don't want five hundred young men armed with semi-automatic rifles doing that. (There were incidents in SF bases, there were fights, and at least one case I know of where a soldier shot another soldier.) So we were worked in a way that kept us just the right side of exhaustion. When we weren't on our feet outside – that weird dancing through the city, the scanning, the sudden sprints, the squatting in doorways by the empty milk bottles – we ate, smoked and slept. The only privacy was in the sangars where, for an hour or two, we watched the comings and goings of strangers through a pair of binoculars. Even in the toilets you heard someone in the next cubicle. The showers were all open stalls. The smell of each other, the hiss of sleep breath from the bunk above, the way somebody hummed or cracked his knuckles or cleared his throat. I'd find it unbearable now, though when it was over and I was home, I remember walking on the Levels and being completely alone for the first time in what felt like years. It frightened me! I was afraid I would drift apart, my limbs float off over the fields like zags of straw. By then, of course, I was full of strange imaginings. I was a house you would not want to visit. A house with an alarm going off in it.

They briefed us. They told us to be nice to the RUC. I don't remember getting ready but it would have been the usual – check your kit, load your weapon. And we would have been in a good mood because a house search was a break in the routine and there was always the chance of something interesting happening. We picked the RUC up on the way, then the whole convoy swept up the Crumlin Road and into the Ardoyne. A summer's day, breezy but warm. A day to go fishing, to sit in the garden of a country pub. We'd been shown on the map in the briefing room where we were headed, but as we were being driven there and driven back I doubt I paid much attention. It wasn't a long journey. Belfast is not a big place and the parts we dealt with were all close to each other. The Falls, the Shanklin, Short Strand, the Ardoyne. The expression 'a stone's throw away' has a fairly straightforward meaning in that city.

We pulled up along the road. Two army Land Rovers and two belonging to the RUC. Everybody got out – debussed in the unlovely language of the army. A straight east–west street of two-up-two-down houses, neither old nor new. Front yards mostly just for parking a car but some with a paddling-pool, a swing, a stab at a garden. The RUC didn't seem to be in much of a hurry. They stood in that way they liked to stand, or how I always remember them, hands tucked into their body armour. Were they waiting for some final permission to come over the radio, a last piece of intel? Was somebody watching from the top of the hill? We had a young officer with us, a second lieutenant, probably no more than a couple of years older than me. He joined in with the chat and I could see John France didn't like it much. Lots of people equals lots of targets. A drive-by shooting – we called them shoot and scoot – was definitely going to hit somebody. He went to speak with them. He wouldn't have been in awe of a young officer or the RUC. Anyway, whatever had been holding things up was sorted and the police, one of them carrying what I picture in memory as a Sterling submachine gun, went through a metal swing gate and down to the front door. John France came back to give us our orders. You, by the wall, you at the corner, you by the pillar box. When it came to me, Private Rose, he looked me over, paused, then sent me to the alley at the back of the house. I don't suppose I was pleased about that. Alleys had an evil reputation and on foot patrol we passed them quickly, peered down and passed them in a stride as if they were crevices in the pavement we had to take care not to fall into. But John France wouldn't have been interested in whether I liked my part. We were standing in the open and we needed to shift. Also, the back of the house needed to be covered. Why not send me? I had given him, in the last three months, no reason to think I'd do anything stupid.

I about-faced and jogged to the end of the street, turned left, passed a wall decorated with the portrait of a hunger striker (I don't remember which one, not Bobby Sands) and came to the mouth of the alley. Brick walls and wooden doors on both sides, a concrete path, rising slightly and ending in a slotted view of the hills. There was no one there. I checked over my shoulder to make sure there wasn't some local dicker – a look-out – taking an interest in me, then doubled about ten yards into the alley and went down onto one knee next to the wall opposite the one I was supposed to be watching. More shadow on my side, more light on the other. There were some bins out but I don't think there was one near me. I had no cover other than the shadow (not that a dustbin would have been much use). I started counting off the doors until it occurred to me I wasn't sure if the house being searched was the ninth or tenth in the terrace. So – the white door or the green? As I could see both of them clearly I probably decided it didn't matter much, but the doubt would not have helped. It would not have made me calmer.

And here's something I've spent thirty years trying to work out or remember. When, in all of this, did I cock my rifle? As I ran around? When I took up position? The moment is lost, and no hope of getting it back now. But what I know, or what I think I know, is that for the minute or so I waited in the alley the weapon was in a state expressly forbidden by the yellow card in my pocket. 'Unless you are about to open fire no live round must be carried in the breech and the working parts must be forward.' That's what it says. I've checked it online. You'll know enough about weapons to understand. People did it, of course. It was not unknown. If your corporal saw you he might bollock you or he might think you were showing initiative. Depended on the corporal. I don't believe John France would have approved but he wasn't there to see it. No one was.

And the safety? It's a switch just above the pistol grip, and on the SLR you can work it with your thumb while your trigger-finger stays where it's supposed to be. Clearly, I switched it off at some point. I honestly can't remember when. My best guess is I did it when I heard the shout – a man's voice cutting the air and coming, as far as I could tell, from the direction of the house. My first thought was that it was one of the RUC laying down the law, putting the fear into somebody. It was only afterwards, listening back across wider and wider spans of time, I began to have the idea that what I'd heard was a name. His name. So maybe not the RUC but someone who lived in the house. Father, uncle, brother. A sharp, clear, aimed shout. The kind you'd use if you saw a child about to follow a ball onto a busy road.

Let's say I flicked the safety then. Thumb on the lever and off it comes. That would make sense. The rear sights would have been up (I'd learnt my lesson in Tin City) but I didn't need them. The distance between me and the doors was only fifty feet or so, about the same from where I'm sitting now in the study to the aspen tree at the bottom of the garden. An infantry soldier who can't shoot fifty feet in broad daylight and hit the target, who can't do it quickly, doesn't know his work.

As for what was in my head then, between the shout and what followed, I'm tempted to say your guess is as good as mine. Adrenalin shuts down the kind of thinking that takes place in words and at the pace of speech. You're living in the far reaches of yourself. What guides you is the training, those months in basic, the weeks at Tin City, the hours and hours of drill. If you could be said at such a time to be interested in anything – I mean beyond staying alive – then it has to do with not letting people down. The battalion, the platoon, the brick. Thoughts about right and wrong, about whether I should have been there at all with a cocked rifle behind someone's house, I don't remember that voice. If it spoke it spoke in a whisper.

It turned out to be the white door, and it opened inwards, so that it seemed simply to disappear. In its place was a boy, a young man, a mop of brown hair, T-shirt, jeans, trainers (did people wear trainers then? In the Ardoyne? Perhaps they were plimsolls, gym shoes, daps). He stepped out – took a stride or half-stride into the alley – saw me and checked himself. He was in full sunlight, or that's how I remember him. Quite a tall lad, lightly built, rangy. We had, at best, two seconds to take each other in. He saw what he needed to – no way past, no way through. I saw brown hair, a pale, expressionless face. And I saw something else. His hands were not quite empty. He was holding something in his right hand – small, dark in colour, part of it protruding beyond his right fist. I couldn't see what it was, I wasn't close enough for that. And I'm not pretending I thought it was a gun or some sort of bomb, that's not my defence. I'm just saying that in the second we faced each other his hands were not quite empty and I saw that at once.

Why had he run from the house? Did he think the RUC would take him off to Castlereagh police station and give him a kicking? One of those interrogations that ended with a trip to the hospital? But the detectives who interviewed me later that day were very clear. He was not a terrorist. He had no police record. He had a cousin in the Fianna, which was a sort of Republican youth group, part Boy Scouts, part IRA, but everyone in Belfast had a cousin mixed up in something. Those detectives, RUC men, almost certainly Protestants and Loyalists, no friends of the Ardoyne, had nothing to say against him. So I don't know why he was running. He might have feared his innocence would not protect him. Who knows what stories he had heard, some of them true. And he would not have had much time to weigh it up. One moment in his bedroom listening to music or doing his homework, the next the police coming through the front door and all hell breaking loose. Perhaps he was having a joint up there, a sly smoke beside an open window, though nothing like that was ever spoken of.

But seeing me, fifty feet away, why not stop then? My best answer – the best I've been able to come up with in thirty years, and God knows I've given it some thought – is that he was used to it. He was sixteen years old. Have I said that? He knew us. Soldiers on foot patrol, in Land Rovers, behind riot shields, at vehicle check points. It's likely, given where he was growing up, he had been stopped before, perhaps multiple times, questioned, searched, one soldier frisking while another stood across the street with his rifle raised. I would not have been the first to point a gun in his direction. I might not have been the tenth or the twentieth. So he would have seen it very differently – seen me very differently – from a kid stepping out of his house in an English town and seeing the same thing.

His plan was to outrun me. I think that's right, though that isn't necessarily what I thought at the time. He couldn't go the short way to the road any more, so he'd have to go the long way, towards the hills. His trainers against my NI boots. He'd have a good start, and though I was probably at least as fit as him he wouldn't have needed to win the race by much. He would have known very well that a soldier on his own would only pursue so far, that he would not, in a place like the Ardoyne, risk isolating himself. As I said, he knew us, and familiarity breeds the inevitable. In the looking-glass world of the Troubles he might have felt almost safe.

* * *

At the Factory, before the RUC interview, I made a statement to the Royal Military Police. Redcaps we called them, and maybe they're called Redcaps in the RAF too. While I waited for them I was in a room with a lance corporal for company. I don't think he was there to guard me. As far as I know I wasn't under arrest or anything like that. If I was, no one had told me so. I think he was there to keep an eye on me, see I didn't wander off. He might also have been there to help me get my story straight. For my sake and for the sake of the army. I had never seen him before. He spoke in a low voice out of the corner of his mouth as though we were two cons in the prison yard in a film. Had he done this before? Was it one of his special duties? A wiry, tough-looking character, all bone and gristle, a little moustache on a pock-marked face. The sort of man I don't think you'd ever come across outside the army. I never have. He asked if I'd given a warning and when I shook my head he nodded as if he'd expected that. He urged me to keep coming back to the threat, because if I'd believed my life was in danger then I'd had every right to do as I did. Split-second decision. No time to think it through. What anyone would have done. Any soldier.

Something devilish about that lance jack, a whiff of sulphur, but he was right. You come back to the threat because it's very difficult to argue with what someone says he felt. So that's what I did, first with the Redcaps, then with the RUC. It wasn't lying. Every time I left the Factory I felt threatened. Out there, a hard Republican area, the thirteenth year of the war, alone in an alley with a young man, something in his hand, some object I couldn't identify in that second we came face to face, of course I felt threatened. But when the yellow card said you could open fire if there were no other means of protecting yourself it wasn't talking about that, some generalised sense of threat. It meant something specific. It meant a high degree of certainty. It meant you'd bloody well better be right. And I knew that. We all knew it.

As for getting my story straight, there wasn't really the material for one. At the Saville they were keeping track of scores of soldiers and hundreds of civilians, of comings and goings all over the Bogside. Lines of command, lines of sight. Hundreds of pages of testimony from people who couldn't remember and people who couldn't forget. They were dealing with crowds, with folk memory. They had expert witnesses – men I imagine bowing to each other when they met in the corridors – who talked of the limits of what could be said, the behaviour of rounds, the nature of wounds, who had examined the hands of the dead for signs that they had fired a gun or carried explosives.

Ambrose Carville won't need any of that. It's why he tells me it can be done in a day. I'd say it could be done in an hour. Two people, one red line between them. Witnesses? They might have found some. There would have been a sort of view from the upstairs windows of nearby houses, though to have seen both of us, to have seen us clearly, to have seen exactly what happened, they would have needed to be in the alley with us and they weren't. And what could a witness add? What's disputed? I was there, he was there. A range of about fifty feet.

John France was the first to arrive. He came full tilt around the corner. He couldn't have known what he was coming to but that didn't slow him down. I try to picture sometimes what he saw when he looked at me. He must have said something to me but I couldn't tell you what it was. He might have asked if the boy had been armed. He might have asked if I was wounded. There had only been one shot but in a city the sound of gunfire is confusing.

Was that an echo or a second shot? I remember him grabbing my arm, and shoving me forwards, telling me to cover the end of the alley. Given the new situation it needed to be done, and quickly, but I assume he also wanted me out of the way, not to be standing there when people started looking round for who was responsible. I ran, knelt by the wall again, the shaded side, the aim position. And because of that, because I had my back to it all, I heard more than I saw. I don't know if that's easier. I heard a woman screaming. I heard a man repeating the same words over and over. I heard John France and the RUC sergeant trying to keep order while at the same time trying to give first aid. Our kits didn't have much in them. Bandages basically, some sterile dressings, iodine swabs. Faces began to show themselves at the end of the alley. They saw me and kept their distance, but the truth is they could have walked down there and lifted the SLR out of my hands. I don't know if John France realised that or not. I heard the ambulance siren. I seemed to hear it from its setting out, its whole journey across the city. A helicopter started to circle. Then a bottle, launched from one of those back yards, somersaulted through the air and shattered on the wall above me. When I looked round it was only soldiers left in the alley. The family had been taken back to the house or had gone to the hospital. Another bottle came over. I wasn't even wearing a helmet, none of us were. I was afraid for my eyes. I was afraid that someone was running to fetch a grenade. There would have been a grenade in the Ardoyne somewhere. A grenade or any kind of bomb, its blast contained by the walls of the alley, would have cleared it.

What can I tell you about those final minutes? An August day was falling on our heads like a tower block. At some point I heard John France shouting my name. He had to shout because of the noise of the helicopter. He waved me towards him and covered me as I ran. I leapt over the litter of dressings. I leapt over his running shoes that had been taken off and then forgotten. I leapt over the black web that crossed the whole width of the path. One of the Land Rovers had reversed to the mouth of the alley, rear doors wide. We tumbled into the back, everybody wild-eyed and heaving for air, somebody up front bawling Move! Move! Move! APCs had arrived and troops in riot gear but people knew or guessed who was in the Land Rover and they let us have it. As we turned up the street a petrol bomb burst across the windscreen grille and for three or four seconds we were just driving through fire.

At the Factory they took away my rifle. I suppose they needed it for ballistic tests. I followed the colour sergeant to the room I mentioned, a sort of office with metal filing cabinets and plastic chairs, a metal table. When the colour left, the lance jack came in. He gave me a cigarette. He asked where I was from and I told him. I could feel him taking me in. I was a story he would tell to other lance jacks. Then the sound of boots and the door opening and two Royal Military Police with briefcases came in. I'm not sure of their rank. NCOs, I think, or one might have been a warrant officer. When they were ready they told me to sit in the chair on the other side of the table. The lance jack disappeared. I never saw him again. The Redcaps looked like men not entirely at home with pens and paper but they did everything thoroughly. One of them, the bigger one, a real prize-fighter, laid blue carbon paper between two sheets on the statement pad. He did it once, then, not quite happy with it, did it again.

They wanted me to start at the moment we left the base to go on the search. I spoke and the bigger of the two wrote in black biro. Was he writing everything I said? It didn't look like it. Perhaps part of his training was just to write the stuff that mattered. When he got to the bottom of each page he tore it out and put the carbon paper underneath the next. So it was a story told with pauses. I would look at him and when he was ready he would glance up and nod. I can't say now how long it took. Less than an hour. At the end I was told I could go to the canteen and eat. After that I was to report to the CO's office.

It was many hours since I'd eaten but I didn't go to the canteen. The thought of sitting with other soldiers, some of them, perhaps all, already knowing what had happened or having heard some Chinese-whispers version of it, the thought that someone might ask how it felt.

I went to the NAAFI instead, bought biscuits and a can of drink. The woman who served me was the only woman on the base. Kath? Kathleen? She was a local, so if she didn't hear about it from a soldier she would hear when she went home. I ate some of the biscuits, drank the tin, then brushed the crumbs off my lap and went to the CO's office. In the outer office people were doing clerical work. It was a busy place, phones ringing, people scurrying about with files. They all knew what I was doing there and all of them at some point took a good look at me. When I went through to the CO I came to attention and saluted. These things, as you know, become automatic. He asked if I was all right, and I said, Yes, sir. I saw there were two other men in the room, dressed in civvies. These were the RUC detectives. The CO said they would interview me at a police station. He said he was sure I would give them my full co-operation. I went out with them to the yard. They had a civilian car, unmarked, just an ordinary car, or that was what it looked like to me. One of them took a long coat from the boot and told me to put it on to cover my uniform. I sat in the back. They didn't speak a word on the journey, either to each other or to me. In the interview room they had a green folder with his name on it. When they opened it I could see a photograph, and although it was upside down it looked like the sort of photograph kept on a mantelpiece in a frame, and I assumed they had taken it from the house. The hair I had seen, thick brown hair, was cut short in the picture. And he was younger, more obviously, more definitely, a boy. They took my statement. I said what I'd already said to the Redcaps. When I was done they informed me I was not at that time being charged with an offence but that I might be later. It would be a decision made by others. We all smoked and used the same ashtray. I didn't break down or anything. I don't know what they thought of me. They were both somewhere in their forties and with that deep tiredness you saw often enough in Belfast among people who were there full time, who weren't going home after four months, who were already home. I'd say they were neither for me nor against me. They did their job. That and no more.

I got a lift to the Factory in an army Land Rover. I assumed someone would be waiting for me – the colour sergeant, the lance jack, John France, someone, and they would tell me where to go and what came next. I hung around in the yard. I might as well have been invisible. In the end I went up the stone stairs to our room. It was empty. I curled up on my bunk and slept. When I woke they were back, taking off their gear, putting rifles in the rack, lighting cigarettes. I wondered who the new fourth man was and if I would ever patrol with them again. When they saw I was awake they nodded to me. Someone asked how it had gone, meaning the interviews. I said they were OK. I understood I was on the other side of something and that they were looking at me across a street, a river. They could not join me, I could not join them. It was early evening by then. I wanted to call Dad. I could feel things getting away from me, and if there was anyone in the world who could put it right, it was him. I was still thinking in those terms, you see, putting things right. There was the usual queue for the phone but the soldier at the front gave me his place and when the booth was free I went in. I started dialling the number. It's the same one I have now. At some point, in the middle of dialling, I understood I couldn't begin to tell Dad anything at all about the day. I went out and said, No one home. Actually, I might have said, Wrong number.

Upstairs the others were dozing or asleep. I slept for a while, then woke and lay there, rigid, as if I'd come round in the middle of an operation. Lots of things that became familiar later began then. The chaos in the head, the chaos in the heart. I sat up to watch the TV, one of those detective shows they made hundreds of episodes of, all of them basically the same episode. The room wasn't cold but I was shaking, my arms wrapped round my chest. In the squat in Bristol I saw a man like that who was coming off hard drugs. I stared at the screen as if my life depended on it. I don't know if I was making any kind of sound, I might have been. John France got off his bunk and came over. In some degree or another he too must have been in shock. He told me to lie down. When I did, he put the Walkman earpieces in my ears, put the Walkman on the blanket by my hand, studied me a moment, nodded, and went back to bed. I had never listened to music in that way before – music that seems to play inside your head. It was Motown stuff mostly. I listened to Marvin Gaye and Smokey Robinson and the Reverend Al Green. I listened to Stevie Wonder and Gladys Knight. I listened to the Temptations. I listened to Wilson Pickett singing 'In The Midnight Hour'. It means I can't listen to any of that any more. If I hear it playing somewhere I have to leave at once, even now. But it got me through. It carried me. And what he did that night, John France, the loaning of the precious machine, the perfect timing of it, I'd say it's one of the kindest things anyone has ever done for me. It's nice to be able to tell somebody about it at last.

In the morning I was sent to the CO's office again, and that afternoon I was at Aldergrove airport. By nightfall I was back in Germany, the old Luftwaffe barracks. For the next few weeks I was given simple duties. I mowed the grass around the trees that shaded the parade ground. I painted the whole length of one of those long wide corridors upstairs in the old building. I did not go out on any border patrols. I did no guard duties. I did not handle any weapons. Other soldiers, those who knew why I was back, the gist of it, looked at me with a mix of curiosity and respect. Some avoided me. Some spoke to me in a low voice as if I'd been bereaved. Even that crew of older men, veterans of Operation Banner, even they nodded as they passed me, acknowledged my existence in a way they wouldn't have bothered to before. I looked for places to hide. One I found was the old air-raid shelter with the concrete eagle in it, *Luftschutzraum*. Sit there for fifteen minutes and smoke. Whenever I could get out and drink I did. I walked deeper into the town to bars where I was unlikely to find another squaddie. The best was a place called the Ratskeller or the Rathskeller. Very simple and homely. An old couple ran it. The man had a very fine moustache. I would drink until my money ran out. I was never any trouble to them. I think they understood what was going on or some part of it. People are not fools, and what had Germans of their generation not seen already?

The padre had a talk with me. He was the only person from the army who seemed to think I might need some help. He was the Catholic padre and he told me he had once been a monk. We met in his room. It was cosy, full of books. We sat on armchairs. He made me tea. He asked no questions about Belfast, about what had actually happened. Anyone listening at the door would have been none the wiser. He told me the story of the disciples frightened by the storm. Do you know it? They're crossing the Sea of Galilee and a big storm blows up. Jesus is asleep in the boat. The disciples wake him. They are, in the language we might have used at the time, bricking it. And Jesus chides them. Where is their faith? Have they not understood yet who he is? He commands the storm to cease and it does. You can picture the faces of the disciples. Mouths slack, brows furrowed. They often seem slow-witted in the stories, comic stooges of the great magician, but I don't think we'd do any better. You don't expect a man to be able to command the wind or make the waves lie down. I listened to the padre talking, this ex-monk whose hands, whose whole body perhaps, smelt strongly of coal-tar soap. I leant and nodded. I wanted him to have the impression he was helping. When it was done he stood and said I could come to see him at any time. His door would be open. I thanked him. I don't think I saluted. The padres were officers but as far as I remember you didn't have to salute them.

A letter arrived from Dad. The CO in Belfast had been in touch with him, though from the letter it was hard to know what had been said, what exactly. He knew I'd been sent back to Germany. He knew I was in trouble. It was quite a short letter and I could feel the anxiety in it. He would have written it up in here, sitting where I am now. He said he was relieved I was out of harm's way. He urged me to get in touch. I phoned him the same evening. It was easier than I'd thought it would be. We both spoke calmly. I told him what I was doing, the simple duties, the painting and the mowing. I can't say how I sounded to him. Normal, not normal. At the end of the call he said I should come home as soon as possible and I said I would.

That night, in the Rathskeller, I got spectacularly drunk. I have no idea how I got back. My first true blackout? I should have been put on jankers, confined to barracks, but they looked the other way. By then I was dreaming pretty fluently. Night blooms, the news read by a maniac. But in their way the dreams were a relief. They had an honesty I couldn't find in waking life or couldn't face. They showed me where I was.

In October I came home on leave. I had already applied for a discharge. No difficulties were put in my way. I don't know if they were relieved to see me go. Leaving takes about the same length of time as getting in. Technically, I was still in the army when I went to Bristol in the old ambulance and still in it the night I met your mother in the snow.

Maggie, the dead boy's name was Francis Harkin. It's taken me a while to get that down, hasn't it? Two words. I'm guessing it's painted on a wall there or carved into stone in some garden of remembrance. I hope it is. All I know about him I learnt from the RUC detectives who took my statement, which is to say I know almost nothing. He was sixteen, still at school, had no known connection to any paramilitary organisation. I also know he was asthmatic because that was what he had in his hand when he ran out into the alley, an asthma inhaler. One of those blue or grey ones you use to spray medicine into your lungs. In a race then, even with my boots and clobber, I might have caught him.

In the end I was not charged with anything. They told me that before I left Germany. I was summoned to see someone called Major Holly, a middle-management type, pink as a sausage, and I stood in front of his desk while he read out the decision of the public prosecutor. The matter would be taken no further. My defence – the one offered by the army on my behalf – was that I had acted reasonably in the circumstances and that this was the case even if I had, in fact, been mistaken. It was the standard defence and it usually worked. The major asked if I understood and I said I did. Even so, he felt the need to explain it to me. You're in the clear, Rose. Case closed. You can put it behind you now. You can get on with your life. He had a slightly puzzled expression on his face. Perhaps he'd expected me to look more grateful.

I believe the family received compensation. I couldn't tell you how much. When a boy in the same neighbourhood was killed the year before by a soldier in an observation tower (he heard gunfire, looked through his sights and thought he saw things he might not have seen) the family received sixteen thousand pounds.

I get hung up on details. His T-shirt, for example. It wasn't plain. It had some pattern on it, a design. Darth Vader? Rocky? And was it red? Black? Black with red lettering? I have rerun it so many times he's sometimes like an actor I dress for the part with whatever I can find in the props basket. All of us are like that, in fact. A travelling theatre company with only one short play, pulling on our costumes for the ten-thousandth time. But each time we play it there's a small alteration. The RUC walk up the front path in a different order, perhaps jostling each other like a pair of comedians. There's a different hunger striker painted on the side of the house. The wall I have my shoulder against in the alley is warm from the sun or it's cool from the shade. Sometimes I completely forget to imagine the hills.

*   *   *

He'd be forty-seven now. Brown hair thinner and peppered with grey, the light frame broadened by solid Irish food. He'd remember, of course, the day the house was searched, his wild decision to run. He'd remember the soldier behind the house. He'd remember it and shake his head. *Thank Christ all that's over.* Then he'd pick up his keys, call to someone that he'd be home soon, step out his front door and greet the day.

Did I set out that day to shoot an Irishman? Payback for the dead bandsmen and the dead horses in the London parks? I have examined my conscience more than most. To sift your intentions is hard, whatever your friend Nagamudra might say. The mind is not a box you can just empty out. Do we, at any given instant, know all that is in our heads? *All* of it? Do you? And suppose there is, in some fold of the brain, some crevice, unlit and unvisited, the thought of doing harm, some small idea of it, very small, does that count as an intention? Even when the rest of what's there is different, is opposed, means no one any harm?

I've spent thirty years trying to say something to the woman who keened over him in the alley. I have tried, drunk and sober, to find the words. At some point I began to imagine the words as a spell that would release me from a curse. I broke her heart that day. I know that. I knew it at once from the sounds she was making. I think now that my heart must break too and only then will I know what to say to her.

It's Saturday afternoon. My watch is AWOL but I'd say it's about seven. There's a blackbird in the garden trying to keep the night off with a song. Someone should tell him it's a bit late in the year for singing. I don't have any more to write. I look at the pile of paper on the desk and my main feeling is that at great length and with many hours of work I've somehow managed to miss it all. At least you know his name now. I'm glad to have put that down.

Will you try, at a meeting one Sunday, in the silence there, to hold him in your thoughts for a while? I don't have a picture of him to give you so you'll just have to imagine him, someone who seems like they could be him. Maybe a friend from school, some boy you knew, somebody without blame. Though I've told you I don't believe in the dead I think it would soothe him, the old anger. I think you'd be the right person to do it. Anyway, I'd be grateful if you'd try.

I wish I had a different story to tell you. I would have kept it from you if I could but it turns out that wasn't possible. It cannot be made less and it cannot be made safe and it cannot be hidden and it cannot be forgotten. So there it is. Make what you can of it. I'd ask for forgiveness if I thought there was any chance of having it but it's not an option. I know that. It's not in anyone's gift. There is, in truth, no one to ask.

I'm sorry, Maggie. I'm very sorry.

Dear Maggie (if I may),

Though we have seen each other on a number of occasions at the meeting house we haven't yet managed to exchange more than a few words. That is very remiss of me and I hope to put it right soon. I wanted to slip a note under the door of your splendid-looking tea rooms to say how sorry I am about Stephen. He was doing so well! And now, alas, this, and seemingly out of the blue. I want you to know that you can, at any time, contact me or any of the other Friends and be sure of a sympathetic ear and, wherever possible, of practical support. Stephen is very dear to us, and not simply on account of his father – your grandfather – who was such an important member of our community for so many years.

My telephone numbers are below, the landline and the mobile. Tessa Douel has asked that I include hers also. Please don't hesitate to get in touch.

Yours in Friendship,
Sarah (Waterfall)

STOP

It occurred to me I might be dead and I think it's possible that I was, that I'd crossed the line or was crossing it, was in some kind of limbo where the brain is busy trying to make sense of what it doesn't understand at all, trying to see itself, what's wrong, then doing what it always does, putting together a story of some kind, however unlikely. I saw things – heard them too. They seemed real enough at the time. I was lying under the aspen tree and Mum was kneeling beside me. She was talking to me but I couldn't get it, not quite. Or I couldn't get the words but I understood the sense. She wasn't able to help me, she wasn't able to look after me, that place was taken, there was somebody else she had to take care of. I knew who she meant and I saw the rightness of it but I was frightened. I would have clung to her but I had no strength at all, couldn't lift a finger. Then I felt myself tipping backwards – quite slowly – and there was an ease to it I was tempted by. After all, what was I trying to save? But something nudged me the other way, some instinct, something reptilian, the last of life's gatekeepers, and I began to will myself upwards, spent everything in a last effort to reach the surface and the light.

And then the light was there, directly above me, and I opened my eyes and I was in the back of an ambulance in the company of a pair of volunteers. They had on those crude homemade hoods, the eye holes frayed. They didn't speak to me, didn't introduce themselves. I could smell the drink on them, as if they'd had a few to get them in the mood. The hands of one looked like those of an old man, like talons. The other had smooth skin, very white, and I thought this could be a girl, a woman, one of those whose picture I studied at the Factory. We were travelling recklessly, some maniac up the front hurtling us down country roads, no streetlamps, no sounds of other traffic. I knew of course how it would end, the crossroads or whatever it was they were aiming at, some place with nothing nearby except foxes and sleeping farmhouses. Given the nature of my offence there might be a beating first, they might want to break something, but headlights can be seen from miles away in country like that, so wiser just to kneel me down at the edge of the road and get on with it. They wouldn't need their hoods any more. My hands would be tied. I'd feel the dampness of the road through the cloth over my knees, and by the light of the dipped headlights I'd see hawthorn and campion, perhaps part of a gate, the mud rutted by tractor tyres. And everything would be interesting, wouldn't it? The mind's last big stretch. And all of it irrelevant, already half a galaxy away. And then the boots come closer, stop an arm's length behind you. Nobody says anything. In your head you have the word 'okay', you have the word 'now'. You tense your back, stiffen the muscles in your neck. As if that'll help.

When I woke in the hospital – woke properly this time – there was a lot of confusion. I'd been drugged, wired up, floating, and in the space of a heartbeat I was back. No smooth return. It was a jolt, like someone had the defibrillator pads on me. For half a minute I had no idea where I was but it wasn't my first night on an ICU. I heard the machines, the hissing of compressed air, and from something else, another machine busy keeping someone alive, little electronic peeps, like a van reversing out in the car park. I think the first thing I did was groan. The next was to scratch about for a buzzer or alarm but my fingers found only the sheets and I had no voice. In the morning or at the nurses' shift-change, I tried again and this time I got some attention. I asked what was going on, what I was doing there. How had I got here? The nurse went away and came back with a pill in a paper cup. That's one way to deal with questions.

When I'd slept it off I realised I'd better ask in a way that didn't make me look like I needed sedating. I found my buzzer, got a nurse, a different one, very sympathetic, but beyond being able to tell me I'd been there for three days she didn't have any answers. She said she would find somebody who could help but night came again and I was still none the wiser. I stopped asking. I waited for the police to show up but that didn't happen either. I had cannulas in the backs of both hands. Stuff leaked into me from clear bags, diluting the poisons. If there had there been a wall to turn my face to I would have done it but I was, as you saw, somewhere in the middle of the row, and even the people at the end are well away from the wall. I dare say they think about things like that when they design those places.

There was a whole day when I wept without bothering to wipe away the tears. They looked at me then, shrewdly. They were not interested in a drunk's self-pity, but in ICU tears are a sign you're on the mend. I remember a staff nurse on the night shift, cheery and battle-hardened, beautifully Irish, telling me, as a kind of joke, that I was condemned to live. She was right. The slow hours in that place did their work. I dried up, began to eat. Turns out I don't quite have the character to die of *feelings*. The character or the courage. Eventually they kicked me out. A porter arrived with a wheelchair and pushed me along a mile of corridor to an observation ward. This was an old part of the hospital – big windows, high ceiling, wobbly linoleum – but here at least I hoped I might get a visitor. I did. I came round from a doze to find Dr Rauch at the end of my bed. We just looked at each other for a while. I said I was sorry. I felt like a child there with her. A child who has failed many times, who has promised to improve and then failed again. The only comfort was that I could see she had expected it, that she knew us well enough, knew me. She asked if I wanted to go into rehab. There was a place in Bristol, a local-authority centre called Virgil House. She had sent people there before. She could refer me if I wanted it. I said yes, immediately. I knew I couldn't face going home. I couldn't think of anywhere I'd be more lost. She nodded, said she'd take care of it. She didn't wish me luck or say any nonsense about getting well soon. I do believe she called me Stephen. I think she did. Then she left and I watched her, her slightly stooped back, and thought how it's always me who leaves. She's small and burdened. A doctor who cares more than is wise.

And it's where I am now – Virgil House. Where I've been for almost two weeks, the last residential treatment centre in the city – Austerity has done for the rest of them. I'm sitting on a bench in the courtyard behind the house. A lot of pot plants out here, succulents and so on, a smokers' zone that's always busy. We're in a smart but anonymous area off Whiteladies Road. Wide streets, big grey villas, most of them packed with university students, kids from all over the world. Opposite us is a dental practice with blinds in the window. There are no shops on our street and no pub.

They've done their best to make the house welcoming – more B-and-B than hospital – but all the guests are addicts, detoxing from booze or hard drugs or both, and there's this smell that seeps out of us, in our breath and through the pores of our skin, which can't be covered up by disinfectant or the cooking steam from the kitchen. It's only men here (I've no idea what the women are supposed to do) and we're asked to think of ourselves as brothers. I share a room with two of them, one about my age, public school voice, here on his third stay. He runs a restaurant in the city and worries someone will steal his chef while he's in. The other is much younger, a Bristol lad, Hartcliffe. I don't think he's spent much time in restaurants. From the look of him I'd say there wasn't quite enough food on the table when he was a boy. I think they call it 'food insecurity' now, but it might be better just called hunger. He wears a Bristol Rovers hoodie, has a tattoo of a blue tear beside his left eye I think he probably did himself. I know quite a lot about both of them. I suppose they must know a lot about me.

About half the brothers suffer with depression, and on my second day I was asked to fill out a questionnaire. Do you keep reasonably cheerful or have you been low-spirited recently? How would you describe it? Does it come and go? Have you wanted to cry? Does crying relieve it? Do you feel beyond tears? Each answer carries a score. They tot it up and make their diagnosis. I must have been just the right side of the line, though there was a section about guilt – Do you feel you've let your friends and family down? Is your condition a punishment? – I couldn't have done so well on. At breakfast I watch people lining up the pills next to their cereal bowls. Seroxat, Cipramil, Efexor. I was on Librium in the hospital (10 mgs four times a day) but here I take nothing stronger than vitamin B. I haven't wept since coming here. I haven't had a panic attack. Am I OK? Obviously not. The staff here are suspicious. They want more from me. They accuse me, very gently, of holding out on them. They're waiting for a wall to give and I suppose I am too. My guess is they have a white box with my name on it in the office and the hour will come when I'll stand at the office door with bloodshot eyes and trembling hands and ask for it. So be it. If it's what needs to happen maybe I should welcome it. Why put off the inevitable? But until then I have this spell of days, a gap, an opening, I might be able to do something with. Don't ask me what. But *something*.

I pieced together the story of what happened to me that night at home by lying in my hospital bed and waiting for the world to send its messengers. Tess Douel was the first. She came the day after I'd seen Dr Rauch, the early-evening visiting hour. I saw her coming down the ward looking at the beds, at the heads in the beds. Did we all look the same? I wanted to call out to her but I choked up and had to settle for feeble waving. It's only when you meet someone from the outside that you realise how weak you are.

The food trolley was working its way through. Visitors – entire extended families sometimes – settling themselves at the sides of beds. I told Tess I didn't know how I'd got to the hospital. I didn't know what had happened or who had called the ambulance. I said I didn't know anything, though that wasn't quite right. I knew some things. I had, for example, a pretty clear memory of myself standing in the Spar in front of the booze shelves and feeling a rush of black joy.

I asked if she'd seen you. The sister in ICU had told me you'd been in – twice on the day I was admitted and three or four times the next day, but after that, nothing. Tess shook her head. I had the sense she was weighing up how much she should tell me, what I'd be able to manage, what was best left. Then she drew the chair closer, settled those large brown eyes on mine, and began to speak.

The first she knew of any trouble was when she went to Plant World to order flowers for a wedding. She took her list into the office. Only Debbie was there and she asked at once if Tess had heard the news. I'd had some type of seizure, at home, and been taken off in an ambulance. She didn't know how I was, how serious it was. Tess said the news shocked her. She felt guilty. The day we spoke outside the shed and I told her I was afraid of losing you she'd had a premonition of trouble. She'd done nothing about it and now things had turned out as she'd feared.

She left the office and drove over to my house. It was only when she was parking that it occurred to her there was no point in being there. I had been taken to hospital! The house would be empty. Unless I was already back? What if it had looked a lot worse than it was? Or the whole thing was just gossip, a town rumour? One way to find out. She walked up to the front door and said she had her finger an inch from the bell when the door opened and there was Lorna! They recognised each other from the meeting house, and after getting over the surprise of being suddenly face to face like that it was obvious to Tess that Lorna wanted to talk. I've told you before how Tess has something that draws people out. She looks honest. She looks like she *will* listen. And Lorna may have felt she owed some sort of explanation for being there, inside my house, on her own. They went in together to the kitchen. Tess made a pot of tea, then they sat with their mugs while Lorna told her about the two of you ringing my doorbell on Sunday morning and getting anxious when no one answered. You'd obviously forgotten your keys (though haven't I told you where I keep the secret one?). And then my neighbour Frank coming over with the news of what he'd seen – the ambulance, and me under a blanket hurried into the back of it, middle of the night.

The next part of the story – some of it at least – you'll know much better than I do, though it feels important to try to get it straight in my head. It's also what I'm supposed to be doing here, at Virgil House. Getting clear, facing into, taking responsibility for. They want us to be like men standing on some exposed headland staring into the wind. It's what they call being accountable. That's a word I hear twenty times a day.

So – you drove to Bath and found me in ICU, tubed up and perhaps, to look at, more dead than alive. Someone would have explained why I was there, that I hadn't tripped over the stair carpet or slipped in the shower. Did you get a flashback to the time you came with Evie to see me in the hospital in Yeovil? Did you think you were seeing what you'd imagined you'd see then? And I wonder what else they told you. That I'd pull through? That I might? That I wouldn't? (When Dad was near the end, Dr Brompton, his GP, took me aside one morning and said, You do understand that your father is very ill? I thought he was an idiot but I suppose he just assumed that with all the drinking I might not have realised what was going on.)

The next morning you went over to my house, the pair of you. Had the keys this time. You wanted to pack a bag for me. I don't know if the hospital asked you to do that or if it was just something you thought might be necessary. Either way, thank you. As for what followed, I think I guessed it before I heard it. After all, why not look around? I might have left a window open and some room was filling up with rain and birds. And so you came to the study, leant in and saw the pile of paper on the desk. How much did you read? Did you see your own name, get some inkling of what it was, that it was aimed at you, was, perhaps, about you? And then what? Lorna calling you from the hall and you putting down a half-read page and setting off for another visit to a man who might have been made of wax for all the sense you were going to get out of him?

I kept asking Tess for details she didn't have. What time did you leave the hospital that day? What time did you get back to the Silk Shed? How long after that did you leave to go to my house again and carry on with your reading? I wasn't at my sharpest. There was still some brain-blur, brain fog. And to have everything third hand! Like watching a film in a mirror. Tess was patient, went over things again when I asked her to. She saw what she was dealing with, a sick man speaking to the world, trying to make sense of it. But she stuck to what she knew, what Lorna had told her. I don't think either of them – Tess or Lorna – is the sort of storyteller who makes stuff up to plug a gap.

But why go on your own? Why not, I suppose. You're not joined at the hip. You were going there to read and you don't need company for that. Maybe Lorna had duties at the Silk Shed. Anyway, you were gone for hours. Lorna said she rang your phone a couple of times but got no answer. After midnight before she saw you again, and when she did she was frightened. You were silent, thin-lipped, furious. You wouldn't answer her questions. She told Tess her instinct was to give you space, let you take your time, but somehow she couldn't do it and she followed you from room to room until, just before bed, the pair of you exhausted and Lorna asking for the hundredth time, What *is* it?, you said – you shouted! – Stephen's been lying to me!

Were those really your words? Tess spoke them quietly, almost a whisper, but I heard them – seemed to – as Lorna had. They went in like a blade.

I missed the next part of the story. I was deaf, stuck, had a taste in my mouth like reflux acid. Tess waited. There's not much more, she said. I must have nodded or waved her on. It didn't seem like there could be much else to lose.

When the morning came nothing had changed. Lorna started her questions again but all she got for her troubles was a warning to 'Leave it!' She'd seen you in moods before but never like this. She told Tess she decided to put her faith in work. If you were busy, did the normal things, all those things you need to do to get the Silk Shed ready for opening, you would find yourself again. And for a while it seemed to be helping, but then, of course, you dropped the tray of crockery and though none of it was valuable stuff you wouldn't be comforted. Was that the moment you made your decision, or had it been made already? You swept up the broken china, went to the flat, came down fifteen minutes later with a case. You were going north, home, to Evie. You wouldn't say when you'd be back, you didn't know. Lorna told Tess you wouldn't meet her eyes, that you said sorry to her but said it as if to a stranger. There were tears then – in my kitchen, and I assume at the Silk Shed too. A few minutes later she saw you go by in your car and you were hunched over the wheel as if headed to the far ends of the earth.

For a while Lorna was lost. She had no idea what her next move should be. She told Tess she had a ten-second crisis, then shook herself into action. She called the hospital to make sure I was still alive, put a 'closed due to staff illness' card in the tea-room window, hunted down your keys and drove over to the house. She was afraid you might have taken it with you, whatever it was you'd read, but she hadn't seen you come in with it so guessed it was still there. It was. A little scattered and shuffled but clear enough. She sat and worked through it. And she did what I think you didn't do. She took the Commission's letters from their hiding place on the bookshelf and read them too. She didn't know if she was justified in doing that, if it was some sort of violation of privacy, but she did it anyway. She needed to know what was going on. It was self-defence.

She was cagey with Tess about what she'd read but when Tess asked if any of it was about Belfast she opened up. They sat in my house for the best part of two hours and when they left they hugged on the doorstep. That hug was the first thing in the whole story I liked.

Tess stayed with me until the ward emptied and the staff were settling us down for the night. I think she felt she'd been unwise to say so much but short of not coming in at all I don't know what else she could have done. She said something about you and me reaching the place we needed to get to, that there would be a far side to it and it would be better because there would be no more hiding anything. As she spoke about it, I had the sudden feeling she might be talking about something of her own, her own experience, something I'd failed to notice. I worry about that – that I've spent a lot of my life not noticing what other people are going through. The ward lights were dimmed and she stood up to leave. I caught her hand. How had Debbie known? She shook her head. She hadn't stopped to ask. It hadn't occurred to her. Sorry, she said. And she squeezed my fingers and left.

* * *

A long night after that. The shadows of the night staff, their whispers, the now and then sound of a curtain being drawn around someone's bed. You always wonder if the bed next to you will be empty in the morning. Some idea of the night as a body of black water you have to swim through and not everyone guaranteed to make it. I thought of you, of course. I don't know what the inside of Evie's house looks like so I imagined you in rooms I mocked up and then decorated with things I remembered Evie having in Bristol. The Georgia O'Keeffe, the picture of Yeats, the paperbacks, the rugs. I had conversations with you, pleaded with you. Was I talking to myself? Disturbing the neighbours? One of the nurses came over. She asked if I needed anything. I shook my head. She did something with the pillows, the covers, smiled and slipped away. Like I said, I was on Librium in the hospital, and the point of that class of drug is to make the mess you see, and that is in fact your life, bearable to you. I forget who makes it. There are probably factories in India that churn it out now, millions and millions of little black and green capsules. It would be easy to get hooked. I've known people hooked on similar stuff. But I was grateful for it that night, understood its purpose. I wanted to be dull.

I did in the end find out who called the ambulance, who, in fact, saved my life. It's not who I would have chosen. A couple of days after Tess had been in, Debbie Levett showed up. She was wearing a wig I'd never seen her in before, short, silvery-grey, slightly luminous. I suppose she buys them online. There's certainly nowhere in the town you could get anything like that.

Tim says hello, she said. I actually laughed at that. I said I assumed he'd fired me but she answered, very firmly, she would make sure he did no such thing. For a few minutes we had one of those hospital conversations that seem hard to avoid. What was the food like? Not bad. Had I made any friends? I said the man opposite waved once in a while. We both looked at him, and he, obligingly, waved. When that was done with I asked what I hoped she had, in part, come to tell me. Who, on the town grapevine, had given her the news? How had she known about me? She cocked her head and I thought she was going to be mysterious about it, that I'd have to play a guessing game. Then she came out with it – Annie Fuller.

The instant the name was spoken I saw Annie in her coat sitting beside me in my garden. Sometimes you can *feel* the connections being made. Synapses – is that what they are? – touching like ears of corn. I thought I was going to get the rest but that was all. Three or four seconds out of an entire night.

When I explained how little I could remember, that the drinking and whatever came at the end of it had wiped the tape, she promised to tell me all that Annie had told her over cups of coffee in Shrubs. Turns out the two of them are pretty thick together. I'd no idea. Those times I saw Annie at Plant World she was probably just there to see Debbie. I was an afterthought.

It begins on the high street with me stepping out of the Spar carrying a bag rattling with bottles. I know what I bought. Two big bottles of cider and a bottle of vodka, Spar's own brand. The moment I was outside I put the bag down, took out one of the cider bottles and had a good long drink. The shock of it! I'd been dry for nearly four years, Maggie. The poor body had no idea what was coming. The world grew thinner – seemed like it might fade out entirely – then seeped back. I was OK after that. Not much anyone can teach me about the abuse of alcohol. I sank half the bottle – half a litre – screwed the cap back on, returned the bottle to the bag, picked up the bag and marched into one end of a blackout.

Back home I went into the garden. I know that because it's where Annie found me. She'd seen me coming out of the Spar. She'd been in the window of her parlour doing whatever she does there on a Saturday, rearranging the urns or dusting the old hand bier. She had a front-row view of my first pull on the cider.

I have never told her I'm an alcoholic but she knew. I assume Debbie had told her. That or it's just common knowledge. Anyway, she watched me from her window. She didn't rap on the glass and make don't-do-it gestures, which might, I suppose, have looked strange with a background of urns. And if I wanted to stand in the high street drinking cider wasn't that my business? A grown man? So she went on with her work, finished it, locked up the office and went home. She was starting to cook her tea when she suddenly switched everything off, put on her coat and walked the half-mile between her house and mine. She knows my address. She'd used it to send that invite for the folk night in Wedmore.

It was dark by then. She tried the bell, looked through the front windows. Another person – most – would have settled for that. Not Annie Fuller. She started round the side of the house, came to the garden door, found it unbolted and went through to the garden. The light was on in the kitchen and that's what she headed for. Don't you think that's extraordinary? She was going to knock on my back door, ask if I was all right, perhaps smuggle the bottles away from me. You need a certain confidence for that. But I wasn't in the kitchen, I was lying on the grass, dark clothes on dark ground, and she almost tripped over me. I claimed – and this is Annie to Debbie rather than anything I can remember – that I was stargazing. I did not, apparently, then or at any other time, ask what she was doing in my garden. She sat beside me and we talked. I had – it makes me cringe to think of it – a great deal to say for myself. After a while she persuaded me to sit with her on the bench by the back door where we had some light from the kitchen window. I was on the vodka by then. She told Debbie she wasn't frightened but understood I was not myself any more and would need careful handling. In this she was wise. I've never been a violent drunk but she wasn't to know that. Does this dog bite? It looks like it could. She thought if she kept me talking I would drink less or maybe just exhaust myself and fall asleep, but by this point in the proceedings it would have taken something like death itself to stop me, which is more or less what happened. I finished the vodka and launched the bottle into the dark of the garden. Then, maybe fearing it wasn't quite empty, a few drops to be wrung out of it still, I wanted to find it again, insisted on it, wouldn't be put off. Now, as you may or may not know, my house has quite a collection of torches in it, also a lantern or two, but Annie had been smoking and I borrowed her lighter and followed its flame to the bottom of the garden. She stayed on the bench. She was starting to think she might need some help. She knows Frank. She buried his wife a couple of winters ago. Between them they might have been able to chivvy me into the house and up to bed. But as she watched the little flame (I imagine it weaving about like the fireflies I used to see in Italy) I made a noise like I'd been punched, and the flame went out.

She called to me, got nothing back, then worked her way down the garden, a woman in the dark on her own with a very drunk man she knows only slightly, and who is, at this point, quite possibly no longer among the living. She found me under the aspen tree, face down. She turned me over. I was what they call unresponsive. I was breathing but my breathing was 'odd'. She thought I'd had a heart attack or a stroke. She ran to the house (falling over a watering can on the way and bruising both knees), found the phone in the kitchen and called 999. Then she went upstairs, stripped a blanket from my bed, found one of the torches, and came out again to do what she could for me. I don't know whether funeral directors receive any training in first aid. It wouldn't seem like a priority for them. From what Debbie said I got the impression she just tried to make me comfortable, put the blanket over me, that kind of thing. She also, apparently, spoke to me, and I can't help wondering what she said. I've also wondered if in that dream I had, that hallucination or whatever it was that Mum was beside me, it wasn't Mum it was Annie. That's quite a strange feeling. Anyway, the best part of half an hour passed before help arrived, which is a long time to be with someone as she was with me, the two of us under the tree, my odd breathing, the rustling of the aspen leaves, the way they always sound like rain.

The first to arrive was a paramedic on a motorbike. He took my pulse, shone his pencil torch into my eyes, tried to rouse me by calling my name. He spoke to Annie in a calm, slow voice. He was clearly worried.

By the time the ambulance came the neighbours were out. We don't get sirens down our road very often. There was, among the ambulance crew, some confusion as to who exactly Annie might be. Was she Mrs Rose? She wasn't. A partner? A relative? She told them I had a daughter, presumably my next of kin, though she didn't know how to reach you. All this might have been fairly unsatisfactory. Who did I belong to? Anyone? But they didn't hang around. They would have been very used to hoovering up Saturday-night drunks and bringing them in for a pump or to have their heads stitched, but I was clearly well past all that. They trolleyed me along the side of the house, packed me into the back of the ambulance and took off for the bypass. The neighbours dispersed, no doubt with a bit of head-shaking, and Annie's evening ended with her shutting my kitchen door, shutting the garden door and walking home to her uncooked tea.

And there it is. I owe my life to an undertaker, a woman I have had ungracious thoughts about and have spoken about in that way. Did I, while we sat on the bench together, lecture her about her politics? Did I tell her I was going with the Co-op rather than Fuller's Funerals? I don't know if I'll have the nerve to ask about it when I see her. What *should* I say to her? I mean what beyond 'Thank you'? Because whatever I intended when I pulled those bottles from the shelf, whether or not I meant to be found on Sunday morning stiff in the grass with the dew on my face, I am glad now it didn't happen.

Or I'm glad most days. Three out of four. Four out of seven. That may be the national average.

Maggie, when I put down my pencil that Saturday at home and headed out to the Spar, the one satisfaction I had, maybe the only one, was that I wouldn't have to write any more. I'd started to hate it. You said to Lorna I'd been lying to you and I think sometimes that's what writing is. I should have found a language with a suppler wrist. I should have written music for you. Anyway, I thought I'd finished with it but when I told Zoë – she's the addiction counsellor here – what I'd been doing, the 'letter' to you, she was excited and wanted me to keep it going. I told her I thought writing was dangerous. She said I seemed to have survived it. So here I am again, your father the escape artist, writing to you at a distance. If nothing else, it lets me keep something alive between us, or some hope of that, or maybe just the illusion of it, like when I read the books in Dad's study after he died. It's not like I really think you're going to read any of this – why would you ever read anything of mine again? – but I can send it out on the breeze like those prayers we say here, believers and unbelievers together. Something to comfort, something for now. A way of tricking ourselves into going on.

Here's how we spend our days at Virgil House.

Up at six thirty, which is more or less sunrise at the moment. Then a half-hour of stretches with someone called Terry, who tells us 'The issues are in our tissues.' I believe it. Breakfast is at eight. Porridge, toast, tea (but no coffee). There are catering tins of peanut butter that people dig into. Eat enough of it and you might get a buzz on. Then housework. This is practical but also a kind of training. Some of the brothers have not, I think, done much of it before. I was on the hoovering today. Yesterday I cleaned the toilets. Tomorrow I'm on veg chopping. An hour of this and a man called Brendan comes round with a wooden clapper. He's one of the team here, the fixer and go-to man for anything practical. He sorted me out with a pencil, and this notebook, which is all recycled paper. On the cover it says, 'I used to be something else'. He sorted me out with clothes too, because the bag you packed wasn't a bag for a man who would be away for a month. They have a deep cupboard, like the stockroom of a charity shop, and with the same smell. I got everything I needed out of there, including a coat of black and white wool that had a rail ticket in one pocket (Liverpool Lime Street to Bristol Temple Meads, one way) and in the other, a small pine cone that I've put on the sill of our bedroom window as a weather gauge. Like the notebook, Brendan used to be something else, a teacher in a secondary school until he burnt out and retrained. Easier, apparently, to deal with a houseful of addicts than a class of fifteen-year-olds who may or may not throw you out of the window.

After housework we gather in the big room downstairs. It's called the community room. We stand in a circle with our hands on each other's shoulders and sing the 'Serenity Hymn'. Those who are new to the house can read the words off a big poster on the wall. Those who can't read – and there's more than one here – just muddle through for the first couple of days.

Then the talking begins, which is the day's real work. Group therapy, speaking circle, one-to-ones with the addiction counsellor, the visiting psychiatrist, the visiting nurse or doctor. Talking is muscular. I've lived alone for so long I'm out of practice. Listening is less physical but not much easier. I've heard versions of these stories before, the stories the brothers come out with, but I think my skin's getting thinner. There are men here who have walked through fire. Much of the damage went on at home. The assaults, the horror shows. The abusers were often members of their own family. Is this well known? Is this something everybody understands? The fact that I wasn't sexually abused as a child puts me in a minority here. They talk, they shake, they sweat, they weep like children. And you don't need to be Sigmund Freud to understand that it *is* the child weeping there. It is the child.

As for what you're going to say when you sit down in the circle, you might think you know but you don't, not really. And that's strange, isn't it? Who's in charge here? Who's making the decisions? My first morning I meant to say something about Dad, what I felt about having let him down so spectacularly, what he must have felt about me, but instead I started talking about Mum and the two or three memories I have of her. They're like pieces of old cine film, fragments that have survived not just one fire but many. Mum in the kitchen framed by the window. A young woman! She puts down a saucer of milk for a cat. I don't think we had a cat. Maybe a neighbour's cat? In another sequence we're in the front room of the house reading a book. I think she was teaching me to read. It was a book about a whale in the zoo that's too big for the pool and gets sunburnt. I ended up telling the brothers most of the story. It ends happily enough with a trip back to the sea. I can remember the illustrations in the book – the men with the crane hoisting the whale out of the pool. I can remember the colours. I must have been looking hard at the turning pages and I wish now I'd been looking hard at Mum instead.

I haven't said anything about Belfast yet. I skirt about it. And I haven't mentioned you – not in the groups – though I came close to it on Monday. For some reason I balked. I felt their eyes on me, the men on the plastic chairs, these veterans of bad living, the kindness in their faces. I fell silent and stared at my hands. After ten seconds or so the facilitator moved it on. Thanks, Stephen. The circle turned and another voice began.

Painted on a corridor wall upstairs opposite my bedroom: 'You learn everything fighting your fear.' It's from an American writer called Norman Mailer. He was a drunk. He stabbed his wife with a penknife, though happily she survived.

* * *

At the evening meal we have readings. Brendan or one of the brothers reads while we eat. Improving literature! Last night it was a book by someone whose name I can't remember and wouldn't be able to spell if I could. Part of it was this – inside everyone is a garden and we have to go back to the garden and take care of it. When I write it down it doesn't seem very deep but something about it caught my attention.

It's half past four and we're waiting for the start of art class. The last art classes I attended were in Shepton Prison. The governor was keen on it. I wish I could remember what I tried to paint there, I don't, but I remember some of the old cons, lifers some of them, taking it very seriously and becoming pretty good at it. There are lots of things you can't be in prison but an artist isn't one of them.

Aafter tea I'll go to AA. I'm working the steps again. Hi, I'm Stephen, I'm an alcoholic. It's Step Four today – 'In which we make a searching and fearless moral inventory of ourselves.' I'll take my usual seat, closest to the door. My roommate with the restaurant (David) will likely take the seat beside me. Then we let down the net and haul up some of the disgusting things we've done. And don't let anyone tell you confession isn't competitive. No one is going to stand up and talk about stealing paper clips from the office. You don't have to speak, you're not obliged to, but the longer you stay silent the harder it gets. They want us to live out loud. If you feel it, say it. Spout! And it makes me think of this place I saw a programme about once, a Buddhist temple in Thailand or Burma, where they treated heroin addicts. Much of the treatment consisted of physical purging. The addicts – skag thin and not wearing much in the heat – drank great jugs of something that turned their stomachs. I couldn't tell you what it was but they seemed eager enough to have it. They emptied their jugs then threw up like fountains while the monks watched them.

The young lad in my room, the young Bristolian, calls himself Snout. David asked for his real name, which is Alan, and that's what we call him. Snout is not a name, said David. It's part of an animal. They're an odd pair together. David says it's the democracy of failure, though probably we're supposed to think of it as the democracy of addiction. We get along. David is encouraging Alan to change his socks and underwear and generally to take more care of himself.

Alan cries at night. It's not loud and it doesn't happen every night but more often recently. Most nights now. I've wondered if I should try to comfort him but if he's in a dream and I wake him I'm not sure what I'll set off, and if he's awake and I go over he may think I'm coming on to him. I know enough of his story to know that wouldn't be a good idea. So I lie there and do nothing. I wait for it to stop. I assume, on the other side, David's doing the same thing.

Beside the tea urn today in the break between community development and a talk called Facts About Addiction, a brother I've noticed because I've noticed him noticing me – stocky, in his forties, mostly bald, crazy amounts of violence in his eyes – asked if I'd ever been in the army. I know he was in the army because he's talked about it several times in AA and speaking circle. I would have known anyway from the tattoos on his arms. He was in the first Gulf War and says he has Gulf War syndrome from the injections they were given to protect them from chemical-warfare agents. He has told stories about the Gulf War, only some of which I believe. I think some of the stories he tells belong to other people or are things he's read online. It doesn't matter. I don't have a problem with that. In some way he feels them all. He uses the C-word a lot and has been asked to use it less. I don't know what he's seen in me or thinks he's seen. What can be left of my time in the army? Three years thirty years ago? I said no and said it immediately. I didn't want to feel we shared anything, had a bond between us. That was stupid of me. It's something I'm going to have to put right one day and I will. But not today.

A new arrival last night. David says he's seen him before on one of his previous stays. A professor from the university, a world expert on the ancient Assyrians. How's that for a job description? He has long grey hair he keeps in a ponytail. He has already made quite an impression. In speaking circle today he talked about watching a nature programme on television when he was a boy, some film of lions bringing down an antelope, picking off the one that had stumbled or become confused or was just slower. When the antelope knows the lions are close it puts on a spurt but there's already a sort of hopelessness. And then they have it and they bring it down and one of them goes by instinct for the throat and you see – he saw as a boy, sitting in his comfortable home in North London – the expression in the antelope's eyes. Everything is ending in the long-dreamt-of disaster. It's beyond fear. It's the next place. He said it might have been wolves and a caribou, he wasn't sure, it was a long time ago, but he remembered the animal's expression perfectly. He said he saw it more and more often on the faces of the people he met. He saw it in some of his students' faces. He was becoming afraid of the shaving mirror in case it showed him the expression on his own face. There was total silence when he finished. We all seemed to know very well what he was talking about.

I had an appointment with the doctor this morning. A check-up. Everybody gets one. He was a young doctor, and was, I decided, an example of what a person is supposed to be, how they're supposed to turn out. While he was examining my tongue and listening to my chest I had this fantasy of changing places with him. He would walk back to some group confessional with men who could all, to one degree or another, be described as desperate. He would sleep in a room with a man who cries. And I would be out in the world, stethoscope round my neck, yes Doctor, no Doctor, thank you, Doctor. I imagined a nice car, I imagined a nice girlfriend. I imagined being able to have a drink, just a few on a Friday evening, perhaps with other doctors. I imagined visiting my father and him patting my back, leading me into the house where we would have a very friendly and respectful conversation. Of course, the young doctor examining me might have a life nothing like the one I imagined. His father might be a drunk. He might have lost his mother. His girlfriend is cheating on him with a slightly more handsome and brilliant doctor. He called me Stephen several times, made a point of it. He talked about my tummy and my poo. Emilia Rauch would never talk about poo. But he was a good lad, I thought. If I envied him, I was also pleased to be in his company, this successful human being. At the end I shook his hand and immediately realised he didn't really want me to do that.

Today, Saturday, I was passing the door to the kitchen when Brendan, who was carrying a couple of ten-kilo bags of potatoes, had them on his hips like children, said someone had phoned to say they would be coming to see me tomorrow. Sunday is the day for visitors. Other than AA there are no meetings or classes. When I asked him who it was he frowned, shuffled through his thoughts while the potatoes got heavier, and said, finally, Jenna. He spoke the name as a question and I for some reason said, Ah, Jenna, as if I knew exactly who he was talking about. There was no time for anything else. He made a face, tilted his head towards the kitchen and went off with his load.

Jenna? Who was Jenna? Someone from the meeting? Some long-unseen relative from Langport? In the end, having to hurry to catch the minibus to the swimming-pool – we go up there every Saturday morning, an outdoor pool – I decided she was probably from the hospital, Dr Rauch's number two coming to see how I was getting on, or some social worker required by law to follow up on anyone found unconscious in his garden from the effects of alcohol. Anyway, I settled on that and had put it away and was halfway down a length of the pool when I had a kind of vision – it was like a picture on glass held up to the sun – of a young girl with hennaed hair. Of course I know a Jenna! The girl in the back of the ambulance the day I hitched to Bristol. The girl from the house on the hill. Was *she* my visitor? Skinny Jenna with her patchouli oil, her feather earrings? She played no big part in my life in Bristol. I can't even remember if she was still in the squat when I moved out to be with Evie. Would she want to see me? Could she have tracked me down? And then I had this idea – very paranoid – that Ambrose Carville had stuck my face all over the internet like a wanted poster. But even Carville can't possibly know that I'm here. Can he?

I thought of finding Brendan again and asking for a surname but it wouldn't have meant anything to me even if he'd had one. None of us in the squat used surnames. Surnames were for squares. But she's the only Jenna I know, and however strange it is, now that I've thought of her I can't get it out of my head that I'll see her tomorrow.

I'm writing this on Monday. There was no chance to write yesterday. You'll understand why.

On Sunday morning I was in the community room waiting for my visitor. There were a half dozen others waiting for theirs. David was hoping to see his chef, who he says is 'going cold' on him. Alan, in a freshly laundered hoodie, was expecting a visit from his mother (or someone he calls his mother, it's complicated). Every now and then Brendan would come in with a visitor and there'd be hellos and hugs. I found it quite difficult. The waiting, the looking up. I wasn't sure I was ready to have an ordinary conversation, one that wasn't a type of confession. And I was tired. I'd spent half the night thinking about Jenna and the squat, and then, of course, about Evie and you, and I'd got myself into a tangle at the prospect of meeting her, of not recognising her or, throughout the entire visit, never working out what she was doing there. I picked up a book from the half-dozen on the table beside me and tried to distract myself. It was called *Ego and Soul.* I read the first page, read it again. How should I greet her? Shake her hand, kiss her cheek? Or would we just stand there staring at each other, too shocked by what the years had done to speak at all?

I suppose it's possible you've already been told what happened next. I heard my name and looked up from the book and there was Brendan smiling down at me. Next to him, her red hair dyed black as an old telephone, was Lorna. Hi, Stephen, she said. Weren't you expecting me?

We spent a minute unravelling the confusion. There had, of course, never been any Jenna, no wild child grown stout and middle-aged and wanting to 'reconnect'. Jenna had always been Lorna. Brendan made a sort of yoga-style apology with his palms together. Did we want tea? Lorna lifted the bag she was carrying and said she had everything with her. Great, said Brendan, fantastic. He left us. As soon as he was gone I asked Lorna if you were with her. You could have been outside, perhaps in the car. She shook her head. I wasn't surprised. I might even have been relieved. God knows I want to see you, Maggie, but to have had you suddenly there – I think I would have frozen.

It was about half twelve then. It had been drizzling all morning but a breeze was tidying away the clouds and it looked like a half-decent day. Lorna asked if I knew a quiet place for us to go and after thinking for a moment I said I did. I saw David's chef arrive, a small neat man in a dark suit and tennis shoes. Alan was still waiting, and as I left we gave each other a thumbs-up.

I went with Lorna to a place in Clifton called Birdcage Walk. I hadn't been there in years but it hadn't changed much. Perhaps it's been tidied up a bit, the boozers excluded by some by-law that's sent them shuffling off to somewhere more hidden. At one time there was a church up there but it was bombed in the Bristol blitz and burnt to the ground. The graveyard is still there, some very old stones peeping out from long grass and ivy. And there's a paved pathway between pleached lime trees, benches on either side of it, most of them when we arrived already spoken for, but the last one was free and I wiped the rain from it with my sleeve and we sat down.

Lorna unpacked her bag. There was a flask of tea and some home-baked scones. She'd brought china cups and saucers. She even had a bowl with sugar lumps in it. She poured the tea, screwed the top back on the Thermos. On the walk up I'd told her about Virgil House, the routine there, some of the people, whether or not it could be said I was making progress. All that was out of the way and now it was her turn to speak. She said you were still with Evie. She hadn't seen you since you left after dropping the tray. More than a month! She had spoken to you on the phone, twice. That was OK, it was friendly enough, but both times she had finished the call feeling the distance between you had grown. Then Evie had called. I'm guessing you know that, that she had your permission. She gave Lorna a crash course in those years before the two of you found each other. Your girlhood, your growing up. It's the sort of call I could have done with before you moved to Glastonbury. I don't know what it would have spared us but we might have been less unsure around each other. I would have been less in the dark. Anyway, the long and the short of it was you needed time. How much time wasn't specified. And she wanted to see what you'd read in the study. She asked Lorna to send it on, and she'd done that, parcelled it up and sent it north. She hoped I didn't have a problem with that. I said I didn't care what happened to it. Evie could make a bonfire out of it if she wanted.

I asked if I should call you.

No, she said.

And the Silk Shed?

Closed, she said. She could do it on her own but she didn't want to. Couldn't find the enthusiasm, didn't see the point. I said I was sorry. She nodded, and said that when she met me for the first time, saw the two of us together, you and me, she had understood that something would follow, that things wouldn't just be patched up. She had understood, then forgotten.

We sat quietly for a while. A pair of gulls fought over the remains of someone's sandwich. On the other side of the green a man on his own was having an imaginary sword fight. Elegant little thrusts and parries. Sudden dance-like movements towards his shadow on the wall. I think he was practising something. It didn't look like madness.

When we spoke again we spoke about you, but no theories, no attempt to explain you. We just traded stories. She, of course, had many more of them, things I'd never heard before. At one point we were both laughing (the ballroom-dance classes in Stockport). Then the storytelling seemed to make us sadder and we stopped. A bell struck somewhere down in the city. She glanced at her watch. We'd drunk the tea but hadn't touched the scones. She started to pack things away. She said Sarah Waterfall had been in touch and that she was a nice woman. I agreed. I said I thought my father and Sarah might have been lovers. I don't know why I told her that.

We walked down the hill together and said our goodbyes on the pavement beside her car. Close to and face to face, I could see how the last weeks had pinched her. She was wearing no make-up. She looked younger, not as tough, not as sure of herself. I don't really know a great deal about her. You told me she grew up in a Croydon tower block, a council place with so much mould and damp on the walls that a TV company came to film it for the local news. And then one day she meets a nice girl and gets the courage to reinvent herself a little. If I can't fix it up between us, Maggie, if that's beyond me, beyond anybody, then God help me I intend to do whatever it takes to make it right again between you two. I almost said that to her, though as I've no plan of how to do it, it wouldn't have impressed her much. Maybe the only useful thing I can do is keep my nose out. Become small. Disappear?

She wanted to know how much longer I'd be staying at the house. Another week, I said. And how would I get home? I said I'd walk down to the bus station. No, she said. She would arrange something.

And that was it. She had the car keys in her hand. I bit back a second apology, which I thought would just needle her.

Evie, she said, thinks this is all about trust.

Trust?

She shrugged, smiled a sad smile and left.

I walked for a while then – just up one street and down the next, not going anywhere. I wondered if this was going to be the moment when it all came apart. The moment I just knelt down in a corner and waited for people to collect me. There was the shadow of something, like the shadow of a cloud on the sea. I couldn't tell you its name exactly. I couldn't even say what I felt about it, whether I was afraid of it or in some way wanted it. I tried to distract myself with what was around me but the area didn't offer much. The grey houses, and now and then a band of students, who I think it unlikely saw me at all. When you're nineteen, a man my age, a man with a face like mine, his life is unimaginable.

One last turn and I came out at the junction opposite Virgil

House. It looked normal enough, Sunday-afternoon sleepy, Tibetan prayer flags fluttering above the courtyard fence, one vehicle in the staff car park. But as I crossed the road I heard a door slam somewhere in the body of the house and I looked up and saw a face at one of the upstairs windows. It was only for a second. I couldn't see who it was. Now, I thought, the front door will open and someone will run out with his clothes on fire, his hair. I went in. The office door was open but there was no one in there. There was a shout from upstairs. It's natural to hesitate when you hear a shout like that. Then I went up, I ran. At the end of the landing four or five brothers were crowded round the open door of one of the bathrooms. When I reached them they stood back a little to let me see. In the bathroom, Alan was lying on his back on the floor. Brendan was kneeling on one side of him, David on the other. Both David and Brendan had blood on their hands and there was blood on the floor, shiny fat slicks of it. There was also a knife that I recognised as one from the kitchen. When not in use the knives are kept in a locked drawer. Or the door is usually locked. It's supposed to be locked.

Brendan looked terrified, sick with it, but David seemed calm. Or not calm, but like he knew what he was doing, was in control of himself. You never know who'll rise to the occasion. You don't know about yourself, not before it happens. Each of them was holding up one of Alan's arms trying to dress a wound on his wrist. Beside me, the ex-army brother whispered that the blood on the floor was arterial blood. I knew it was too. I know the difference. Then David looked up, saw me, and asked me to come in. He got me to kneel down by Alan's head and showed me the place on the inside of the elbows, a pressure point to slow the bleeding. I think I was taught something like that in

Tin City. I took hold. Alan had his eyes not quite fully shut. The skin of his face was slack and grey. There was a bubble of saliva at one corner of his lips that moved with the rhythm of his breathing. And that was how we stayed, the three of us trying to keep his life inside him while the others looked on and spoke in whispers. We all heard the siren at the same time. In the city, of course, you have to listen for a while to know if it's coming your way, if it's yours or someone else's. We decided to lift him and carry him down the stairs. We could save a minute or two like that and a minute or two might be important. The others came in then, and there were so many of us we filled the room. The Assyrian expert was beside me, supporting Alan's head, cupping it in his hands. I still held his elbows. I didn't dare let go. We edged down the landing. Christ himself could not have been carried more carefully. On the stairs, those at the front with his legs lifted him up, those of us at the back kept him low. At the bottom of the stairs we laid him on the hall floor, very gently. People moved away a little. Alan's eyes flickered open but I don't believe he saw anything. Some of the brothers called encouragement to him, promised him he'd be OK. The paramedics arrived. One, a woman, took his arms from me and said, That's fine, love, well done. They were swift. They got him out and away. Their first suicide of the day? Their third? The siren kicked off again, grew fainter. We stood around in the hall. Now that he'd gone we didn't know what to do with ourselves. People started to drift off. I saw Brendan in the office crying on his own. I should have gone in to comfort him but I didn't. I went back upstairs. I was exhausted. I felt like we'd carried him not just down the stairs but right across the city. The bathroom door on the landing was still open. I stopped there a moment. Blood on the lino, footprints in the blood. Blood on the wall too and up by the sink and in it. You might imagine I was thinking then about the alley in the Ardoyne, and of course I did think about it, though in some part of my head I'm always thinking about it, it's always there, so it wasn't like it suddenly *came* to me. What did come was something else, something I hadn't thought about in years, a story I was told at the Factory by a soldier on his third tour. It was about a mobile patrol ambushed with heavy-calibre weapons that had been set up in a house where the residents, an old couple, were being held hostage. The lead Land Rover took the worst of it. These weren't the sort of rounds that bounce off the outside. Afterwards, the Land Rover stood empty in a corner of the SF compound. Before going to the workshop it needed to be cleaned out, the inside needed cleaning, but no one would do it. Those tasked with it refused. In the end, very early one morning, a regimental sergeant major, wearing an apron of bin bags and carrying a bucket of steaming water, opened the rear doors and climbed in. He was later seen pouring bright red water down a drain. Anyway, that story came back to me and I wondered why the soldier told it to me. To frighten me? Warn me? Or because he couldn't get it out of his head and putting it in mine helped him a little?

I closed the bathroom door and went to my room. Alan's bed was as he'd left it in the morning, neatly made in the way you learn in prison. I lay down on my own bed and was asleep very quickly. Almost dark when I woke. I didn't move. I lay there letting the dark fall on me like rain.

Today there's been a big effort at making normal and we're glad of it. The staff have met. They will have a protocol, of course, what to do in the event of. It certainly won't be the first time this has happened. The only shift in the routine was a visit from the top man, a doctor, silver hair, the look of an ex-rugby player, a reassuring smell to him if you got close enough. He addressed us in the community room after the 'Serenity Hymn'. He told us Alan was in hospital and in a stable condition. He spoke about shock and sadness. He wanted us to look out for each other, to be sensitive to anyone who seemed to be struggling. He said he was proud of us and knew we'd put on a first-class show. Actually, he didn't say that last bit and I'm being unfair to him. He was very sincere and did well what he was there to do. When he left someone suggested we sing the 'Serenity Hymn' again. I thought it was a joke but people stood and we sang it a second time, much louder, as if hoping the sound of it might reach the hospital.

In speaking circle people were queuing up to say their piece. There was a lot of energy to let go of, a lot of adrenalin. All the suicide stories came out. Everybody had witnessed something or had had a go themselves. Pills, rope, high leaps. One attempt at electrocution involving a hair-dryer and a bath. At least four of the brothers knew someone who had jumped off the Clifton suspension bridge. All those attempts, of course, successful.

Zoë wanted to see everybody, whether or not it was their day with her. A rota was pinned up on the board in the hall. There was some speculation that those being seen first were the most at risk. I was about halfway down.

When I sat in the chair opposite her – it's two chairs and a little round table with an orchid on it (a white moth) and a box of tissues – she asked me what I assume she's been asking everybody. How had yesterday's incident made me feel? Had it given rise to any suicidal thoughts? I said it hadn't, which was the truth. I thought it was a strange question in some ways. Do you need to see someone eating before you know you're hungry? I told her about going out with Lorna, and something of the conversation we'd had. I told her about coming back to the house and the scene in the bathroom. Basically, I told her what happened and what I'd seen, though by then she must have heard it a dozen times, and she didn't want a description, she wanted to know how I felt about it. I shrugged. She waited. I said it had made me feel tired. Tired, she said. All right. And what else? The difference between talking to someone like Zoë and talking to a regular person is that they will not let you look away. It's understood that you're hiding something. You're choosing to hide it or you don't know it's there or you know but you don't have the words. Is hiding the same as lying? I don't think it can be but sometimes I'm not sure.

I said – and you find yourself saying things just to break the silence – that what mattered yesterday was being given the chance to be useful. David, she said. I nodded. He called you in, she said, but you didn't have to go. You could have refused. You could have walked away.

I said I'd thought about that.

You thought about it, she said, and you still went in.

I said I couldn't think of what else to do. Or perhaps I went because the others were there and they were watching me. I might have lost face.

Was that what it was about? she asked. Losing face?

I shrugged again.

You played a part in saving a life, she said.

I don't think so, I said.

But you did, she said.

And I found I wanted to deny it or to make it as small as possible, my contribution. And this, of course, was noticed and pointed out to me. I spread my hands to show that whatever the game was she had me beaten. Oddly, given what had been going on, what was still very close to the surface, I found myself at the edge of laughter.

So now it seems everything is on the move, though I get stuck on questions like who and what. After I finished writing yesterday – I'm already halfway through this notebook – I went to AA – Step Eight, 'in which we make a list of all persons we have harmed and become willing to make amends to them'. As I have no worthwhile secrets from you now you'll understand the trouble I have with this. Sometimes it's difficult to make amends, sometimes it's impossible. I wasn't alone in struggling with it. There are brothers who appear to have harmed every single individual they ever had contact with. Betrayal was a big theme. Once the word showed up it never went away. The Assyrian expert had betrayed his father. The ex-army brother had betrayed his mates, fellow veterans. He had stolen from them. He had lived on the streets and stolen the few poor things other rough sleepers had. David spoke about his wife and children, about the lies he'd told them, how easy it had been in the beginning to fool them, the kick he had got out of that. Trust, he said, getting it back, was like creating a beach one grain of sand at a time. He sat down. There was a pause, a taking of breath. I got to my feet and spoke about you. I've spoken about you to Zoë but not in the groups. In the groups it's not a conversation, you're making a statement, you're speaking your truth. I said I loved you but I wasn't a fit father. I said I'd tried, but too late. I didn't say anything about the writing and how that had hurt you. That would have taken us somewhere else. But as I went on I got a bit lost and heard myself talking about us in ways that didn't have much to do with betrayal. I described the day we went to Exmoor when the heather was out and we picnicked in the lay-by above the sea. I mentioned the famous opening of the Silk Shed. I said we went to Quaker meetings together. This wasn't quite the point, not what we were there for, and to get back on track, make my story about us the right sort of story, I finished off by saying you couldn't possibly have faith in someone like me. I said the moment to have made amends with you was twenty years ago when you were still a child. The damage was done and the moment had passed. I sat down. I got a little round of applause. Someone patted my shoulder. Ezra (who runs the group and is also an alcoholic) said, It's never too late, Stephen. Then the brother beside me got up. He's a very mild-looking man, softly spoken. He told us about selling his son's mountain bike to buy gin.

It was a long session and we didn't break until about eight. I was knackered but you can't go to bed at eight even in rehab so I made tea and sat in the community room. I think I told you there are books in there, mostly of the self-help variety, but I didn't want that. You can get sick of it, this business of working on yourself. I'm not here looking for a cure. In one of the cupboards I found a coffee-table book of photographs, old black-and-white pictures of cities – New York, London, Delhi, Milan. The buildings were sharp, in focus, very detailed. The people, where there were any, blurred and feathery. I don't think anything was intended by that. I think it was just to do with the techniques they were using, length of exposure and so on, but it felt accurate, the way we exist on some sliding scale between stone and air.

I flicked through it, finished my tea, and went to bed around nine. Half nine is curfew. Everybody has to be up in their room by then. The bathroom where Alan cut himself has been thoroughly cleaned but no one wants to use it, so there was a queue at the other bathroom. In the bedroom, David was doing his exercises. He tells me they're Chinese and maybe they are. After exercising he puts creams on his face and has tried to persuade me to do the same. I can't honestly see the point. It takes me long enough to get to bed as it is. As a boy I could be ready in thirty seconds. So much work now just to lie down.

Once the lights were out we talked in whispers for a while, or he talked and I listened. He told me about when he first decided to run a restaurant. He'd done lots of different jobs before, none of them anything to do with food or catering. He was on a winter holiday in Italy with his wife – now his ex-wife – and they went to have lunch in a place at the side of a canal. They hadn't known about it before. It just looked nice and it was close and they were hungry. It turned out to be a good choice. Family run, three generations working there, the walls covered in pictures of people, perhaps locally famous, dining at the restaurant. Then a child came in, a boy, ten or eleven years old, wearing a school uniform, a satchel on his back. It was a cold day, a winter fog that hadn't lifted. The boy, perhaps the youngest member of the family, was known to all the customers. The father warmed his son's hands between his own. A place at a table was found for him. The grandmother brought him out a bowl of soup from the kitchen, and when he'd finished that another plate was brought, a set menu of simple food. And the boy was thoughtful and calm and had good manners. When he was done and it was time to go back to school there were more kisses, more exchanges with the customers, and out he went into the fog, loaded with love and good food. And David, whose marriage was already ending, who was having an affair with someone he didn't like very much, who was becoming distant from his children, decided he would try to make a place like that, somewhere that was about the food but also about a lot more.

And have you? I asked.

He sighed. I heard the beginning of his sleeping, that little fall. I wasn't far behind. And I should have dreamt of cities or restaurants but instead I dreamt of the Levels. I think it was the Levels, though it was night in the dream too and nothing much to go on but a sense of familiarity with the emptiness around me. There was a fire in the distance, an orange light pulsing across a whole arc of the horizon. It might have been Glastonbury burning down but I think the dream belonged to a time even before Glastonbury, some catastrophe of the young planet, a meteorite strike, something like that. Animals fleeing from the fire ran past me, great herds of deer, almost invisible, rushing past like flood water. I thought I'd be trampled, that sooner or later one would collide with me. But gradually I came to understand that the animals were reading the darkness ahead of them, that their movements, even in the midst of panic, were very delicate, very precise. They sensed me and made the adjustment. I had nothing to fear. I just had to stay still and trust them.

I can't say how it ended, if there was much more to it. What came next was like a shift in music. Daylight, fine weather. I was in the town, on the high street, could see the shop fronts or some version of them, could see the entrance to the library, not as it actually is but as I have dreamt it before. And there, on the opposite pavement, striding towards me, was Peter Irving. Remember I told you about him? The poor man who found he couldn't remember how to carve the Christmas turkey? I don't know in reality if Peter is dead now, but in the dream he looked in perfect health. He was tanned and had grown a beard but I knew it was him. I called to him and waved. He waved back but didn't break his stride. He had things to do. He was a man with appointments to keep.

I woke – my bladder woke me. I went out to the landing still mostly asleep, and by force of habit went into the bathroom we'd all been avoiding. I was already peeing before I realised where I was. It didn't bother me much. It was just a bathroom, it wasn't haunted, though I kept my eyes on what I was doing. I had this idea they must have missed some of the mess, that you can't clean it *all* up, that behind a pipe or right at the edge of the lino there would be something, a red line.

It was quarter past five in the morning. David was fast asleep. I got dressed very quietly and went downstairs to the hallway. A member of staff stays in the house at night but no one patrols the place. The office door was unlocked. I went in and riffled around until I found some photocopy paper and an envelope, one of those thick brown envelopes I associate with official notices, On Her Majesty's Service, that sort of thing. I took a biro from a box of them, then carried everything through to the community room. For a few minutes I stood in the dark at the big bay window. It was the new moon, but the street lamps made it hard to know what kind of sky there was, if there were any stars out. Nothing moved.

I put on a side light and sat in the same armchair I'd been sitting in before bed. I used the book of cities as a desk, laid it across my lap. There was no agonising. I knew everything I wanted to say and all of it fitted onto one sheet of paper. I folded it, put it in the envelope, addressed it from memory, licked the gum and sealed it.

I could have given the letter to Sandy, who does admin in the office in the mornings. She would have posted it but I wanted to do it myself. They don't like us going out on our own – easier to give way to temptation – so I grabbed David and we walked up to the post office in Clifton. He asked about the letter. I said it was just some business I had to take care of and left it at that. He didn't ask again. In the post office I inquired – stupidly, I suppose – if letters to Belfast needed a special stamp, maybe an airmail sticker. No, no, said the woman, Belfast was still the UK. Same stamps as anywhere else. First or second class? First, I said. She stuck on the stamp and I watched her twist in her chair to drop the envelope into the grey sack behind her. David was waiting outside. He'd bought a family-size bar of milk chocolate and we ate the whole thing on the way back.

We are asked to look inside ourselves and I do. You must do it too sometimes, and I wonder what you see there. I find it hard to say what I see. Something that might be the creation of the world, or just an old television screen with the signal coming and going, flickering between channels. I see flags rippling in a wind, a path winding through a forest, people walking down a city street, somewhere I suppose I must have been to once. And if I stick with it, try to tune in, to slow the film down so I can see something clearly, it doesn't get any bigger, this inside of mine, it flattens out, gets smaller, until I'm just listening to the rain on the window, the hot water bubbling in the urn. So this whole business of an 'inside' is very confusing. And a lot depends on it. It's where we're supposed to find ourselves – our real selves. Which is something else I have a problem with. Are the men here not already real? Am I not? How can anything be more or less real, I mean, if it exists at all? I'm being too literal, of course. I get that. They mean conscience, or what Quakers sometimes call our inner teacher. The still small voice. That kind of thing. But my point is, we're all here trying to fix ourselves up, busy with it every day, and we don't even know what we are, not really. How do you fix something when you don't know what it is, what it's *supposed* to be? Because if I'm honest, Maggie, I couldn't tell you what I am. I could tell you a lot of things about myself, could drone on for hours, all the things I've done, my 'character', but I'd come to the end of it eventually. And then what? Then I'd have to sit there in silence and the only truth would be 'I don't know'. Is that a good place to be? At fifty-one years old?

Three more days here, counting today. This morning Brendan gave me a feedback form and asked me to strip my bed on Sunday morning, put the sheets in the laundry bags. Some finality to that. Stripping my bed. I could have asked to stay longer. There are people here who stay for months. One brother's been here almost a year. But I think if I stayed another month it wouldn't be easier to go back, it would be harder. I think I might go past whatever is useful and start curving back to what brought me here. But what am I going home to? A house I was carried from in a scene lit by blue lamps. The town will know, of course. Local drunk falls over. I don't mind that. It's not like I had some great reputation to lose. Nor am I really afraid of drinking again. And don't worry! I'm not kidding myself, I know what I am – I have to say it out loud every day. I have learnt for the hundredth time, and hopefully for the last, that however deeply you think the wanting has been buried, the days, months and years you pile on top of it, it burrows back to the surface and waits there, just under the skin. But that night when I drank in my garden I swallowed it down like bleach. No pleasure, barely even the memory of pleasure. So it's not *that* I'm afraid of so much as the loss of a routine, of a shape to the days, something to hand me through. Here, we are moved about by bells and wooden clappers. There's a timetable pinned to the noticeboard in the hall. People sit in rooms expecting me. If I don't show up they'll look for me. And I have to make an effort to get on with people, to bear them and make myself as easy to bear as possible. All that will go. It'll be a relief not to have to get out of bed at six thirty every morning and have as the first thing I see the view of another man getting out of bed, but I'm going to have to be very careful I don't spend my time hanging around the house doing nothing. Despite what Debbie said, I'm not sure I will still have a job at Plant World. I think this last train wreck is all the excuse Tim needs. Maybe it's for the best. There's a new supermarket at the edge of town and they might need somebody. Driver, shelf-stacker. It's usually a fast turnover in those places. And there's a Quaker community up in Derbyshire I've been thinking about. A big house, communal living, the life of the spirit. Would they have me? Fresh from rehab?

Beyond all this, of course, is you. To miss someone in a place they've never set foot, that's one thing, but at home I'll see the signs of you all over the house. Your handwriting on the white-board, the straw hat you left on the peg by the back door at the end of last summer, and which is still there. The little vase in the study you gave me for my last birthday, just big enough for a couple of sprigs of honeysuckle. The power of those things. That does frighten me. The thought that I've been carefully protected here, more, probably, than I realise, and that there's an evening waiting for me I cannot possibly prepare myself for.

Not that I will, in the weeks ahead, be without any direction. The letter must have arrived in Belfast. I assume someone's read it.

I have set things in motion, wheels, that will, one way or another, shape whatever future I have. They may shape it completely. I'll know that soon enough.

And there's the tea bell! What will tonight's improving literature be? Last night it was an old Persian poet telling us to greet trouble at the door, treat it like an honoured guest. The dark thought, the shame, the malice, meet them at the door laughing. And fourteen men at four tables listened and cut up their food and squeezed ketchup onto their plates and – who knows? – one of us may remember to do it.

There's this tag they have here, a set of initials that everyone is taught at the beginning of his stay. FEAR. It stands for Face Everything And Recover. The other reading, the alternative, is Fear Everything And Run. When I sat with Zoë today – wise, blue-eyed Zoë – my last session with her, we talked about that, which reading I'd chosen, which I felt capable of. And we talked about the practicalities of the coming weeks. I was asked to visualise myself at home being positive. What are you doing? she asked. I said I could see the house but couldn't see myself in it. Keep trying, she said. Maybe I'm in the garden, I said. Good, she said. What can be planted in September? I gave her a list – onions, broad beans, radishes, spinach. I said, I've been slow to speak, Zoë. She said she knew that but I had at least kept turning up.

We sat. She let the silence grow. Through the window of the room the day looked like a summer's day, perhaps one of the last of the year. I could see the full head of a city tree, a sycamore, I think, a little dusty, and in one or two places beginning to turn, but still mostly green. Something hypnotic about a view like that. Can a tree make a man braver? I don't see why not. Anyway, with half an hour to go I launched into it, fourth of August 1982. No tears, no raging, and as much detail as I dared. And I told her about the Commission, and the letter I'd written in the early morning. I more or less quoted it to her.

There was something sly, I suppose, in telling her like that, so late in the game. If she'd thrown up her hands and cried, Oh, for f*ck's sake! I would have thought it no more than fair, but they're not there to react as you and I might. She thanked me for speaking. She said she was sorry I'd had to carry it for so long. I wasn't sure if she meant here at Virgil House or in life generally. I said there were people in Belfast who carried much more and I was the cause of it. What they carry, she said, is different. It isn't a question of more or of less. All of you, she said, are carrying the weight of that day between you.

And that nearly did for me, Maggie, the thought of us carrying that day together. What I saw in my mind's eye was something like our carrying of Alan down from the bathroom, except now it was Francis Harkin we held. Though I had no right to touch him, of course. I had to separate myself. I had to watch them go.

She said there were treatments now that weren't available thirty years ago. Treatments for trauma that had a very good success rate. She outlined a couple. One involved eye movements (sounds too simple, she said, but it gets incredible results). Another was a sort of theatre that lets you play out the moment again, take control of it. I said I didn't think of what happened that day as an illness that needed a cure. That's not how I thought of it. I said I couldn't imagine any treatment that would make it go away and if there was one I wouldn't want it.

She said it wasn't a case of making it go away but of making it something I could live with. I think she said 'live alongside'. I said that was what I'd been doing most of my life, and she reminded me of how I had come to Virgil House. Ambulance, ICU, touch and go. She spoke back to me something of the history I had given her over the month, the succession of collapses, hospitalisations, slow recoveries, then new moments of crisis, of panic, the whole wheel turning again. If I wanted to take that on myself, OK, but what about *you*? You would have to watch it happen.

I shook my head. I said you wouldn't be watching, you'd already seen enough. You were off.

She leant forward a little, closed her pad and put it down on the table. Our time was up and we'd both heard someone on the stairs, both knew someone would be waiting in the corridor for his turn with her. Stephen, she said, we have to be careful not to get trapped by our stories. That's one of the things we can learn. To tell the story differently, even to let go of it completely. To do that for a single minute and see what's in the space we free.

She walked me to the door, squeezed my arm. We thanked each other for a last time. When I opened the door one of the brothers was sitting on the chair out there. He held out a hand and we tapped palms, like football players swapping over on the touch line.

I was meant to go to art class after Zoë but when I went down to the hall the front door was wide open, there was no one in the office, and I just walked out. Warm out there, shirt-sleeve weather, which was how I was dressed. I thought Brendan or someone would call me back but I reached the end of the road and felt I'd broken an invisible cordon. I kept going. I crossed Whiteladies Road and started walking towards the Downs and the suspension bridge. There was no plan. And as I walked I started to remember the day I ran away from home when I was, I think, eleven years old. Is eleven an important age? It was near the end of the summer holidays. Dad was working and I was at home on my own. I took a half-packet of Digestive biscuits, some clothes, and set out. I walked towards the Tor. I suppose I must have been unhappy about something but I can't remember what it was. It might just have been the prospect of going back to school. I sat in a field and ate the biscuits. I was probably away four or five hours. When I got home it was dusk. Dad was there. He asked if I'd been for a walk and I said I had. I was worried he'd mention the biscuits but he didn't. I put the clothes back into the drawer and we carried on. I've no idea if he understood what I was doing that day. And that's an odd thing, isn't it? You grow up and really you've no idea what the adults are thinking. It's only when you're an adult yourself you can start to take some guesses. By then, of course, it might be too late to ask.

I didn't go on to the suspension bridge. I went close but I didn't go on to it. I saw that they'd raised the height of the side-rails. It used to be you could have climbed over them as easily as a farm gate. Now it would take some agility. And it would take longer, perhaps long enough for someone to grab an ankle and hang on.

I followed the path onto Sion Hill. This was territory I'd known very well once, my old stamping ground, but all my memories of it seemed ten degrees or thirty yards out. I kept expecting to find myself somewhere I wasn't, or not quite. Shouldn't there be a cut down to the Portway here? Where was the house with the round window? And what about the old chemist's shop where we bought Collis Browne's mixture for the morphine it had in it? I passed a pub we used to go into. That at least was where I thought it should be, though now it looked like a place for good meals, somewhere that might not let in the sort of people we were then. I steered left, away from the gorge. It was time to start circling back to Virgil House before they began a full-scale search. The art teacher would have reported my absence. Brendan would have gone round the house. He would have looked in the bathrooms. The place was still jittery. Nobody forgets any more to lock the knife drawer. Perhaps Zoë would say, He's OK, he just needs a little time alone. Would she say that? What did she think of me? How much trouble did she think I was in? How many different kinds of trouble? Anyway, I was walking above the city, Georgian real estate, glimpses into big rooms and small gardens, and suddenly the world I was walking in and the one that belonged to memory mapped onto each other perfectly and I stopped and looked up at the building at the side of me. Oh, it was smartly painted now with cream paint, a blue front door, the brass handles and knocker polished and shining in the sunlight, but it couldn't fool me. The glass in the big sash windows was sparkling, and behind the windows there were shadows that were also, somehow, clean, shaken out like linen. No one was sleeping off their cider dreams in those rooms or brewing a tea of psilocybin mushrooms. Somewhere in there would be a grandfather clock that actually worked. And the bathrooms would be warm and the air would smell of furniture polish rather than joss sticks and patchouli oil. Had they kept the sundial in the back garden? It had a year carved into it – 1819. And was there, under the floorboards or down in the cellars, something left over from us? Someone's UB40 card, one of Jenna's feather earrings? Things do hide, they do get missed. I stared at the house for a good ten minutes – long enough to make my neck ache – and I was still staring when one of those sash windows on the first floor was raised and a man's head and shoulders appeared, someone about my age. I shaded my eyes and squinted up as if I might recognise him. Maybe Marcus had bought the place with his inheritance. It would take that sort of money. But it wasn't Marcus. It wasn't anybody I knew. Can I help you? he called. By which he meant, of course, bugger off before I call the police.

Brendan had told me a Mr Nigel Moody was coming to collect me but I was wise to him this time and had worked it out. On Sunday morning about eleven thirty Nagamudra rang the doorbell. I was waiting in the hall with my bag. David was waiting with me. He had already given me his business card. The restaurant's called AsaNisiMasa. He said if I came there he would treat me like that schoolboy in Italy. In fact, he said *when* I came. He hugged me. Brendan hugged me. I tried to hand back the coat but he said to keep it. Then I saw the ex-army brother coming through the swing door of the kitchen with a mug of tea and a sandwich, and I followed him into the community room and told him I'd lied to him and that I was ex-army too. He said he'd known it, could always tell, was never wrong. Something about the way a man holds himself. Was he flattering me? We exchanged the names of our regiments. They weren't the same. He'd been in armour. Then he put his tea and sandwich down and we hugged too. He's quite short so the top of his head was just under my chin. I could feel all the uncalm in him, his fizz of old suffering. God knows what he felt in me.

It was harder to leave than I'd thought. Nagamudra left me alone for the first part of the drive, no questions, no small-talk. When we did start to talk it wasn't about rehab or drinking. He was in his overalls, had come off a job in Glastonbury renovating a place on Paradise Road, and would be going back to it later. His van was full of what looked like Victorian plumbing, so we discussed plumbing and wiring and roofing and plastering, and I can't tell you how good it was to talk like that, the ins and outs of useful work. I got him to tell me, in great detail, about a floor he was tiling, the brown and white tiles he'd found in the reclamation yard in Frome, how slowly it was coming but how nice it looked. I said if he needed someone to fetch and carry I was his man. He laughed, gently, said he'd remember that, might give me a call.

We were halfway home before I got up the courage to ask about you, and even then I somehow shied away from it. I asked if they'd been keeping him in the loop. They? I suggested Lorna. He said she'd called to find out if he could pick me up, had explained where I was and why. And he knew the Silk Shed had been shut, had driven past and seen that for himself. He thought it would be opening again soon. *Good*, I said. He agreed. I waited to see if he'd say any more but he didn't. Maybe he was waiting to see if I'd ask any more. I didn't. Sometimes better to hope than to know. But I also had the idea that he was playing the part of the loyal servant, the old family retainer (or even the honest squaddie) who hasn't been told much and what he does know he doesn't gossip about. It might have been much simpler than that, of course. He might just have preferred not to be any more involved than he was.

We came round the edge of Shepton Mallet. Another mile and I caught a glimpse of the Tor. I felt myself clench, felt the lurch that comes at the start of an anxiety attack. I asked Nagamudra to stop in a lay-by. When he pulled in I got out and walked a few steps, stood between a pair of thorn trees doing my breathing exercises. I closed my eyes. I grounded myself. I sometimes think that's what it comes down to, techniques, ways of keeping yourself on the surface of the earth, of buying the minute or two you need to let the shadow pass. I wondered what might happen if I asked Nagamudra to drop me at a railway station somewhere – Gillingham, Castle Cary – loan me the price of a ticket. I thought he would probably do it. Then I thought he probably wouldn't, and I got back in the van and we went on.

I had been away six weeks, give or take a couple of days. The house, when we arrived, looked as if it had spent the time filling with silence. I thought I might peer in at a window and see a tree inside, like a place I dossed in in France once, a house in a forest, long abandoned, old wallpaper hanging from the walls, the smell of rot and damp and foxes, a 1950s fridge in the kitchen like an unexploded bomb.

I had no key with me but the spare is under a brick by the bins. I told Nagamudra I was going to fetch it, and he pointed to the car parked behind us and said, Isn't that Evie's? He went and rang the doorbell while I stood examining the car. It had a National Trust sticker in the windscreen and I was about to say, I don't think Evie's a member of the National Trust, that she wasn't the sort of person who would ever join it, too middle of the road for her, too middle class, when the front door opened and there she was.

Did he know she was there? And how does he know what her car looks like? None of this was explained. It was a conjuring trick. He said hi to Evie, shook my hand, went back to the van, turned it in the road and took off for Glastonbury. Evie and I faced each other across the doorstep. She had a tea cloth in her hands, looked perfectly at home. I'd no idea where to start. I grinned. She grinned back.

I followed her inside. Laughably, I wanted to see myself in a mirror, check myself. Was I presentable? Forget attractive, I wanted to see if I had toothpaste down my chin or if I could flatten my hair, which had grown pretty wild in rehab. I glimpsed us in the hall mirror as we passed. For a second it held us both, then just me, then whatever it holds when no one's there – the opposite wall, the nothing, the slow clock of the light in there.

In the kitchen there was the smell of coffee, and from the Rayburn something savoury. How's that for a welcome? And were you going to appear? Come in from the garden with your straw hat on? I must have been looking around expectantly because Evie shook her head. Only me, she said. We can talk about all that later.

We ate at the kitchen table, a shepherd's pie, a good one. She asked questions about Virgil House and I answered them. I showed her the card for my friend's restaurant. I was babbling, light-headed. I was so grateful to have her there but so unsure of what she was doing or how I should behave. I was in disgrace. Was I in disgrace? When have I been anything else? I tried to remember how long it was since I'd last seen her and realised it had to be your passing-out parade. I felt I was in a play and at any moment she would stand, smile, walk out the door and disappear. I thought I might wake up in hospital groping for the buzzer.

When we'd finished eating she started collecting the dishes. I said I'd do it but she shook her head, said I was probably tired. I told her I wasn't, though I was. The thought of the coming conversation made me tired. The truth-telling. The need for honesty. God knows I should have been ready for it after rehab but it was different there, there were rules of engagement. My only inspiration was to start the thing myself, and as soon as the last plate had been put away and there was nothing more to fuss with, I said, Evie, please, where is she?

She said you were at the Silk Shed, or that was where she'd left you. Shall we talk in the garden? she said. A pity to be inside on a day like this. She was right. The thermometer by the back door said twenty-three degrees. The sky was cloudless, a low, splashy sun. The garden was at the edge of a wildness I liked very much. The unmown grass was dry on top and damp beneath. The bindweed had flourished. Some of the unpicked beans were eight or ten inches long. As for the dahlias, I should leave them alone more often. There was a thicket of them, bright as bandsmen.

We started walking slow circuits together. The air had the scent of things going over, early autumn in the little gardens, the dark muck of the beds. It distracted us, and I might have been glad to keep it that way, Evie and me in the garden, end of story, beginning of. But that wasn't what we were there for.

She told me the two of you had driven down two days ago, each in your own car. She said she had taken care to arrive a couple of hours after you so you'd have time alone with Lorna, and when she did arrive the pair of you were busy in the tea rooms as if nothing had happened, no emergency, no trouble. They looked at me, said Evie, like cheeky girls daring me to say something. And did you? I asked. She shook her head. We ate cake, she said, lots of it, something extreme that Lorna had made with passion fruit and pistachios and a lot of cream. Those girls, she said, will be twenty stone each if they keep that up.

I said I was afraid I'd ruined things between you, that you and Lorna were either side of a confusion I was the cause of. Evie shook her head. The girls are fine, she said. It wasn't ever about them. She said perhaps I forgot that people other than myself have a past, that even a girl in her twenties has the whole of childhood to look back on. And what's bigger than that? She said that when you first came home – your old home in the north – you sounded, even looked somehow, thirteen years old again. She had no idea then what it was about but it was clear you'd had a shock and the shock had sent you back in time. It took half a week to tease it out of you – what had been going on, what you'd seen. Her instinct then was just to leave you as you were. She didn't try to wake you from it. She let you be and mothered you. Later, of course, she spoke to Lorna, and soon after that the parcel arrived with the pages inside. She said she tried to read it with your eyes. What had you seen there that so disturbed you?

You *know* what, I said. What else *could* it be? I felt the same frustration I'd felt with Zoë at Virgil House. I'd come out with something that seemed undeniable and obvious – a fact – and then, somehow, it wasn't. She'd find a loose thread and start to tug . . .

Evie stopped us, our walking. We turned to face each other. We were standing between the runner beans and the gooseberry bush. She looked up at me in a way I remembered so well from our old days together that I smiled – I couldn't help it. Her face is thinner now than my memory of it and time has made the usual marks, but her eyes, I swear, are entirely unchanged from those that looked at me across the table that morning after the snow party.

I don't believe it's that, she said. Or, at least, that wasn't the heart of it. It was finding out I'd been hiding the truth. It was the rejection.

I said rejection was the last thing I'd intended. That everything I wrote had exactly the opposite aim.

But why not speak? she said. Couldn't I have trusted you? It was time I understood how hard it had been for you to take the risk of *any* kind of relationship with me. That when you were a girl – when, in fact, you were about thirteen – you told her you had decided, once and for all, to live without a father. You weren't going to waste your time thinking about me any more. You had a mother and that was all you needed. To hell with fathers! And you meant it. For years after that you barely mentioned me. You'd agreed to my coming to the parade but you needed some persuading. It wasn't until your early twenties that things began to shift. You decided to tiptoe a little closer. You would try it out. You were more confident then, perhaps because of Lorna. But the fear and the anger were in you still. The shame too. The shame of being the girl whose father didn't want her, didn't love her. To show yourself, to uncover what you had carefully hidden, to run the risk of having it fail, of being in some way betrayed, that was the high-wire you walked each time we met.

And it was going so well, said Evie. Every week you'd call her from the Silk Shed and it was a rare call that didn't have some mention of what we'd done together – the meeting house, a lunch out, a walk. Small things that had given you pleasure, that had reassured you.

Oh, Maggie! I was stunned to hear about those calls. Hearing about them gave me no pleasure. I sagged. I felt stupid. I said I knew I'd lost you, that losing you was the price I had to pay for Belfast. It was justice.

But you're not listening! she said. Will you listen, please? She touched my arm and started us walking again, the silvery path through the grass we'd already made together. She told me that when she believed you were ready, the two of you sat down at the kitchen table one evening and went through the pages together. She pointed things out – things you had hardly noticed or not at all first time round. She read pages aloud to you, made sure you heard them, what was there and the voice that went with it. You did not, that evening, want to go to the end of it – why would you? – but next morning she came down to find you with it again, saw tears on your cheeks but knew at once these were not a child's tears. You had found yourself again, and what you read now you read as an adult. Your judgements would be an adult's judgements.

In truth, she said, it wasn't as simple as that, or that wasn't the end of it. You still needed time to adjust, to think it through. It's very interesting, she said, to watch someone doing work like that. She saw how you comforted your old self. She was proud of you. I wanted to say I was proud of you too but I didn't know if that was allowed. Can you be proud of a person recovering from the things you've done to them? I'm not sure. I'd need some time to think about that.

We made one last circuit of the garden, in silence this time, and as we came back to our starting point I asked Evie what they were, these adult judgements of yours. Oh, she'll tell you herself, she said. I said we'd have to meet for that to happen, and that's when she explained this business Sarah Waterfall has dreamt up. We will meet at the meeting house. Where else? You will come there tomorrow with Sarah. I will come with Evie. Eleven in the morning.

I said I thought it sounded like a cross between a wedding and a hostage exchange. And what's it got to do with Sarah Waterfall? But apparently when Sarah suggested it – it came through Lorna

– you liked it, liked it immediately, so I suppose I must try to like it too.

We finished our talk beside the aspen tree. Evie rolled a cigarette and smoked it while I told her about the tree, how a crown of its leaves allows the wearer to visit the underworld and return safely, how I can never look at the tree without some thought of my own mother. She finished her smoke and buried the dog-end in the earth, then reached over and picked something out of the long grass, a blue latex glove, inside out. It must have been one the paramedic was wearing that night. It made me shiver. I stuffed it into a pocket and we went back to the house.

Ten thirty now. In Virgil House the lights will be off. A new brother in my old bed? God knows I wish them all a peaceful night. Evie is in the bathroom. I can hear the drain gurgling with her bathwater. We went on talking of course. It became easier and easier. What made us good company for each other in 1982 has somehow survived all the changes. At dusk we went out to the garden again, saw a crescent moon somewhere over the Quantocks, already close to setting. I'd imagined she'd be going back to the Silk Shed but she said the plan was to stay with me. She'd texted you to say I'd agreed to the meeting. She had her toothbrush and nightie in the car. Unless I wanted to be alone? I said I didn't. I said she was very welcome.

I lit a fire in the front room, the first since April. I cooked fish fingers and peas out of the freezer and we ate with plates on our laps either side of the fire. I told her about the photo of us on the suspension bridge. Turned out she knew all about it, had seen the picture on the dressing-table of your bedroom at the Silk Shed. The dressing-table! That, too, I wish someone had told me about before.

And we strayed, filled gaps in time, half a dozen years in a sentence, jobs, relationships (about Ray she said only, 'In the end we were better off apart'). We didn't avoid what was difficult but neither did we keep prodding it. We talked about our time in Bristol. When I apologised for my young self (see Step Eight) she said she wasn't so impressed with her own part, and for a moment or two her eyes grew dark and glistened. We talked a lot about you, of course, the kind of conversation most parents have all the time but a first for us. Better late than never? I hope so.

She'll be in the spare room tonight. A long while since anyone was in there. The beds, like the wardrobe on the landing, came from Granny and Grandpa Rose's place in Langport. You've seen them. Those headboards are solid walnut. They were probably made nearby and can never have been cheap. The high days of Rose's Boots & Shoes! Despite the warmth of the day the room was chilly. I offered to put a heater in there and she reminded me she was a northerner and not afraid of a little cold, but she accepted a hot-water bottle and I gave her the one in the red wool cover. It's a bit ancient but I think it's the best.

And have I mentioned there were letters waiting for me? From the Commission? The first was written before they received mine, the other afterwards. I showed them both to Evie. She asked what I knew about Ambrose Carville and I was about to tell her – give her chapter and verse – when I remembered I knew nothing about him at all. I may bring the letters with me tomorrow, the second one at least. You may want to see it.

I can't stop thinking of tomorrow as a test, and one I'm quite likely to fail. Will we be left alone? Will the others stay? And if they stay, will it be some sort of group discussion, everybody putting in their two-penn'orth? Or will they sit in silence like a jury while I . . . do what? Plead? Apologise? Shake like a tree? I have a part in a play but I haven't learnt my lines! I'm not even sure what the play is about. I'll stand in front of you opening and shutting my mouth like a goldfish.

And there's the bathroom door. Evie's out. I'll go and clean my teeth in the steam of her bath. She just called to me, Don't sit up all night, Stephen! I called back, I'm on my way. And so I am.

I lay awake a long time – thoughts you only have at night, alone. Among other things I thought about prison, and saw myself, broom in hand, sweeping a landing on the wing, a slow, methodical sweeping.

On my night trips to the bathroom I looked at the door of the spare room and could hardly believe Evie was in there. Tempting to go close and listen, try to catch the sound of her breathing – but don't worry, it was just a thought, I didn't do it. The last time I was up, the night was thinning, though it was still properly dark. Dark and foggy. I heard a car pass. Who goes to work at four thirty in the morning? Early even for a farmhand. Was there some emergency out there? A sick child, a woman about to give birth? I curled under the covers and finally slept. When I opened my eyes again Evie was sitting on the side of the bed with a cup of tea in her hand. She had on a morning face, a little pale, pale shadows under her eyes. Did *she* lie awake all night? Those old headboards like tombstones? She left me with the tea, and while I sipped it, I considered pretending to be ill. Perhaps I was ill. Was I ill? Then I finished the tea, went to the bathroom, filled the basin with cold water and lowered my face into it, kept it there as long as I could hold my breath.

By the time I was downstairs she'd already set the table and put the porridge on. I had dressed in the clothes I wore at your birthday party (no teeth in the pocket this time – I checked, carefully). I asked Evie if she thought it would do. She looked me up and down and said it was fine but she was going to trim my hair after breakfast. She did. We had no hurry. We did it outside. I carried one of the kitchen chairs into the garden. Evie wrapped a towel round my neck and snipped away with the scissors from the sewing box. She circled me, looking for new bits of hair to attack. When she was satisfied she dusted my shoulders with the towel, wiped the back of my neck.

Because we had time to kill, and sitting around made me fidgety, we walked up to Dad's orchard. The last of the mist, gauzy – when exactly does fog become mist? – was snagged in the tops of the tallest trees. I felt a strange fierce pride in it, that damp, untidy acre of Somerset. I have seen deer and foxes there, badgers, courting teenagers. A bull got in there once and stood very still, watching me from the corner of his eye, may blossom all over his face from pushing through the hedge. I've slept many nights there. I have been drenched, been drunk, been right at the edge of what I could bear, and at times filled with a sort of simple hopefulness that seems to flow out of hedgerows and from the tips of grass. I suggested to Evie – none too seriously – that she might move down here too, the West Country. She smiled. She didn't think so. She had projects. I got the impression one of these might be romantic but I'm just guessing. She told me about the group she belongs to, northern women writing the histories of northern women. Making little films too. And tapestry, she said, and laughed at herself. We spend whole afternoons sewing. It puts us in a trance.

I told her how nervous I was about seeing you. She said you would be feeling nervous too but that it would be all right. She had raised you to be loving, and you were. I said, At least she knows what I am now, though even I didn't understand quite what I meant by that. Later I said, She owes me nothing. Evie nodded. Tell her these things yourself, she said. She just wants you to be open with her.

As we walked the orchard, climbed it and turned at the top, I remembered when she took my hand in Bristol. I knew – I'm not entirely lost to reality – that nothing like that was going to happen but I wanted *something* to mark the moment, so I stopped to pick up a faller, a really good-looking apple, all glossy from the wet grass, and made her a present of it. It's a cider apple, I said. You'll find it on the sharp side. She thanked me, touched the apple to her cheek and said she'd save it for later. It was time to go. We walked into the town. I grew solemn and silent. I couldn't help it. When the roof of the meeting house came into view my heart did something, some skip in the rhythm, that made me think of the defibrillator on the wall of the library, if I should mention it, casually, to Evie.

Ned was waiting by the steps. He waved, we waved. While we were still out of earshot I said, Is everyone in on this? What's *he* doing here?

You're the first, he said. Well done. I'm sure the others won't be long. Hello, I'm Ned. He shook Evie's hand and led the way into the building. It was chilly inside. Out of habit I sat where I always do, back to the door and facing the windows. I saw Evie sniffing the air. I forgot to ask but I don't think she's ever been inside a Quaker meeting house. I wondered how she'd react to it, with her history. But once she'd had a look round she seemed comfortable enough. I tried to settle into the quiet. Evie came and sat next to me. Ned was on the bench the elders use, peering at a booklet. All sorts of stuff was pouring through my head. At one moment I had a very vivid image of John France. He was staring at me, puzzled, slightly suspicious, as if I were a camera, and he, on his way elsewhere, had suddenly found himself in front of the lens. And I thought of how he must be now, the reality of it, a man with part of his leg missing, and I felt, somewhere in my chest, a little flash of anger and grief. Then I heard the creak of the outer door, the sound of light feet. I turned in my seat and there you were, also looking rather solemn, Sarah Waterfall just behind you. Evie went over and hugged you. Sarah smiled at me and nodded. I smiled back. I felt suitably foolish. Also, I suppose, grateful. People were trying to help. I understood that.

At some point all of us were looking at Sarah, and she, in the voice she uses at the meetings, said, We will leave Stephen and Maggie together now. And out they went, a sort of procession. The door was closed. Later we heard, once or twice, their voices in the burying ground.

For a few seconds we avoided each other's gaze. When our eyes did meet we nearly burst out laughing. I almost wish we had. I would have liked them to hear that. I would have liked Ned to look slightly pained. But the room commanded us to be serious. Two hundred years of men and women moving through the dark of themselves in the hope of a voice that knows them. You don't lark about in a place like that.

We weren't sure where to sit. Our usual places, side by side? How would we speak like that? How would we look at each other? It would be like talking on a bus. In the end we settled on the same row but with a space between us. That was quite good, not too formal. Then we did the classic thing of starting to speak at exactly the same moment. After you, I said. No, you said, you first. And what did I start with? I told you about Evie cutting my hair in the garden and how at the end she held up an imaginary mirror so I could admire her work. It wasn't very relevant. You told me she used to cut your hair when you were younger and you'd gone to school with some fairly strange styles. You asked me if I was feeling better. I said I was. I told you about Virgil House, one or two of the characters there. I said nothing about the young man and what he did to himself in the bathroom. I asked how it was with Lorna. Good, you said, very emphatically, and I knew that was the truth. You asked if I was going to drink again. I said – I hope not pompously – that an addict cannot promise not to go back to his addiction, that I didn't want to drink and didn't think I would but it was a deep illness and to make promises would be wrong. You nodded and slowly turned the ring on your thumb. I think both of us might have had the feeling that some of what we'd meant to say, perhaps even the most important things, didn't need saying any more. And as we went on the pauses between our speaking grew longer. Did you notice? It wasn't awkward. It was like we were slipping back towards what we were used to in that place. I thought you might ask about Francis Harkin but you didn't. I imagine it's not an easy thing to ask about. What would the question be? But you did ask about the Commission, so I took the last of their letters from my jacket and passed it to you. You read it carefully and I watched you carefully. I said something about going up to the library later in the week, checking flight times, maybe booking a hotel room. You nodded. You seemed to be thinking about it, so that when you opened your mouth I was expecting something practical about the arrangements, advice on budget hotels. Instead, very steadily, and in a way you must have been practising in your head for days, you made your offer. You stunned me, Maggie. God knows what I looked like. You must have thought I hadn't heard or hadn't understood you. Anyway, you repeated it and added, If that's OK, if you're allowed to have someone with you.

I don't think people want to see their father in tears. I never saw my own crying. He must have done after Mum died but I didn't see that and I'm not sorry. I stared at the elm floorboards. A wave of heat passed through me, and when I looked up and looked at you, your waiting face, I felt I was wearing all the room's light and wondered if *this* was how we were supposed to feel before we stood at a meeting to minister. In the end, of course, I had no grand message for you. No poetry or speaking in tongues, just yes and please and thank you. You smiled – were you the parent then? – and looked as if your work for the day was done. And then, suddenly, we were two swimmers too long under the water and needing to break the surface again. You said you were going to use the Ladies. I explained the slight problem with the cistern. I don't think you wanted us to walk outside together and be stared at. Better one at a time. So I went out alone and found Ned giving Evie a tour of dead Quakers. I stopped by the oak tree and waited for her to join me. Well? she asked, and I grinned and nodded.

At home I lay down on the bed, told myself I would shut my eyes for two minutes, try to catch up with myself, then woke an hour later to the sound of voices downstairs. I picked out yours, then heard Lorna, Sarah, Ned. I couldn't hear what anyone was saying, just the voices lapping over each other like water in a cellar. When I got up and looked from the bedroom window I saw the kitchen table had flown outside and settled under the aspen tree. Evie was down there having a sly smoke while she decorated the tablecloth with things she found in the garden – wild marjoram and lavender, some leaves from the vine. The mist had melted into the air and we were in that gap, those few hours before it started to roll in again. A cooler day than yesterday but bright as crystal. A day of long views. Were we celebrating? Celebrating what? I started thinking about it, then backed off for fear it would be bad luck to name it, like the old story of the cider barrel that never empties until the day someone squints through the bung-hole and finds it full of cobwebs. Sometimes we get more than we deserve, much more. It's very hard to make sense of.

Lorna had brought a hamper from the Silk Shed. Lorna will bring a hamper to Armageddon. Picnic food, Famous Five food, but all of it changed a little, reinvented. And what was that drink made of, that iced tea? I tasted fennel in there. It was delicious – though I suspect at the Silk Shed you drink it with a shot of gin or mescal in it.

We sat wherever there was a free chair. You were between Evie and Lorna. I could see nothing but happiness in your face. As for me, I spoke and laughed and ate my gala pie, but I was also somehow still watching from the bedroom window. Sarah was at the head of the table, her grey hair long as a girl's and worn loose today. I understand why you and Lorna took to her. She *is* impressive. She gazed down the table approvingly. I don't think the elders will be kicking me out just yet (though I always know where my sleeping bag is, my pack, my boots). And then her little toast, if that was what it was. Take heed, dear friends, to the promptings of love and truth in your hearts. And she raised her glass and we raised ours. The whole garden held its breath. But I didn't dare look at you. I didn't look at anyone.

You all took off after lunch and I don't know when that hallway has ever seen so much kissing and hugging. Evie, who I held in my arms for the first time in nearly thirty years, said I should get some rest, and once I was alone and the air had settled, that was what I longed to do, creep back upstairs, an old dog to its basket, but there was one more job, one last piece of business to take care of before the day ran out on me. I went into the garden with the scissors Evie had used on my hair and cut twelve of the best dahlias. Dahlias have playful names. I know some of them. 'Bishop of Auckland', 'Snowstorm', 'Wine-eyed Jill', 'Roxy', 'Labyrinth'. I didn't have any nice paper to wrap them and didn't want to wrap them in newspaper so I just tied them with some twine, snipped the stems and set off for town. I was far from sure the place would be open. Do funeral parlours keep regular hours? But when I pushed at the grey glass of the door it opened and I went through into the office. There was no sign of Annie. I wondered – what a coward I am! – if I could leave the flowers on the desk, scribble a quick note, but she came through a door from the back, saw me, saw the flowers and smiled broadly. The flowers started a hunt for a vase. I want you to know I resisted the urge to suggest she use one of the urns in the window. If you're busy, I said, I could come back later. No, no, she said, Mondays are quiet. I found that a bit mysterious. Does no one die on a Monday?

We sat together on armchairs in a sort of lounge area on the other side of the office from her desk (a box of Kleenex on the glass-topped table between us). I said that in some traditions when you save a life you become responsible for it but that I wasn't going to hold her to that. She laughed and said it was the ambulance that had saved me, not her. I pointed out that without her there wouldn't have been an ambulance.

We talked for the best part of an hour. I won't pretend I didn't enjoy it. We were very open with each other. You can't be too formal with someone who has knelt by your unconscious body in the dark, speaking to you. And, yes, we even touched on her politics. It didn't fluster her at all. She said she'd left the BNP years ago and was now, she reckoned, somewhere in the middle ground of the Tory Party. I said, Another five years and you'll be a socialist. Do you think so? she said. She seemed quite struck by the idea, something unexpected from the library of possible Annie Fullers. And you, she asked, where will you be in five years? Various words came into my head and I might have come out with them if the phone hadn't interrupted us. She excused herself and answered it. It's always interesting to observe someone at their work. I think it was a call about a service later in the week. Annie sounded kind and practical, and I got the impression she was probably very good at what she does. When she finished I stood up and said I had to go. We shook hands, and I was turning to leave when she said she wanted to show me something. OK, I said, though I was a little nervous. What do *you* think goes on in the back rooms of funeral parlours? But we went outside, out to the yard and the garage, and she unlocked the wooden doors and there was the old Wolseley hearse her father had bought when he started the business, a car the size of a motor launch, and polished so hard it shone even in the gloom of the garage. She opened the driver's door and invited me to sit inside. I thought the car had the same smell as Grandpa Rose's wardrobe. It can't go faster than thirty, she said, but it doesn't need to. On the front passenger seat there was a top hat with a red and a yellow ribbon tied round the crown. I wear that, she said, and walk in front of the car for the last part of the journey. It's what we offer them, whoever's riding in the back. Slowness, stillness, our best words, then silence. She asked if I had a driver's licence and we both laughed. I do, I said, though I'm a bit rusty. I didn't mention anything about putting cars in ditches. I rather fancied driving that old Wolseley. Nor did I mind the idea of following behind Annie with her hat and ribbons. I put my hands on the steering wheel. It's made of some kind of superior 1960s plastic, a narrow rim, black and hard as bone. I'll fetch the key, she said, and you can have a listen to the engine.

START

This is the most purple room I've ever been in. Purple carpet, purple curtains, a little purple sofa, a purple bedspread. Is purple restful? The colour of emperors, you said, though I don't think an emperor would stay in a room like this. Yours down the corridor is identical except for the view. More of the city in it. Rooftops, spires, cranes, rainclouds. I looked out, expecting to be able to recognise some landmarks. I recognised nothing.

Noises of the city night now, dulled by the thick glass of the window. I'm in bed and glad to be so. I've got the Virgil House notebook resting against my knees. Though this is a budget place the bed's a big one, lots of pillows and cushions. Across the room, the TV takes up most of the wall. I've got it on with the volume low, a sports channel showing a grand prix, in Japan I think. Looks like it rains as much in Japan as it does in Ireland. Or in Somerset for that matter.

Did you enjoy the day? Are we here to enjoy the days?

You were pleased when I told you the flight was on Saturday because it meant we'd have all of Sunday to look around the city. You wanted, you said, to get the feel of the place. That hadn't occurred to me – I mean that you would be curious, naturally curious about it, would want to know where you were, see it for yourself. And I remember puzzling over whether the 'feel' was evenly distributed, or if it was heaped up in certain parts of the city. When I asked you if there was anything in particular you wanted to do, you shrugged and said, Not really. You didn't want museums or anything like that. You didn't want to go on an open-topped bus, which was a relief. OK, I said, hoping I'd understood you. So this morning we set out like a pair of tourists, in search of the feel of the place. I was watching you but I was also watching myself, catching myself in whatever reflected – mirrors and shop windows and so on. It all looked normal enough. I seemed well disguised as a middle-aged man, a fairly harmless sort, and anyway, who would be looking at me? It would be the young woman beside me they'd notice, dressed for the city, a little bit of city smartness. It wasn't Samarkand or Kyoto but it was all new to you and you were alert to the small differences, pausing now and then to take a second look, sometimes getting your phone out to take a picture. Getting the feel.

And what was I up to? I wasn't sure at first, then realised that among other things I was keeping a street map in my head of the route back to the hotel. This is what I did when I patrolled the city with John France, though then it was how to get back to the Factory. Quickest route, safest route. The fear was always of finding yourself out on your own, of looking down and looking up again and no sign of the others, of people seeing that and passing the word along.

When we'd been out a while you asked me how much I remembered. Very little, I said, and that was the truth. It's not like I was expecting troops and burnt-out shops, but the changes were more than just the absence of all that. The Belfast I knew was black and white, like an old postcard. This place was shiny, well-heeled. The big stores were open, the Sunday streets thronged with people carrying shopping bags. There were almost as many buskers as you'd find in Bath, and almost as many tourists – a whole coach-party of Chinese folk photographing each other beneath a statue of Queen Victoria.

The only uniforms I saw were on the backs of a pair of police patrolling near the city hall (one building I did manage to recognise). A man and a woman, probably in their twenties. Not, of course, the Royal Ulster Constabulary any more, though to my eyes the uniform looks much the same, and I assume a lot of the old RUC just stayed on, same people, different cap badge. They were wearing stab vests and carried pistols on their hips but didn't look like they were expecting any trouble. It's been a few years now since anyone's taken a shot at a policeman.

And I began to tell you about some of the RUC characters I'd known. You've asked me to be more open, to share more, and I'm trying to do that, though I'd say it's a fine line between telling old stories and just banging on about the what-was, becoming the pub bore – albeit a sober one. And what I remember, when I say it out loud, doesn't always convince me. Was it really like that? Did he say that? Did he say that *exactly*? It makes me worry that when I stand in the offices of the Commission tomorrow I'm going to sound a lot more unsure of myself than will be comfortable, a lot more evasive. I don't know, sir. I can't remember. It was a long time ago, sir.

Well, the rain arrived, swept in on a breeze, and as we'd forgotten to bring one of the purple umbrellas from the hotel, I bought a solid-looking black one from a street seller, one of those men who magically appear with the first drop. You chose a café for us, walls white as a meeting house and staff who took the business of making coffee very seriously. You asked for the Wi-Fi code and dialled Lorna, smiled at me and retreated to a private corner to speak to her. I leafed through a book of fashion shots, boys and girls, skinny and very young, children really, pouting at the camera in the kind of clothes I've never seen anybody wearing.

When we set out again I decided the city had nothing to say to me, not now, not any more. I had confused a place with a time, as if our flight from Bristol would return us to the 1980s. Instead, it had brought us somewhere that wanted nothing to do with any of that, had turned its back on the past, on *that* past, and done it pretty thoroughly. The ambition – and you can imagine the conversations in City Hall – was to be like anywhere else in the UK, somewhere to make money, to go shopping, see a film. A place Chinese tourists could come for the shopping and the craic, and they might know nothing at all about what happened here for thirty years and that would be fine. How much do I know about what was happening in China in those years? Something to do with Mao. The Great Leap Forward? I'm not sure. Important things, world-changing things. So we strolled, snug under the umbrella (it was only when I opened it that I saw the Guinness toucans), chatting a little, turning this way and that, no particular route in mind, just where our feet took us, a day out, a strange day out, father and daughter in curtains of Irish drizzle, until we found ourselves at the end of a wide road that cut through the city to the hills, and I looked down it and knew exactly where we were. I stopped, like a man who's seen himself coming from the other direction, his own ghost.

This is the Falls, I said.

You had a map from the hotel. You traced our journey with your finger. Divis Street, you said. I said Divis Street leads onto the Falls Road. I pointed to the tower block, all that was left of the Divis flats complex. It's been painted, smartened up, looks half decent now, but the thought of going any closer to it made my mouth dry.

I would have turned back but you were interested. A month ago I doubt you'd even heard of the Falls. Or the Shankill and the rest of them. But you've been busy. You've been doing your research, mostly online, I think, YouTube and the like. Old news broadcasts, documentaries, feature films, odds and ends people have put up. You were even watching something while we waited in Departures at Bristol, a little film on your phone. You had the earphones in but I could hear a small angry sound like an insect trapped in a jar, and when I looked over your shoulder could see what looked like a bus burning in a street. That might have been the Falls. So you've been building your own story, your own version of the Troubles. And it makes me think of that phrase Evie used in the garden about you reaching an adult judgement. What is your judgement, Maggie? Who has your sympathy? Who are you with? Who are you angry with?

I have this theory – and it's only a theory, it might well be wrong – that most of what's out there, online or off, is pro-Nationalist. Not pro-IRA, that's not the same thing, but a view of the Nationalist community as a people hard-done-by, a community oppressed and provoked over many years. Lots of reasons for that. The main one is that it's true. But it may also be that Nationalists have been more ready to speak up, have a clearer story, one they're good at telling. The others – people holding on to a flag not much valued on the mainland, who ran the police force, government, business – that's a harder sell, though when we were here we saw them as our natural allies, trusted them, felt relatively safe in their neighbourhoods. As for the British Army, when is it ever possible to watch film of soldiers on the streets, armed men moving among civilians, some of those civilians children, and not have doubts about the rightness of it? You won't have missed the Bloody Sunday stuff. That doesn't get any less shocking. The thing itself and the lies afterwards.

You've expressed no views, or not to me. You certainly haven't accused me of anything. You've asked a couple of questions (one about internment, which was long before my time in Ireland) but we've had no big discussion yet about what happened here. I've wondered if your time in the RAF – wearer of a uniform, taker of orders, swearer of an oath – might shape your thinking about it, but I'm pretty sure it's the pink triangle tattooed on your arm that shapes it more.

Anyway, you wanted to see it, the famous Falls Road, so we started to walk. The rain let up and the hills came closer. There weren't many people about. Those we did pass I imagined looking at us and knowing very well we were strangers. I kept quiet. I didn't want anybody to hear our English voices. And I knew it was stupid, that nobody cared. It was Sunday on the Falls Road. A good deal of not much. Some traffic, the fast-food shops open, a garage, a newsagent selling Sunday papers. But the further we went, the less I could shake off a sense of the place having, deep in its brickwork, a shadow of menace like a damp stain impossible to remove.

We passed the turning to the Factory. I didn't say anything. I didn't want to be seen gesturing in that direction. Anyway, it's all gone now, pulled down years ago.

We passed the turning to the street (named after a spring flower) where John France was shot by a bullet that had already passed through the body of another soldier.

You asked how I was doing. I said I was all right but suggested we didn't go much further, that the road didn't really lead anywhere, just went on and on. OK, you said, but could we go in here? You pointed to the shop beside us. I'd not been paying attention, had been walking in some shuddery dream of the past and couldn't work out at first what it was. I had to stand back a little, go to the edge of the pavement. When I did see I couldn't believe you were serious. You wanted to go into the Sinn Féin shop? It's Sunday, I said, it'll be closed, but you tried the door, the door opened, and with a quick backward glance of encouragement you went in. I followed. What else could I do? Loiter outside? Disown you?

At first the place looked empty. There was a security camera on the ceiling, so we were on view somewhere, the offices upstairs probably. Then that woman appearing like a sprite from beneath the counter, a box in her hands, giving us the once-over but greeting us politely enough. What was she? My age? You asked if we could have a look round. You're welcome, she said. She started unpacking the box, taking things out and pricing them, exactly as I used to do at Plant World, though there we didn't stock mugs with Gerry Adams' face on them. There were posters for sale, DVDs, T-shirts, flags, books. I hid myself behind a display of Republican fridge magnets – little tricolours, Easter lilies, a lot of Bobby Sands with that nice smile he had. You browsed, I sweated. I had the voice of some old politician in my head, some big rubbery face, part Margaret Thatcher, part Ian Paisley, barking Sinn Féin/IRA! Sinn Féin/IRA! In the end you chose a book of poems by prisoners at Long Kesh, and a poster of Countess Markievicz wearing a hat with black feathers and carrying a revolver so big I think it would have blown her off her feet if she'd pulled the trigger.

You chatted to the woman while she took your money. There was no difficulty. What difficulty would there be? Your northern

English voice, her northern Irish one. She didn't have a bag for the poster, she was sorry, there were none of the big bags left. You said we had an umbrella and not to worry. And that was it. I hurried through the door behind you. I couldn't meet the woman's eyes, couldn't quite manage that.

I was angry with you, Maggie. Which is to say I was frightened, shaken up. I told myself you'd put us both in danger, though I knew you'd done nothing of the sort. Did I seriously imagine the woman going to lock the door, point at me and say, We know who you are? That someone was going to come down the stairs? The most dangerous thing we had done all day was cross the Westlink with its lanes of traffic. Even so, it was a good thirty yards down the road before I could trust my voice. I asked what you were going to do with the poster. You said it was a present for Lorna. I said, She'll like it, and I think she will. It will be very at home on the wall of the Silk Shed, maybe next to one of those tea-coloured nudes you told me were Victorian erotica.

When we crossed back into the city centre I looked over my shoulder. No one was following us. We had lunch. You flicked through the book of poems. I didn't ask if it mentioned the men's crimes or if it was just their poetry. I said I was going back to the hotel to have a kip, perhaps a last look through my statement for tomorrow. You walked me there – did you think I'd get lost? – left me in the lobby and went out again to do some exploring on your own. And you asked me to take the book and the poster. You didn't want to have to carry them. So I went up in the lift to my room, an ex-British squaddie with a volume of Republican poetry in one hand and a strange, camp picture of Countess Markievicz in the other. As it happened, I travelled the four floors alone. A slight pity.

* * *

I did have an afternoon kip – just kicked off my shoes and lay on top of the bed. For a minute or two time circled. I was a fifty-something-year-old lying in the filtered air of the hotel room, and a twenty-something sprawled post-patrol on the black plastic of an army mattress, not hearing the soft footfall of the foreign women in the corridor making up the rooms but the thud and squeak of boots on stone stairs, that never-ending coming and going that made up our lives in the Factory . . .

When I woke I showered and fixed myself some tea with the kit they leave in the room, then sat down, put on my chemist's reading glasses, and went through the statement for the hundredth time. Carville advised me to keep it short and that, as you know, is what I've done. The facts as I remember them, a paragraph on what I think or feel now. I have read it out to empty rooms. It takes less than ten minutes.

When I showed it to you in Somerset – the original – you took it away and came back and said you thought it needed to be plainer. I said I didn't see how it could be, and you said, It's as if it all just *happens*. You're there, he's there, and it just happens. You thought it was something to do with the verbs. Lorna apparently felt the same. A problem with the verbs.

So I went back to it, held it up and stared at it as I would a face. It made me feel ill. I couldn't make any sense of it. It was written in a language I didn't know at all. And then, just the other side of thinking I couldn't do anything about it, I began to see what you were on about. Gaps, silences. Me over here, him over there. I needed to join it up. The sky didn't fall on him. It wasn't an act of God. So I wrote it out again with new verbs. I showed you. You read it, nodded, and said yes.

In his last email to me (I've been going up to the library most days to check my new hotmail account, which is already full of people trying to sell me stuff, a lot of it to do with sex) Carville explained that the family would also be reading out a statement. His parents – Francis's parents – are both long gone. It was Carville's understanding that his sister would read the statement. He didn't mention her name though I'm sure he knows it. Older sister? Younger? I'm picturing a woman like the one in the Sinn Féin shop today. A homely-looking no-nonsense woman who perhaps has her hair done in one of those salons there seemed to be a lot of along the Falls Road. She will have imagined the moment times beyond counting, just as I have. She will have imagined me. And I'm hoping it's a look of pure hatred she gives me. I think I could deal with that. Something icy, stone-like. What frightens me is the thought I might see something else – pity, forgiveness. Or just the gaze of someone whose life fell apart thirty years ago and who's never known how to put it back together. I'm more afraid of that than of anything she might say. That part, the words, that's different. I don't know how she'll phrase it, if it'll sound like she's speaking to me, but whatever it is I want to hear it. I'm *longing* to hear it. And when she starts to speak I'll try to open something in myself because I want what she says to go into the deepest part of me. Francis can't speak, so this is the next best thing. This is as close as I'm going to get.

I didn't see you again until you knocked on my door to suggest we go out and get something to eat. You'd spotted somewhere, a restaurant on the same street as the hotel. I wasn't particularly hungry but I put on my coat (not the one Brendan gave me which, at a distance – the distance, say, between where people will be sitting tomorrow and where I'll be standing – looks quite expensive, and not my old beater's jacket that looks a bit military, but the blue windcheater, which shouldn't offend anybody) and out we went through the lobby and the automatic doors. The restaurant was only a couple of minutes away. It was doing a decent trade for a Sunday night. Tell me – was that elfin waitress with all the winding black ink on her arms part of your reason for choosing the place? She liked you too, I think, and took good care of us, bringing over the blackboard and taking us through the night's menu. She told us where everything came from! Lamb from Iona, fish from Ardglass. When did we all get so interested in food? When she asked about wine you got in your no-thanks before me. She took away the big wine glasses and came back with a jug of water (sourced from a tap in Belfast). You told me about your afternoon of exploring. You showed me the pictures you'd taken on your phone. Quite a few were of murals, some of them glorifying the dead of various paramilitary groups. Hard to know what these murals mean now, what their power is, their relevance, whether they're just left up for the tourists. I've heard there are youngsters who think it might be fun to do it all again, put on the hoods, dig up the guns that were never decommissioned. The original crew, those who aren't already just names, will be getting on. Hit men with cataracts, bomb-makers with Alzheimer's. And more than a few I think with chronic drink problems. No point pretending a lot of it wasn't fuelled by alcohol, that people didn't do things they wouldn't have done or couldn't if they'd been sober.

You asked how my afternoon had been but I glided over it. The next table was only a couple of feet away and I didn't want to start talking about the statement or tomorrow morning. Instead we talked about what was on our plates and then, quite gently I hope, about the future – yours rather than mine. Prospects for the Silk Shed, prospects of buying a house, possibly even the one Nagamudra is doing up on Paradise Road. And then, when you'd tucked away a last scallop, you said – oh so casually! – that you and Lorna were thinking of adopting. You were weighing it up still, the pros and cons, but you thought you might. You both wanted to. There were a lot of hoops to jump through but you'd spoken to an agency and they'd been encouraging. I said (like a fool) I hadn't known it was possible, two women. You said the law changed in 2005, that same-sex couples had the same right to adopt as anyone else. I don't know how I missed that. Was I sober in 2005? For all of 2005? I told you it was the best news I'd heard in a very long time and I hope you could see that in my face. I nearly asked the waitress to bring back the wine glasses. You at least could have had a mouthful. I should have ordered champagne for the entire restaurant. In the end I settled on a brief touching of your hand and an offer of babysitting.

And well done for smoothing over that awkward moment when the waitress asked if we were over on holiday. I don't think I could have found a yes half as convincing as yours. And then for five minutes telling us all the places to go! How we should get out into the country – Strangford, Magherafelt, Lough Beg. I liked her for all that. I liked her enthusiasm for where she came from.

We said goodnight to each other at the door of my room. I gave you the countess and the poets. The short walk back in the moonlight had changed the mood. Just the realisation, I suppose, that we were close to it, the reason we'd come. Nothing but a night's sleep between us and a walk up the road with Ambrose Carville. We stood in the purple corridor, both of us a little tongue-tied, as if wondering what was best to say, if there was anything to say. You hoped I'd get some sleep. You too, I said.

See you at breakfast. Then I did that thing, that quick deep look into your eyes that's become a habit of mine. I don't know what I'm expecting to see. Eyes windows of the soul etc, and your soul leaning back a little, as I think a soul must, from the company of a killer.

You're sitting on the end of my unmade bed. I'm on the sofa hoping the room doesn't smell of a man having sweated his way through the night and been unable to open a window to freshen the air. Quite easy when you find that windows won't open to feel the anxiety levels rising. The thought that even the doors to the street might be sealed for the night, air-locked. At three o'clock or thereabouts I crouched in the purple bathroom and thought I would lose my dinner. The moment passed. It all passes. I even got a couple of hours of sleep.

So, this is the arrangement. Carville will collect us. He'll call up from the lobby and wait for us. When I asked him how we would recognise each other, he said he would be the bald man in the fawn raincoat. Is that enough? There might be several bald men in fawn raincoats in the lobby. I should have told him I'd be the man with curly hair carrying a volume of Republican poetry. In fact, I just said I'd be with you. I described you. Right you are, he said. His voice is Northern Irish but not, at a guess, from the city. A country softness to it, maybe one of those beauty spots the waitress mentioned. Magherafelt, Strangford.

You're bent over your mobile, thumbs busy. I assume you're texting Lorna. I wonder what you're telling her. Stephen seems OK. He hasn't emptied the mini-bar (not that there is a mini-bar in here). If nothing else, we'll escape the purple rooms today. That's something to look forward to. After what I say at the Commission the legal machine may blink into life but nothing will happen quickly. I don't expect to be arrested at the airport. Tomorrow we'll wake in our beds in Somerset and life will go on. I have some plans. Writing isn't one of them – unless it's that unfinished essay. I should do that, I suppose. I can't remember the book at all. I'll have to read it again. As for you, if I have anything to tell you, I'll just tell you. I won't write it.

And here's something I could start with, though I think I'll save it for the flight home. I spent a piece of last night, the last hour before the light showed between the curtains, imagining the child you and Lorna might adopt. I seemed to have a pretty clear picture of him. It might be a girl. I've no idea why I decided it would be a boy. I imagined myself taking a walk with him out on the Levels. I could see his small shadow at my side, one of those breezy mornings of big skies, the willows flickering their leaves over the water. I will, I promise you, tell him no unhappy stories. We'll spot moorhens and coots, and maybe a kingfisher, you never know your luck. And when I say to him, 'Your mother', in my head I'll hear 'My daughter'. It made me happy to think about that. It calmed me down a good deal, though whether you would ever let me be on my own with him, whether I'd ever have the nerve to ask, I don't know.

It could be me, of course, that little boy. That thought's occurred to me. In my picturing of him he was about the age I was when Mum died. I could be taking myself out for a walk. It's the sort of thing Zoë would have suggested. She's got me into that way of thinking, turning over the stones to see what scuttles away.

And there's the purple phone! You answer – Hello, yes, OK. Five minutes? And now you've left to fetch what you need from your room. You look so pale! I couldn't get you to eat even a slice of toast at breakfast. I wanted to lean across the table, take your hands and say, You're innocent, love, you're innocent of all this, it's not you they want. I thought again of how wrong I was to accept your offer, how selfish. But too late to stop any of it now. We've come to the end of it, the spool of thread. In the offices of the Commission Francis Harkin's sister will be taking her seat. She has her statement, I have mine. And God alone knows what anyone's going to get out of this, who will sleep easier afterwards. We must get what we can. If we cannot stop the wound from bleeding – and it was a big wound, Maggie, a big wound – we can at least kneel down in his blood together. We can do that much. After all these years. We can do that. And then we'll see.

Acknowledgements

With warmest thanks to my step-brother, Jeremy Hilton, and to my step-sister, former Senior Aircrafts–woman Liz Hilton, for their advice on matters military. Thanks also to my editor, Carole Welch, for her shepherding of this project, and my agent, Simon Trewin, for his usual encouragement and support. The author would like to acknowledge the support of the Royal Literary Fund, an organization that stands by writers in a way many of us have reason to be deeply grateful for. All errors, as ever, are the sole responsibility of the author.